A DANGEROUS HUSBAND

FENELLA J MILLER

B

Boldwood

First published in 2016. This edition published in Great Britain in 2025 by Boldwood Books Ltd.

Cover Design by Colin Thomas

Cover Images: Colin Thomas and Shutterstock

A CIP catalogue record for this book is available from the British Library.

Paperback ISBN 978-1-83678-304-6

Large Print ISBN 978-1-83678-305-3

Hardback ISBN 978-1-83678-303-9

Ebook ISBN 978-1-83678-306-0

Kindle ISBN 978-1-83678-307-7

Audio CD ISBN 978-1-83678-298-8

MP3 CD ISBN 978-1-83678-299-5

Digital audio download ISBN 978-1-83678-302-2

This book is printed on certified sustainable paper. Boldwood Books is dedicated to putting sustainability at the heart of our business. For more information please visit https://www.boldwoodbooks.com/about-us/sustainability/

Boldwood Books Ltd, 23 Bowerdean Street, London, SW6 3TN

www.boldwoodbooks.com

1

Lady Madeline Sheldon was bored. Since the excitement of her brother Bennett's wedding to Grace four weeks ago, things had seemed decidedly flat at Silchester Court. The twins, Aubrey and Peregrine, had taken themselves off to another house party and her younger sister, Giselle, had gone to spend a week or two with her bosom bow, Lucinda Bagshot, who lived about five miles away.

This afternoon Madeline's brother Beau – the Duke of Silchester – was to go to Heatherfield, the home of Lord Grey Carshalton and his grandmother, as he had been asked to visit at his earliest convenience. Madeline was determined to accompany him – not, of course, because she wished to see his lordship again but because she was bored. She had yet to inform the duke of her decision and sincerely hoped he hadn't decided to ride, for if he had that would put paid to her plans.

The weather was clement for early September but storms were forecast and she had no wish to be drenched and catch a putrid sore throat. Perhaps if she was in her pelisse and waiting outside Beau would not have the heart to refuse her. He had mentioned at breakfast that he would be leaving at noon and it was almost that now – no time to change into something more elegant, and barely sufficient to put on her bonnet and still be downstairs at the appointed time.

On her mad dash across the vast hall she saw a lurking footman and called him over. 'I shall be going with his grace. Kindly let the stables know so the carriage doesn't leave without me.' Lottie, her maid, soon found the necessary items and Madeline was running through the house just as the tall-case clock in the drawing room struck twelve.

When she burst onto the front steps she saw Beau lounging against the carriage and he welcomed her with a smile. 'I was about to depart, my dear. You have arrived not a moment too soon.'

'I'm sorry if I've kept you waiting...' She joined him in the turning circle.

'You haven't, sweetheart, I was teasing you. I should have thought to suggest that you accompany me, for you must be lonely rattling around this house on your own.'

'Grace and Bennett return from their wedding trip next month and I'm to visit them as soon as they are settled.' He handed her into the carriage and a footman folded up the steps and closed the door. 'Do you know why Lord Carshalton wishes to see you?'

'I don't, but for a gentleman I barely know to send me such an urgent message it must be something serious. He would probably have preferred to speak to Bennett as they both have a military background, but he must do with me.' Beau stretched out his legs and fixed her with a look she had come to dread. 'Madeline, I know Grace invited you for a long visit as soon as she returns from her wedding trip, but you must not go. A newly married couple need their privacy and space to settle into the married state. They are coming to us for Christmas and New Year, and you may return with them after that.'

There was little point in arguing, as once her brother had made a decision he rarely changed his mind. 'Very well, I did think it a little strange that she extended the invitation. Was she just being polite?'

'I'm certain of it, my dear. Why don't I take you to join Giselle? We pass the home of Sir John on the way to Heatherfield.'

Her heart sank at the prospect of missing out on possible excitement. 'I don't like to call in unannounced...'

He chuckled. 'Silly goose – of course I won't deprive you of a visit to Heatherfield, for I know that you've been hoping to further your acquaintance with his lordship since you met him at the wedding.'

Madeline was tempted to hit him with her reticule but wisely refrained. 'I should love to see Giselle and Lucinda afterwards, if that's possible. Although it depends how long you are detained by this business.'

'I believe that Miss Bagshot gave you and your sister all the pertinent knowledge about our new neighbours. Remind me again what we know about the Carshaltons.'

'He was a major in the army, a career soldier, and inherited the title unexpectedly. His father was the third son and was estranged from his family and never expected the title to go to him, as there were at least two other cousins in line before him.' She screwed up her face whilst she thought what else she had gleaned. 'Ah, yes! It seems that the family estates were left to his uncle but the title and fortune came to him. I wonder why Lady Carshalton has chosen to reside with a grandson she doesn't know rather than at the ancestral home with her son and his family.'

'No doubt she doesn't like her youngest son for some reason. It's not our concern. Although we only met the once I liked the man; he had a direct manner and showed a lively wit.'

'He is certainly an attractive gentleman and was much admired by the young ladies at the ball.' The fact that he had singled her out for the supper dance had not gone unnoticed by her siblings. He had not visited, or made any effort to renew their brief acquaintance, which puzzled her. To have shown her so particular an interest at the ball and to then have ignored her very existence was odd, and not at all civil.

The carriage settled into companionable silence and she was given time to let her thoughts drift back to that evening four weeks ago. His lordship was not quite as tall as her brothers, but was equally broad in the shoulders. Having spent so many years serving King and Country he had a smart, military bearing. His hair was the colour of new-mown hay and his eyes an unusual shade of blue... Her reverie was interrupted as the carriage lurched and turned into the drive.

Although they were expected, neither their host nor their hostess appeared to greet them when they stepped into the hall. The butler bowed them in. 'Your grace, my lady, I shall conduct you to Lady Carshalton.'

Beau was looking concerned. 'I could swear that I heard shouting coming from the front of the house. There's something decidedly odd going on here.'

She had no time to respond as the butler threw open the drawing room doors and shouted at the top of his voice. 'His grace the Duke of Silchester and Lady Madeline.'

Madeline stifled her giggles and Beau raised an eyebrow. 'We can be sure everyone knows we have arrived. Stop laughing, my love, very bad form.'

Her brother offered his arm and she placed her gloved hand on it. Despite the extraordinary announcement none of the four elderly ladies present were paying them any attention. In fact the assembled company were gathered at the far end of the drawing room staring out of the windows.

Beau increased his pace and together they almost ran to join Lady Carshalton and her other guests. 'My lady, is something amiss?'

The elderly lady he'd addressed turned at his words and Madeline was shocked by what she saw. Lord Carshalton's grandmother was paper-white and could do no more than gesture towards the window. Her brother took one look and swore, adding to the distress of the ladies present.

'I'm going out to help. Stay here, Madeline – do what you can to calm things down.' Beau rushed off, his boots loud on the boards as he raced for the exit.

She patted Lady Carshalton's arm. 'My lady, how did the accident occur?' Her heart was thumping painfully behind her bodice and she could scarcely bring herself to view the distressing sight outside on the greensward.

'My grandson and his gamekeeper had been inspecting the woods as there had been reports of poachers. We heard the sound of gunfire and rushed to the window to investigate. As we watched, Mr Bishop's horse galloped from the trees with him draped over its neck. My grandson came after him and managed to catch the trailing reins.' Lady Car-shalton dabbed her eyes with her handkerchief before continuing. 'I never thought to see such a thing in my life. Poor Mr Bishop has been grievously wounded. I must send a footman to fetch the doctor.'

It had been almost impossible to tell one gentleman from another whilst they were all crouched around the injured man – for a heart-stopping moment Madeline had thought Lord Carshalton was the one spreadeagled on the ground.

'Lady Madeline, the duke has now joined them and my grandson's men have gone off at a run. Other servants will arrive with a trestle to transport the patient, so I must make sure the housekeeper has prepared a chamber for him. It will have to be on this floor as it would be too difficult to carry Mr Bishop upstairs.' The old lady paused and shook her head. 'How is it the butler, an objectionable man that my grandson inherited with the house, failed to notice that there had been an incident?'

'I don't suppose anyone on that side of the house would have heard anything untoward, my lady. Now, is there anything I can do to assist you?' It was obvious that the three other ladies would be of no use as they were still twittering and flapping like chickens upset by a fox.

'Perhaps you could reassure my friends, for they are sorely distressed by this incident.' Her ladyship bustled off, having recovered her aplomb after the initial shock.

Madeline moved across to join the fluttering ladies. She had no idea how to address them as she'd not been introduced. 'Ladies, shall we move to the comfort of the fire? I shall ring for refreshments, as I'm sure we could all do with a drink of some sort to calm our nerves.'

* * *

Lord Grey Carshalton was doing his best to stem the blood that was coming from his gamekeeper's chest. He feared the injury was going to prove fatal for his friend – and erstwhile orderly – Ned Bishop. He pressed harder on the folded pad he'd made with his neckcloth and was relieved to see the gore no longer trickled out between his gloved fingers.

'Ned, the doctor will soon be here to stitch you up. Don't kick the bucket, there's a good fellow.'

The man's eyes flickered open. 'I ain't going to meet my maker just yet, sir. I'll be right enough once I've seen the sawbones.'

Grey looked up as two more former soldiers arrived at his side. 'Smith, take Jenkins and scour the woods. The bastard who shot Ned must have left some trace. He was on foot and used a rifle.'

Tom Smith, one of the new men he'd employed, touched his cap. 'We'll get our weapons and take a look-see.'

'Good man. We disturbed a poacher, as far as anyone else is concerned.'

Both men nodded, grim-faced. 'We'll take the nags, sir, in case we pick up a trail,' Smith said.

'Do it. Now get away whilst there's still a chance of catching him.'

His men ran off and as they departed the duke arrived. 'This is a bad business, Carshalton. Why would a poacher shoot your gamekeeper?'

'I can't talk now, your grace, but when we've got Ned comfortable I'd be grateful if you would spare me an hour so I can explain why I wished to see you.'

'Of course, that's why I'm here. Excellent, they're here with the trestle.' The duke stood up and stepped back to allow the four men to carefully move the injured man onto the makeshift stretcher.

Grey kept his hand firmly on the wound as this manoeuvre was completed. 'Right, Ned, you'll be inside and made comfortable very soon.' Bishop managed a weak smile but no more.

It took an unconscionable time to transport the injured man to the chamber prepared for him downstairs. The housekeeper was waiting with bandages, hot water and clean cloths. 'Leave poor Mr Bishop with me. I can take care of him until the doctor arrives.'

The woman appeared to understand the necessity to keep pressure on the wound and as he removed his hand she was ready with a clean pad and applied force herself. 'Thank you, Mrs Humphries, I'll leave him with you. I must get cleaned up and speak to his grace, then I'll be back to see how he does.' As he was leaving she spoke again.

'My lord, Lady Madeline accompanied his grace. She is in the drawing room with the ladies.'

Damnation! This young lady was the very last person he wanted to see today. As things stood he couldn't risk being seen to be paying her any attention. He'd surrounded his redoubtable grandmother with three equally elderly ladies in order to protect her. It was possible that anyone linked to him might be in grave danger. He should never have danced with her twice at the ball, as it could have given

Lady Madeline a false impression. Until this business was settled she must be firmly discouraged.

He met his grandmother in the hall. 'My dear boy, what a horrible thing to have happened. Forgive me for not offering to help, but I am not good with either illness or injury.'

'I didn't expect you to be personally involved, Grandmamma. You have organised the staff and that's all that was required of you. Can you please convey my sincere apologies to Lady Madeline and tell her I'm not able to speak to her?'

'Of course, I understand. I'll suggest that she returns to Silchester Court as no doubt his grace will be some time with you.'

The duke joined them. 'My sister can go to visit Miss Bagshot who is a near neighbour of yours, I believe.'

'Do it.' Grey smiled apologetically at his abrupt order. 'I beg your pardon, your grace, I'm overfond of issuing orders. I can lend you a nag so she has no need to return here.'

'My brother Bennett is similarly afflicted – comes of being a military man. If you could send for my carriage I'll speak to my sister.' The duke strode away and Grey cursed silently. He had offended the man and he desperately needed his help. Lord Sheldon, his brother, would have been better, but the duke must do in his stead.

He would wait in the study and try and marshal his thoughts. In order to get to this chamber he had to walk past the library. As he passed, a slight noise came from behind the half-open door. He froze. Could it be an intruder? He steadied his breathing and crept forwards.

* * *

Madeline settled the ladies as the tea arrived. One of them drew her aside. 'My dear, would you be so kind as to fetch my book? It's in my apartment. I find the stairs a sore trial these days. A footman will direct you there.'

'I should be pleased to get it, Lady Grimshaw.' Madeline hurried off and soon found the rooms she sought. The chambermaid helped her search, but the book wasn't anywhere to be seen.

'Her ladyship was in the library earlier, miss – you could try there.'

'Thank you, I'll do that. Where will I find this chamber?'

The library was on the ground floor and easy to locate. The helpful footman pointed to the door and dashed off on another errand, leaving her to enter alone. As she stepped in a curtain moved at the far end of the chamber. A careless servant had left a window ajar – she would close it, as draughts would not be good for the leather-bound books that filled the floor-to-ceiling bookshelves. She admired the book stand that enabled a reader to peruse a large volume without breaking its spine and paused to scan the titles. Good heavens! There was an entire section in French and another in Italian.

Then she spotted the missing volume on a side table by the fireplace. As she stooped to collect it, something whistled past her ear and thudded into the wall. She staggered back and, unable to keep her balance, fell towards the fire.

2

Grey hurtled through the door as Lady Madeline fell into the flames. He was at her side in two strides and with one hand he snatched a fistful of her skirt and with the other he grabbed a flailing arm and heaved with all his strength. He managed to prevent her head hitting the mantelshelf but couldn't prevent the fine muslin of her gown from dropping into the fire.

As the material caught he threw the girl to the floor and frantically rolled her over whilst beating at the flames with his hands. After a few seconds the danger was over and he sat back. 'Are you burned? Let me see your legs.'

She whispered urgently. 'I'm quite well, sir, but

there's a murderer behind your curtains. He threw a knife at me.'

He moved his head to indicate he'd understood. 'Let me assist you to the *chaise longue*.' The room smelled of burnt cloth and fear.

He pulled her to her feet and under the pretence of helping her was able to slip the poker under his jacket. She understood perfectly and made a great fuss of feeling faint.

'I fear the shock has made me unwell, my lord. Would you kindly open a window for me?'

Once she was seated, he moved smoothly towards the windows at the far end of the library but kept his head turned towards the girl as if unaware of the intruder. 'I'll do so immediately, my lady. What a dreadful thing to happen. It's hardly surprising you're feeling faint.'

His instincts warned him that whoever was hiding behind him was about to attack. In one swift movement he swung round using his momentum to propel the iron poker sideways and his blow found its mark. The intruder screamed and collapsed, taking the curtain down with him. Grey used the material to his advantage and rolled the man inside, then picked the flailing body up and banged the man's head hard against the floorboards. The struggle ceased and the bastard went limp.

'Have you killed him? Do I need to find some cord to tie him up?' The plucky girl was beside him, apparently unbothered by the violence.

'No thank you; the man's unconscious. I'll get my men to take him somewhere so I can interrogate him when he recovers his senses.' She was standing by his side and her ruined skirts were revealing far too much of her slender legs. He was about to suggest she retire and allow Humphries to find her something to wear when she gasped and swayed.

His arm shot out and he caught her as she swooned. What had caused her sudden collapse after being so stalwart throughout the past five minutes? Then he saw a growing pool of blood spreading across the boards. His blow with the poker must have done more damage than he'd realised.

With the girl senseless in his arms he strode down the room and shouldered his way out. He shouted for attention and two footmen appeared at a run. 'Here, take Lady Madeline; she has fainted. Put her in a guest room and let Lady Carshalton know she's needed. Her gown caught fire, but she's unhurt apart from the shock.' He passed her across to the more robust of the two and rushed back into the library, shouting over his shoulder as he did so. 'Send his grace to me immediately.'

He could apologise to the girl later for handing her over to his staff like an unwanted parcel, but now he had to do what he could to save the life of the assassin – he needed him alive if he was to find out who was behind these attacks.

* * *

Madeline recovered from her swoon as she was being carried along a passageway and for a moment was unable to focus her mind. Then shock at her position in the arms of a servant restored her. 'Put me down. I am perfectly well and able to walk on my own.' She was almost dropped, such was the relief of the unwilling footmen given the task of conveying her away from the horrible scene in the library. 'I want to speak to the duke. Where is he?'

The men exchanged worried glances and she was about to speak sharply when one of them looked at her skirts. Her cheeks suffused with colour and she nodded. 'Direct me to a bedroom, but I still need to speak to the duke.'

'I'll conduct you to a chamber, my lady, whilst

Sid here fetches his grace.' The speaker pointed to a hidden stairwell. 'Up here, my lady – it will save going through the main part of the house.'

She followed him in silence. Her thoughts were in turmoil. Someone had tried to kill her, she had almost been incinerated and then Lord Carshalton had grievously injured her attacker. What was going on at Heatherfield? First the gamekeeper had been shot and now this. The footman led her to a guest chamber and opened the door with a bow.

'I shall fetch Mrs Humphries to you as soon as she's free.'

He vanished, leaving her alone in a prettily furnished sitting room. The needs of the injured came before hers and so she settled down on the padded window seat, prepared to wait until her brother arrived. She wanted to go home, not to remain here and be given someone else's garments to wear. Lord Carshalton should have taken care of her himself. It was rag-mannered of him to hand her over so carelessly to a servant.

This morning she had been bored and longing for some excitement, but having a knife thrown at her and then being almost incinerated wasn't what she'd had in mind. If she was honest, she'd rather hoped to renew her brief acquaintance with the attractive man who had danced with her at the ball. Now she cordially disliked him. He was a violent and dangerous man and not a gentleman, for if he was he wouldn't have treated her so shabbily.

A while later a footman arrived carrying a tray with her luncheon, but there was still no sign of either the housekeeper or her brother. Her appetite had deserted her and she ignored the tray and then resumed her seat in the window embrasure.

From this vantage point she could see across the park to the attractive woodland where the shooting incident had taken place. The intruder in the library and the wounding of the gamekeeper had to be linked, but why would she have been targeted? It made no sense. She had never visited Heatherfield before and was a mere acquaintance of Lord Carshalton.

Had she been mistaken for someone else? The more she pondered the conundrum the less she understood it. The only person who could throw some light on this unpleasant business was Lord Carshalton himself, and he was hardly likely to come up and explain. When Beau eventually came to find her, she would get her answers from him.

The time dragged and she paced the floor hoping someone, anyone, would come to explain what was happening downstairs. Until she had a cloak to cover her gown she couldn't leave this chamber and she'd been incarcerated for over two hours.

Eventually there was the welcome sound of footsteps heading in her direction. Beau was coming at last. She ran to the door and flung it open to see Carshalton. Having the man she blamed for her situation in front of her was too much for her fragile sense of control.

'I could have been murdered and it's your fault. How could you abandon me to your staff like this? You are no gentleman and I intend to leave these premises immediately. Why has my brother not come to find me?'

Instead of being offended by her tirade, he merely smiled and gently pushed her back into the sitting room. 'Hush, child, there's no need to shout. I'm not in my dotage.'

Being treated like a schoolroom miss was the outside of enough and she glared at him. 'Don't you dare patronise me, Carshalton. I'm no child and well you know it.' If she'd stopped there all might have been well, but she was too incensed to think clearly. She raised her hand and poked him hard in the chest. It was like pushing at a wall. 'You didn't think me childish when you flirted with me a few weeks ago. I've been waiting for two hours for a cloak to put over my gown so that I can leave here – why hasn't one arrived?' This was accompanied by a second push.

His eyes narrowed and his friendly smile vanished. 'That will do. Sit down and be quiet before I do something we will both regret.'

She backed away hastily until she could position herself behind a solid chair. Without the support of this her legs would have given way. Then she remembered he'd told her to sit but she was incapable of further movement.

'I asked you to be seated. Was there some part of that instruction you failed to comprehend?' His tone was mild but there was steel in his words.

Her fingers refused to release their grip and she was incapable of speech. To her horror, unwanted tears trickled down her cheeks.

His expression changed instantly to concern and he was at her side. 'Come, sweetheart, I didn't intend to make you cry.' He uncurled her fingers and with his arm around her waist carefully put her on the daybed. Then he wiped her tears away with his handkerchief. 'There, that's better. I'm a brute to issue orders as if you were a soldier in my corps. Can you forgive me?'

She sniffed and the soft cloth was returned to her. She blew her nose and managed a weak smile. 'It's I who must beg your pardon. I should not...'

'Enough, it's forgotten.' He folded his length onto the chair she'd been clutching and smiled. 'I'm afraid you will be even more annoyed with me when I tell you the duke has left on a mission for me. The carriage is waiting, so you can leave as soon as my housekeeper finds you something to cover your gown.'

'Beau wouldn't depart without making sure I was unhurt.'

'I told him you were all right and being taken care of. Therefore, there was no need for him to waste time visiting you when there was something more urgent for him to do.'

Her wariness was replaced by anger at his abrupt and unhelpful remark. 'Since I arrived here this morning someone has tried to kill me and then I fell into the fire, and that's the best you can say? You're despicable and I shall depart now – I don't care if I've no cloak. There's no one here whose opinion matters to me.'

She scrambled to her feet and marched towards

the door, but he was quicker and his bulk prevented her escape. 'You shall leave soon, but not until I've told you what happened after you were brought here. Don't you want to know?'

She retreated but didn't resume her seat. 'I'm waiting. Kindly get on with it, as I'm not going to remain under your roof a moment longer than necessary.'

* * *

Grey wanted to shake some respect into the furious young lady who had the temerity to defy him. He clenched his fists and swallowed his ire. 'The man in the library met his maker before I was able to interrogate him, but I'm certain he was part of a plot to kill me.'

She looked less than impressed with his words and he didn't blame her. Good God, the wretched girl was tapping her foot. 'You arrived inopportunely and the man attempted to kill you in order to stop you warning me he'd gained entry to Heatherfield.'

'Is that it? I care not who is attempting to assassinate you, sir, but now I've been made part of this and so has my brother.'

He prepared to explain why he believed he was

being hunted, but she raised a hand to prevent him speaking. 'I don't want to know anything else. The duke will tell me when he returns.' She tilted her nose in the air and pursed her lips. 'Am I allowed to leave or do you intend to add abduction to your list of sins?'

He stepped to one side and bowed. He didn't trust himself to say anything polite. She sailed past him and as he watched her his anger changed to something far more dangerous. A wave of heat surged through him and there was an uncomfortable tightness in his breeches.

The girl had piqued his interest by her rejection and he intended to demonstrate to her that he wasn't a man to turn down such a challenge. He had a moderate amount of success with the fairer sex – indeed was renowned amongst his peers for having some of the most attractive ladies on his arm.

He had no intention of seducing the girl – that would be atrocious behaviour – but he wanted to demonstrate to her that he wasn't the villain she supposed he was. He would keep his lustful thoughts to himself – but that was going to be dammed hard as, without doubt, she was both highly desirable and intelligent. This was a lethal combination in his experience.

By the time he reached the entrance hall, the carriage was pulling away. His charm campaign must wait until he met Lady Madeline again. Ned Bishop should make a full recovery in time, so the doctor had told him, which was a relief as the man was invaluable to him.

Smith and Jenkins had returned from their search and were waiting to speak to him. He'd had refreshments sent to them so they would be content for a while yet. Before he could see them, he must ensure that his grandmother and her friends had suffered no ill effects from the excitement of the morning.

He found them in the small dining room where a cold collation had been laid out as usual.

'Grey, my dear boy, I do hope you haven't upset Lady Madeline.'

'No, Grandmamma, I haven't. I would say that she was enraged rather than upset.' He helped himself to a generous plateful and joined the ladies at the table.

'I'm not surprised she was angry with you. She came for a pleasant visit and was almost burnt to a crisp and her lovely gown was quite ruined.'

'A slight exaggeration, but you have the gist of it. I went upstairs intending to apologise and made a sad mull of it and only made matters worse. The fact that the duke agreed to assist me, and he left without talking to her, added to her annoyance.' He munched his way through several slices of succulent, home-bred ham before resuming the conversation.

'When the dust has settled I shall visit Silchester Court and make amends.'

'That's the least you can do, my boy – you must also replace her gown. We have been discussing this matter and know exactly what you must have made up for her – we've seen a perfect ensemble in the latest edition of *La Belle Assemblée*.'

He put down his cutlery and looked around the circle of expectant faces. 'In which case, I shall leave it in your capable hands. How long will it take to make such a garment?'

'I shall send word to my own mantua-maker today and she will send someone down with samples so we can choose the best material. We think that a Genoese satin would be ideal, as muslin is too fine to be worn in the winter.'

He raised a hand to stop her elaborating. 'I've no idea of what you speak. I'll leave it to your impeccable taste and have no wish to do more than pay the bill.'

The conversation moved on to the latest *on dits* from Town and he hastily finished his food and made his farewells. The ladies didn't know the full extent of the incident in the library and he had no intention of informing them.

The duke had needed no persuading to help when he'd seen the knife sticking in the panelling. Grey half-smiled when he recalled what Silchester had done when confronted with the cadaver. The duke had raised an eyebrow, nodded, then told him he was profoundly thankful that the man was already dead as that saved him the trouble of dispatching the villain himself.

The door to the library was locked and the room would remain so until his own men had time to put things right. He set off to speak to Ned. Smith and Jenkins leapt to their feet and saluted when Grey walked in – old habits die hard. Ned nodded from his bed.

'As you were, men, we've much to discuss. I take it you had no luck in the woods.'

'No, sir, we found nothing useful. Whoever it was made good their escape without leaving any clues.' Smith scratched his head. 'We ain't happy about this, Major. Some bugger's trying to do you in and he's got trained men to help him.'

'The attempts began before I arrived here – in fact, whilst I was still a serving officer. It has to be related to my work for Lord Wellesley.'

'I reckon as you're right, sir.' Bishop scowled. 'There must be something you learned when you were an intelligence officer what could ruin whoever's trying to top you.'

'Sit down, both of you. I should explain that most of the papers I carried from behind enemy lines were sealed. Once I'd delivered a verbal message I removed it from my memory.'

They sat for a few minutes digesting this statement. Grey broke the silence. 'The duke's gone to speak to the militia and hopefully he can persuade their commanding officer to search the neighbourhood. It's a close-knit community here and any strangers would be noticed.'

'I been thinking, sir, and reckon I might know why them varmints are after you,' Bishop told him.

'Go on, I'm listening.'

'Remember, a few months ago we had to go behind enemy lines and were almost captured?'

'I do indeed – that was a damned close thing and the fact that we were betrayed by one of our own made things worse.'

The men exchanged glances. 'It were that, sir,

and them papers you brought were invaluable and gave our troops an advantage when we marched through Portugal.'

'I'm sure you're right; however, I can't see that any of those events are relevant to what's happening now.'

'Captain Rogers was executed soon after for treason, weren't he?'

'Good God! You think this is revenge for that?' Grey leaned back in his chair and closed his eyes in order to collect his scattered thoughts. He had uncovered the traitor and Wellesley had done the rest. 'I know nothing of Rogers' family, but I do know that they were not informed he was executed, but that he'd lost his life in battle.'

'I reckon somehow the true state of affairs got back to his kin and it's them that are seeking revenge.'

'I believe between you that you might have solved the conundrum. The fact that a rifle was used to shoot you, Ned, makes this explanation even more plausible. Jenkins must go to London and visit Horse Guards. They will have the information we require.'

'I've sent for half a dozen extra men, all served

with me in the 95th – a bit long in the tooth but they'll be fine for what you want.'

'Thank you, Smith, that's an excellent notion. A pity the man died before I could question him. I'm hopeful the knife might prove a means to identify him as the design on the hilt is unusual. I've sent it to Horse Guards by express in the hope that someone there might recognise it.'

'Until you get a reply from London, sir, we'll be extra vigilant.'

3

Madeline entered through the front door moments behind her brother. When he saw her he swore. 'God's teeth! Your gown is destroyed – I'd no idea how close a thing it had been.'

She had been intending to castigate him for abandoning her but instead she flung herself into his arms. 'Someone threw a knife at me, I almost fell into the fire and if Lord Carshalton hadn't been there I would have burned.'

His arms closed around her and he hugged her tight. 'Sweetheart, I shouldn't have gone off without speaking to you first, but the matter was urgent.' He looked around and stared at the two footmen who were gawping at them and they slunk away. 'Come, you cannot remain down here as you are. I'll accompany you to your apartment and we can talk freely there without you having to change immediately.'

'No, Beau, I'll join you in the study shortly. I'd much prefer to change my gown and tidy up first.'

Lottie was shocked but held her tongue and did her duty; soon Madeline was on her way to the study. Her brother had sent for coffee and cake – both of them preferred this aromatic brew to tea.

'I expected you to be longer, sweetheart, but I'm glad you were not. I'll tell you everything I know about the incident and why I agreed to leave so precipitously.'

Madeline collected a slice of plum cake, and cup of coffee, and placed it on a side table by the chair she intended to use. 'First tell me why you had to go to Heatherfield so urgently.'

'Carshalton was an intelligence officer and before he resigned his commission two attempts were made on his life. He'd hoped that he would be safe on an estate that didn't previously belong to his family. However, as you're well aware, whoever is trying to assassinate him has discovered his whereabouts.'

'I still don't see how that requires your assistance.'

'He wants me to use my contacts in Town to discover if there are any rumours circulating about him or his family. My errand this morning was to contact the militia – again he thought my request would be taken more seriously than his as he's a comparative stranger in the neighbourhood.'

'I must only suppose that whoever had broken into the library was startled by my appearance, as I can't possibly be involved with this.'

'I'm inclined to agree with you. Whatever the reason for the attacks, it's no business of ours. I've done as much as I'm prepared to and I don't want you visiting Heatherfield again.'

'I've no intention of doing so. Although Lord Carshalton is a handsome man, I could never like a gentleman who can kill another without compunction.' Her brother raised an eyebrow. 'I know that Bennett was a serving officer but he never showed any signs of being a violent man once he returned.'

'Carshalton shouldn't be blamed for what he did, Madeline. If he hadn't dispatched your attacker, I would have done so myself.'

She stared at him in shock. 'I don't believe you. Taking another person's life, unless you are a soldier, cannot be right.'

'I would expect you to feel that way, little one. A

member of the fairer sex is not supposed to understand such matters.' He leaned back in his chair and
smiled. 'There's something I must discuss with you.
I know you enjoy being the chatelaine of Silchester,
but I think it's time you stepped aside and let my
very efficient staff do the job they're more than ade-
quately paid for.'

'If I'm not to be running this establishment in
future, what am I expected to do with my day?'

'Visit your friends, paint watercolours, practise
on the pianoforte – spend your time doing what
other young ladies of your age are doing. You and
your sister will be spending your first Season in
Town next spring and I'm sure you will need to replenish your wardrobes before then.'

Madeline put down her cup. 'Let me get this
quite clear, Beau. From henceforth you expect me to
drift around the place doing absolutely nothing?'

'I expect you to behave as the sister of the Duke
of Silchester. Are you going to eat your cake? If not,
then I'll do so.'

'Take it. I've lost my appetite. I'm going to the
library to find myself a book. I shall not be joining
you for dinner.'

Without giving him the opportunity to respond

to her comment she stalked off, but didn't go to the library; instead she returned to her apartment and changed into her habit. Perhaps a ride around the park would restore her good humour.

Her brother wasn't a stupid man, but sometimes he could be remarkably dense. Did he know her so poorly that he thought she'd be content without a purpose to her life? When Mama had died five years ago, becoming the hostess of this grand place had made her grief easier to bear.

Giselle, her younger sister, was happy being a lady of leisure but this didn't suit her at all. Whatever Beau said about the matter, she was determined to find herself something interesting to occupy her time that didn't involve the insipid pastimes he'd suggested.

Good heavens! He'd been happy to allow her to arrange the house party this summer in order to find Bennett a suitable bride, so why did he think she would be content with nothing to do?

When she got to the stables something prompted her to ask for Beau's recently acquired bay to be saddled for her. She told the head groom there was no need for anyone to accompany her, as she intended to remain within the grounds.

She'd not been out for long when a pheasant

flew out beneath the animal's hoofs. He shied violently, took hold of the bit, and bolted.

* * *

The militia arrived at Heatherfield and Grey quickly explained to the captain in charge what had taken place. He also showed him the corpse stored in an outbuilding.

'My lord, we shall dispose of this body for you and there will be no further investigations. You may rest assured that my men and I will search the area and question the local populace. I shall report back to you with any information I might find.' The man saluted and remounted his horse. The troop split into three smaller groups and began their investigation.

When he'd left his regiment on the Peninsula he'd thought his days of violence and danger were over. He must try and persuade his grandmother to return to the family estates where she would be safe.

Despite her age she'd dealt calmly with the events of the morning as if murder and mayhem were a regular occurrence. He found her and her bosom bows happily chatting together. The topic of conversation was Lady Madeline.

'There you are, my dear boy, are you coming to join us for a dish of tea?' His grandmother pointed to an empty chair and reluctantly he took it. He'd no intention of being involved in any discussion about that particular young lady – he might inadvertently reveal his interest in her.

'No tea, thank you, Grandmamma, I've just come to make sure you ladies are recovered from the shock of this morning's event.'

'Poachers are a fact of life, my boy – nothing to get het up about.'

'I'm glad you are so sanguine, but until we've apprehended the perpetrator could I ask you all to stay away from the woods?'

One of her friends laughed. 'My lord, we seldom leave the parterre, so there's no danger of us wandering over there.'

'Perhaps it would be better if you cut short your visit in the circumstances, Grandmamma, and return to Blakely Hall.'

'I'll do no such thing. I intend to get to know you properly. Your father and I were estranged, but that was between us and has nothing to do with you.'

'In which case, ma'am, I'll not mention the matter again.' He was about to stand up but she prevented him.

'I'm sure you heard us, my dear, talking about the delightful young lady who visited. You didn't tell me you were acquainted with such an illustrious family.'

'I've only met them once before. After her unpleasant experience this morning it's unlikely she will visit here again.'

'Such a lovely girl, don't you think? Isn't it time that you started looking for a wife?'

He'd heard quite enough of this nonsense. 'Absolutely not. I'm in no hurry to enter parson's mousetrap. As I already have an heir in my cousin, there's no urgency to set up my nursery, is there?'

'It's a great shame that your remaining relatives refuse to meet you. They should be grateful the estates were not entailed or they would be living in very modest circumstances.'

'From what the lawyers told me the income they receive is more than adequate and the fortune I inherited is not really needed.' This was a highly unsuitable topic to be discussing in front of others and he drew it to a close. 'Forgive me, ladies, duty calls. No doubt we will meet again at dinner.'

When his ancient relative had joined him she'd come with a positive retinue of followers. As well as her dresser, a hatchet-faced woman whom he avoided, she'd had two outriders and two on the box of her carriage. Exactly what these servants were doing to occupy their time he'd no idea.

He left them to their chatter and went to see how Ned Bishop was progressing. As he approached, the sound of voices made him increase his pace. He pushed open the door to find Jenkins and Smith were there before him.

He waved them back to their seats. 'As you were, men, I've just come to check again how Ned does.' He nodded towards the injured gamekeeper who was looking remarkably robust for a man apparently on his deathbed a few hours ago. 'I'm glad to see you looking better. The militia are searching the area again but I doubt they'll find anything. I expect that their presence will deter another attack – at least for a while.'

Satisfied that he'd done all he could for the moment, Grey dismissed his men; having no further estate business to deal with, he decided to take out his new high-perch phaeton. He'd not had the opportunity until now.

The perfectly matched grey geldings he'd purchased at the same time were also in need of exercise. He sent word to the stables to have the vehicle brought around and then collected his pistol and made sure it was loaded – he could hardly go out with a rifle, but this would fit easily in his riding cape pocket.

When he appeared at the front door he frowned. Jenkins and Smith were mounted and waiting to accompany him.

'There's no necessity for you to mollycoddle me, boys; I don't intend to go far.'

Smith touched his cap. 'You ain't going nowhere, sir, on yer own. Me and Bill reckon you need someone with you until this matter's done.'

There was no point in arguing. He raised his whip in salute and climbed aboard the carriage. He'd not driven a phaeton before and it was damned high – alarmingly so. He gathered the reins, released the brake and flicked his whip; the greys surged forward. It took him a few moments to regain control but once he had, he began to enjoy the experience.

Jenkins rode alongside. 'It's a grand turnout, and you'll be able to see for miles from up there.'

'I can indeed. We'll stick to the most frequented lanes; it should be safer.'

After a couple of miles he saw an open field and decided to turn his vehicle onto it so he could spring the horses. He wanted to know how safe his new purchase was when travelling at speed. He gestured

with his whip and his two men turned to follow him.

'There's no need for you to come with me. You
can remain here, as I'll be in view at all times.'

'We'll go into the middle of the field, sir, then
we're not far from you if anything happens.'

On that cheery note Grey settled himself more
firmly on the seat, pressed his boots against the edge
and snapped the whip. He was almost catapulted
from the box as, instead of going forwards, the
horses veered sideways and the phaeton rocked
alarmingly. What the hell had startled them?

He had barely regained his balance and control
of his team when a massive bay hunter crashed out
of the woods. The animal was riderless and he could
see from the side saddle that it was a lady who had
come off. He managed to calm his team, twisted the
reins around the post, pulled on the brake and
scrambled down.

Jenkins had taken off after the loose horse and
Smith was riding towards him. 'I'm going in to find
the rider. Stay with my horses.'

Although the leaves were turning brown they'd
yet to begin their autumnal fall. He pushed aside
the brambles and moved into the wood. Ahead of
him was what looked like an impenetrable stand of

closely growing trees – how the devil had that brute of a horse fought his way through this without apparent injury?

He looked around and some yards to the left saw evidence that the beast had arrived that way. He cut through the undergrowth, his heavy riding cape snagging the brambles and branches as he did so. He emerged on a narrow path and began to follow the hoof prints, praying that the lady who'd taken a tumble wasn't seriously injured.

'Can you hear me? Are you hurt? Call out and I'll come to you.'

A voice he immediately recognised yelled back. 'Over here, I'm stuck in a hawthorn hedge but otherwise unhurt.'

Grey ran towards the voice and as he rounded the corner, sure enough, there was Lady Madeline embedded in the prickles. Her face was badly scratched, but apart from that she seemed to have suffered no serious injury.

He skidded to a halt beside her. 'Keep still, you're making matters worse by wriggling.' After a short struggle he managed to extricate her. He was tempted to put her across his knee for being so foolhardy as to ride a horse that was totally unsuitable – instead he spoke his mind. 'What the devil were you thinking of? You could have been killed. Surely the duke didn't give you leave to ride his horse?'

Her expression changed from friendly to furious. 'It's none of your business, Carshalton. I don't need your approval for anything I do.'

'Quite true, but as your stupidity not only risked your own life but mine as well I believe I am entitled to an opinion.'

Immediately she was contrite. 'I beg your pardon, I spoke without thought. You're quite right to castigate me – I can't think what maggot got into my brain and persuaded me to ride this horse.'

He delved into his pocket and produced a clean handkerchief. 'Here, let me remove the worst of the gore from your face.' She remained still under his administration but was tense beneath his hands. 'There, that's the best I can do. Fortunately the scratches are superficial and I'm certain they'll not mar your skin.'

'Thank you. I see now that you're not dressed for riding. Is your carriage nearby? I hate to make myself a further nuisance but I fear I cannot bring myself to ride that horse again.'

'You would do so over my dead body, young lady. I'll drive you home and one of my men can lead your mount.'

In all the excitement he'd quite forgot to mention that his vehicle was a high-perch phaeton and that her journey to Silchester Court might well prove to be as eventful as her ride. His opinion of his new team was less than favourable and he didn't trust them to behave themselves.

4

Madeline was relieved that Carshalton didn't offer his arm but allowed her to pick her way through the undergrowth unassisted. She was badly bruised from her fall and dreading the inevitable confrontation with her brother when he discovered her stupidity.

His lordship had been walking in front of her, holding back the branches to allow her to make her way without being whipped across the face. She stepped into the field expecting to see a racing curricle but was horrified to find an even more alarming vehicle awaiting.

'I can't possibly travel in that. I've no head for heights.' His horses were restless, their nostrils flaring and eyes wild. Her heart sank to her boots and unwisely she spoke what was in her head. 'Your team don't look at all steady. I should much prefer to ride one of your groom's mounts. I'm perfectly safe riding astride.'

'Have you completely lost your senses? First you take out a horse that's far too strong for you and then you intend to compound your foolishness by gallivanting through the countryside riding astride. Your reputation would be in shreds if you were seen and the duke would call me out for allowing such a thing to take place.'

'If I go across country I'll not be seen. The other side of this woodland is our land, therefore anyone who sees me will be in our employ, and would not dream of passing an opinion on the matter.'

From his expression he was unused to being gainsaid. 'You'll travel beside me, young lady, or you will walk home. I leave the decision to you.'

She viewed the high-perch phaeton with disfavour and decided a three-mile walk would be preferable to scrambling up on the box. 'I'll walk. I take it your man will return my mount. I bid you good afternoon, my lord.'

Before he could respond she picked up her skirts and dashed back into the wood. She would be footsore and weary by the time she reached her destination, but anything was preferable to having to sit beside that irascible and autocratic man in such an unsteady vehicle.

At any moment she expected him to come after her, to demand that she stopped and return with him, but he didn't. After trudging for ages she bitterly regretted her impulsive decision, and by the time she tottered into the stable yard her discomfort had turned to anger. A gentleman wouldn't have allowed a lady to undergo such an unpleasant experience but would have insisted she accompanied him instead.

The first thing she saw was the horse who had thrown her already rubbed down and comfortable in his stall. She stiffened her spine and, not looking to either right or left, she marched along the path to the house, hoping she still had the energy to get to her apartment.

Somehow she managed to stagger up the stairs and gain the sanctuary of her rooms. Lottie was waiting for her. 'My lady, I've been that worried. I expected you back an age ago. Your face is scratched – did you take a tumble?'

'I did and was obliged to walk home. Please help me remove my boots – my feet are so painful. I should like to soak them in a basin of hot water, but before that I must remove this wretched habit. Such garments are not meant for walking and I fear it's quite beyond repair.'

Her abigail deftly removed her outer garments and helped her slip on a loose morning gown. As soon as Madeline was comfortable the girl turned her back, lifted one boot and pulled it through her legs in order to remove it.

Every tug was agony.

'It won't budge. I think your foot has swollen. Shall I try the other one?'

'No, I don't think I could stand it. If I prop my feet on a stool for an hour or two I expect it will be easier for you to remove them.'

Her maid looked unconvinced but brought the footstool anyway. 'I'll fetch you some refreshments, you must be sharp-set after such a long walk.'

* * *

Grey was tempted to go after her and insist that she accompany him but decided, as she'd so rudely pointed out, what she did was none of his business. 'Smith, drive this back to Heatherfield. I'll ride your horse and lead the gelding. Jenkins, I suppose you'd better come with me.'

He'd selected Smith as he was the better whipster of the two. He mounted and took the reins of the duke's animal. 'I'd better go by the lane; the path's too narrow to accommodate two horses abreast.'

Three-quarters of an hour later he arrived at Silchester and explained his unexpected appearance. He was directed inside where he found the duke in his study. 'Your grace, Lady Madeline went out on that large bay gelding of yours and took a tumble. She was unhurt but refused to remount the horse. She also rejected my offer to drive her home in my phaeton and insisted on walking. I wished to inform you before going out to find her.'

'Serves her right for doing something so stupid. There will be ample opportunity for her to regret her rash decision on the long trek home. No, I don't want you to ride out and meet her and neither do I want any grooms to go.' He waved towards a comfortable leather-covered armchair in front of the cheerily burning fire. 'Take a seat, Carshalton. I'll send for coffee – unless you prefer something stronger.'

Grey was reluctant to leave the girl to walk the

entire distance but he could hardly disagree with her brother. 'Thank you, coffee would be excellent. I apologise for appearing here. I don't want to bring my problems to your doorstep. I can tell you what I think is the reason behind these attempts on my life.'

He spent a convivial time with his host before taking his leave. As he crossed the grand hall he spotted a footman. 'Direct me to Lady Madeline's apartment, if you please.'

It was a breach of etiquette to visit a lady in her rooms but he was determined to discover for himself that she was safely returned. He thought her brother's decision harsh but supposed the long walk might teach her not to do anything so dangerous again.

He had no intention of actually going into the apartment, merely enquiring at the door as to how she did. His knock was answered by a soft call to enter. He pushed open the door and bowed to the figure seated in a chair by the fire.

'My lady, I beg your pardon for intruding, but I wished to ensure that you were safe before I left.'

'My lord, as you can see, I'm perfectly well apart from the fact that I can't remove my boots.'

Forgetting he'd intended to remain in the passageway, he strode in and dropped to his knees beside her. 'Will you allow me to assist you? These boots must come off immediately if you're not to do irreparable harm to your feet.'

He took out a stiletto from his boot top – carrying this was a habit he'd acquired on the Peninsula. 'I'll try and tug them off but if they still won't shift, they must be cut.'

'These are my best boots. They mustn't be destroyed. I'm sure they will come off in a little while.'

Gently he picked one foot up and pulled. She couldn't prevent a gasp of pain. 'Foolish child, you should have sent for help immediately.' He cradled the heel of the boot in his lap and then rammed the blade down the seam at the side and, as the leather parted, she sighed with relief. Without removing it he did the same to the right foot.

'My lord, let me take care of my mistress now.' Her maid had joined them and he was glad of it. 'Do you have a basin of warm water and some clean cloths?'

'Yes, sir, I'll fetch them at once.'

'This will be painful, sweetheart, but I'll be as careful as I can.' He eased her right foot from the mangled boot and his eyes widened. Her stocking was stained red. Her injuries were worse than he'd anticipated. 'Your stocking will need soaking off. Put your foot in the basin and I'll remove the other boot.'

He'd expected her to be upset, to rail at him that she wouldn't be in this predicament if he'd allowed her to ride astride. Her response was quite un-expected.

'It serves me right for stomping off in high dud-geon. Unlike your boots, sir, mine were not intended to be walked in.' She wriggled her toes and the water turned pink. 'I hope I've not done myself any serious damage – I cannot abide sitting about all day.'

'I'll leave your maid to take care of you now, my lady. I'm sure she'll send for the physician if you need his attention.' He'd already spent far too long in her private chambers. He rose smoothly to his feet.

'Thank you for your assistance; I hope next time we meet it will be in more favourable circum-stances.' Despite her scratched face and dishevelled appearance her smile lit up the room. It made him forget his decision to avoid any sort of emotional entanglement until he was free of the danger that surrounded him.

'I certainly hope so, Lady Madeline, and next

time I ask you to drive with me it will be in my curricle.'

'In which case, sir, I should accept your offer.'

* * *

'How bad are they, Lottie?' Madeline asked her maid.

'The blister's burst and that's what caused the blood, my lady. I reckon you'll be off your feet for a day or two whilst they heal.'

'Botheration! Will I need the doctor?'

'Not unless they turn putrid. I'll fetch some of that ointment we used last time you cut yourself, then I'll bandage them.'

The girl removed the discoloured water and replaced it with fresh. The warmth of the liquid was soothing on her injuries and she closed her eyes, allowing herself to drift off. The past few hours had been the most exciting of her life – but she hoped never to repeat any of the experiences.

Lord Carshalton was attractive, and although of a similar disposition to her older brothers she believed she could come to like him. Autocratic, dictatorial men held no fears for her – after all she had learned to live very happily with two such specimens. In fact, if she was honest, she rather preferred a gentleman who took command. The twins, Aubrey and Peregrine, were more like Giselle – that is to say they avoided unpleasantness and were more relaxed about matters in general. This attitude was all very well, but it didn't get things done.

Once her feet were dealt with she was left with the problem of how to move to somewhere more comfortable. She could hardly hop as both feet were equally sore. Lottie had gone to organise a supper tray and the chambermaid was busy elsewhere.

Maybe she could crawl across – decidedly undignified but needs must. She was on her hands and knees when her brother walked in.

'Allow me, my dear.' He leaned down and picked her up. 'Are you heading for the *chaise longue*?'

'The daybed, if you please, Beau.' Once she was comfortably settled he pulled up a chair. 'I've no idea how I'm to manage for the next day or two unless I scrabble about like a crab.'

'I'll have two footmen outside your sitting room and whenever you want to move they can come in and carry you.'

Her cheeks flushed. 'Certainly not. I'd rather crawl, thank you.'

'In which case, my love, I must act as your per-

sonal assistant. I'll remain – no, don't look so horrified – you'll hardly know I'm here.' His expression
was serious but his eyes twinkled.

She reached behind her and threw a cushion,
which he deftly caught before it did any damage.
'Go away, brother. I'll manage without your assistance.'

An alarming racket in the passageway outside
almost caused her to slide from the daybed. Her
brother smiled knowingly and stood up. 'Good, your
chariot's arriving. I've found a bath chair for you – a
bit dilapidated – but it will serve the purpose won-
derfully.'

He opened the door and a footman pushed this
object into the room and then retreated, having at
no time raised his eyes and looked in her direction.
'Perfect! I can manoeuvre myself into it and then
Lottie can push me about. Thank you for thinking of
it. I don't deserve your consideration after my disgraceful behaviour today.'

'I should have realised you were not wearing
suitable footwear and come out to fetch you. Both
Carshalton and I thought we would have a deal of
fence-mending to do in order to regain your
approval.'

'I intend to forget the events of today and I hope

you will do so as well. Lord Carshalton's asked me to drive with him in his curricle. Would you have any objection if I did so?'

'As long as you remain on my lands and have grooms accompanying you then you have my permission. However, until I'm certain there's no danger attached to being in his company you must remain apart. I've told him how I feel and he agrees.'

Her stomach clenched at his words. 'Does he think there'll be more attempts on his life? Surely the arrival of the militia will chase any other villains away?'

'One would hope so, my dear, but one cannot be sure. Our brothers and sister will be returning next week and I thought you might like to arrange an informal supper party to celebrate? Carshalton and his grandmother can be added to your invitation list.'

'Thank you, that will give me something to think about whilst I'm trapped up here for the next two days.'

* * *

The novelty of trundling around in a bath chair soon faded and Madeline was more than ready to rejoin her brother downstairs two days after her accident. Her feet were tender, but sufficiently healed to allow her to shuffle about the place.

'Have you settled on a date for the soirée, Madeline?' Beau enquired when he found her in the small drawing room.

'I have; it shall be the weekend after next. Perry and Aubrey are returning next week and Giselle is coming home tomorrow. I've a list of two dozen names – there'll be sufficient couples for dancing. Do I have your permission to employ musicians?'

'You may do whatever you wish, my love. It's been horribly quiet here without our siblings. I almost think back to the house party with fond memories.'

She laughed. 'I was thinking we might repeat the experience for the Christmas festivities. Bennett and Grace will have returned from their wedding trip by then and I should like to spend time with them both.'

'Let me see who you intend to invite before you send out cards. I don't want my brothers and I to be pursued by hopeful young ladies as we were last time.'

'Have you heard any news from Heatherfield? Is Lord Carshalton progressing with the investigation?'

'I know no more about the matter than you do. The militia are still searching the neighbourhood but haven't discovered any of the would-be murderers.'

'I hope the matter's resolved soon, for it must be decidedly unpleasant for Lady Carshalton to be unable to go about without an armed guard.' Although she didn't mention his lordship, they both knew her concerns were more for him than his grandmother.

5

Grey was worried that his grandmother had been adversely affected by the unfortunate events. Three days had passed and she was almost taciturn and had sent her friends away. He hoped his good news would raise her spirits.

'Grandmamma, we've had an invitation to an informal supper party at Silchester Court next weekend. I hope you will feel more yourself by then.'

She continued to stare into the fire without answering for a few minutes, but then she sat back and smiled. 'How kind of them to think of us, especially after what happened when they were here. I should love to go.'

'Excellent. I'll send an acceptance note immediately. You will also be pleased to know that the area is clear. The militia captain has agreed to send out a regular patrol to ensure there are no further incidents.' He joined her in front of the fire, flicking aside his coat-tails before he sat.

'I would like to visit St Albans, my boy; I believe there is much of historical value to be seen. Although the abbey is in a sad state of disrepair, I wish to see it. I had not liked to ask whilst there was any risk attached to a visit away from here.'

'The weather is set fair, so I suggest we go tomorrow. You must take your maid for company, as I shall ride. The drive is no more than two hours when the roads are dry. If we leave at eight o'clock we should arrive in good time.'

'I should prefer to go next Monday. I have letters to write tomorrow and I don't care to travel at the week's end.'

'Very well, Monday it shall be. Grandmamma, I wish you would reconsider leaving here. Although I love to have your company I'm too busy to entertain you, and now that your friends have gone you will be lonely.'

She nodded and leaned across to pat his hand affectionately. 'That's one of the letters I intend to write, my dear, for I've now decided to depart in November. The weather becomes inclement and the roads impossible after that.'

'In which case, I'll make every effort to spend time with you until you leave. I've been alone for much of my life and I was delighted to discover that I had a loving relative. I just wish the rift could be repaired between my uncle and cousin.'

'As do I. The feud was none of your making and it's ridiculous for my youngest son to hold a grudge.'

A footman appeared to tell Grey he was needed in the study, and he apologised and left his ancient relative to her book.

Smith was waiting for him. He greeted him with a wave, indicating he should take a seat in front of the desk.

His man shook his head. 'No, I'll not be stopping. I just came in to tell you that four of the men I sent for have arrived. I've billeted them with us above the stables. Do you have any orders?'

'They must familiarise themselves with their surroundings and let the local populace see that they are employed here. I don't want them being mistaken for miscreants.'

'They'll be right glad of regular employment, sir, and after a good scrub under the stable pump, and wearing the new togs you've put by for them, they'll look more the thing. They've had a hard time of it these past few years.'

'Once we have a full complement you can mount regular patrols around the perimeter of my estate. Jenkins can leave for London now – there's no urgency so he can travel by the common stage.'

He pulled open the desk drawer and removed a handful of silver coins. 'This should be more than enough to get him there and back, and pay for a night's lodging as well.'

'Right you are, sir. Would you be wanting to meet the new men?'

'Of course, but I'll give them time to settle first. By the way, I'm taking Lady Carshalton to St Albans on Monday and I want you to accompany us. Probably not necessary, but I'm not taking any risks.'

'Best to be careful.' Smith touched his forehead and marched off.

* * *

'A note has come for you, my lady. The groom is waiting for your reply,' Peebles announced.

Madeline took the letter from the butler and

broke the wax seal. She scanned the contents and smiled.

Dear Lady Madeline,

I am visiting St Albans on Monday and as my friends have returned to their respective homes I was wondering if you would like to accompany me? I do not like to travel alone in a carriage. There's no need to bring your maid as I shall have mine.

If you agree then I shall collect you at nine o'clock. We should be home before dark. A verbal response is all that is necessary.

How kind of Lady Carshalton to think to include her. 'Please ask the groom to tell Lady Carshalton I should be delighted to accompany her.'

She had visited this town once before, but a day out was always a treat. No doubt the elderly ladies had departed because of the horrid events last week. If Lord Carshalton had been going then she would have refused the invitation, as her brother had made it quite clear she mustn't associate with his lordship until the danger from these unknown assassins was definitely over.

Beau was in his study and put down the letter he

was reading with a sigh of exasperation. 'Well, my dear, what can I do for you? As you can see I'm busy with estate business.'

Hardly an auspicious start to the conversation. She explained the reason for her visit. 'As you removed the running of the household from my hands, I have nothing to do all day. Once Giselle and the twins come home, I'll be content.'

'Very well, you may go. I believe that Carshalton said his grandmother has her own outriders, so I've no need to send anyone from here. If there's nothing else, kindly go away and let me get on with this wretched paperwork.'

As she was about to leave he called her back. 'I apologise for being so curmudgeonly, sweetheart. I shall be relieved when my estate manager returns from visiting his sick mother and can resume his duties. Shall we play billiards when I've finished?'

'I'd love to. I shall go and practise and hope to make a better fist of it this time.'

Billiards was a gentleman's pastime but when the family were at home alone, she and Giselle were allowed to play.

* * *

On Monday morning she was smartly dressed in a green promenade gown and matching pelisse. Her bonnet was lined with the same material and even her half-kid boots were green. Beau had handed her a small purse of coins before he left to visit an outlying farm, and these were carefully stowed in her reticule.

The carriage appeared at precisely nine o'clock and a footman was waiting to precede her in order to let down the steps and hand her into the vehicle.

Her stomach turned over when she saw that Lord Carshalton, riding a magnificent black stallion, was also outside. She shouldn't go, but it would be uncivil to refuse after they had made a detour to collect her.

The fact that there were three other riders accompanying the carriage reassured her she would be in no danger and that her brother could not possibly object.

'Good morning, Lady Madeline. I'd no idea until today that you were accompanying us to St Albans. I'm surprised that his grace agreed to the jaunt but delighted that he did so.'

She ran lightly down the steps and smiled up at him. 'I wasn't aware that you were coming, but as you have two men on the box and three outriders I'm sure my brother would have no objection.'

His expression changed and she skipped into the carriage before he could send her back to the house. He could hardly drag her from the vehicle once she was safely seated next to his venerable grandmother.

'Good morning, Lady Carshalton. Thank you so much for inviting me. I haven't visited St Albans for several years and I'm so looking forward to it.'

'Good morning, my dear. You look very smart today. Is that a new ensemble?'

'No, I've had it since last autumn.' The carriage rocked and they were in motion. Her heart stopped hammering against her bodice now she was certain she wouldn't be forcibly removed from the squabs.

Madeline had had to take the seat opposite her ladyship, as the space beside her was already occupied by her abigail, Bates. This was a strange state of affairs, as one would expect a servant to sit apart from their mistress.

The maid was hard-faced and unfriendly – not at all the sort of person she could feel happy to have looking after her.

'I was surprised that Lord Carshalton has come

today. I was anticipating an outing without a gentleman in tow.'

The old lady chuckled. 'He insisted on coming with us, my dear, but I'm sure he'll find something with which to occupy himself whilst we look at the sights.'

'I found a pamphlet about the ancient wall, which can still be seen there, and the ruined cathedral. Would you care to peruse it?'

'No thank you, I intend to sleep. I'm not accustomed to rising so early in the morning.'

The maid adjusted the rugs over her mistress's knees and scowled at Madeline as if daring her to speak again.

The countryside they were passing through was familiar, but soon they would turn onto the toll road and then everything would be new to her. They were quite a cavalcade passing down the narrow country lane with three outriders and Lord Carshalton accompanying them.

Half an hour or so later she saw her companion's two servants riding across the fields and wondered where they were going. Forgetting she was supposed to be silent and allow her ladyship to sleep she spoke up. 'Your men are leaving us, Lady Carshalton; why is that?'

A remarkably alert response came immediately. 'They will be going ahead to arrange for refreshments at a suitable hostelry. This is a busy road and it wouldn't do to stop anywhere unless we have a private parlour.'

'I see. I apologise for waking you, but I was surprised to see them go.'

The carriage settled back into silence again and now both her companions were fast asleep. The sun shone through the windows, making the carriage unpleasantly stuffy. The maid should be asked to open the window but Madeline had no wish to wake her so decided to do this task herself.

She slid along the squabs until she was at the far side of the vehicle and then leaned across to unbutton the leather strap. She held on to this so there would be no sudden noise to wake the sleeping ladies.

A cool refreshing breeze flooded into the carriage and then a rider drew alongside and his lordship looked in. He nodded at the gently snoring women. 'Would you care to come up with me for a while?' He spoke softly so as not to wake them. She nodded and he leaned in and opened the door. 'Move forward and I'll lift you out.'

She did as he bid and was whisked from the carriage as if she weighed nothing at all and then she was positioned sideways in front of his lordship. His man quietly closed the door and then both riders reined back and let the carriage move ahead of them.

'I can't tell you how glad I am to be in the fresh air. I thank you for offering to take me pillion.'

He had shifted back in the saddle allowing her more room, but despite him having one arm firmly around her waist she felt extremely unstable balanced so precariously.

'I don't think this was a good idea after all. I'm in imminent danger of falling unless I ride astride and that's impossible in the gown I'm wearing.'

He reined in and once they were stationary lowered her to the ground. 'You're quite right; this was an idiotic notion of mine. Smith, ride after the carriage and get it to wait for us.' His man cantered away.

'Fortunately I'm wearing footwear suitable for walking. I've no wish for a repeat performance of last time as my feet have only just recovered...' Madeline stopped, horrified she'd been so indelicate as to mention her feet.

'I wouldn't have suggested it if I wasn't aware you had on walking boots.' He pulled the reins of his huge horse over its ears and then looped them across his arm. 'You should not have come; the duke will be most displeased.'

'When I agreed to accompany your grand-mother I'd no idea you were coming too. I should have politely declined the invitation if I'd known. I could hardly refuse to get into the carriage once she'd arrived, now could I?'

He offered his free arm to her and she placed her gloved hand on it. 'I gave my word to your brother that I'd keep my distance from you for the sake of your safety, and I'm not happy that I've broken it.'

'I'll explain to him it was entirely my fault. I shall enjoy the stroll, sir. It is particularly beautiful in this lane now the leaves are turning golden. Although I'd prefer to be able to see the surrounding coun-tryside.'

His arm tensed beneath her fingers. He was staring ahead with narrowed eyes. She was about to enquire what was wrong when he leaned down and whispered in her ear.

'There's someone hiding in the woods ahead. I want you to lead my horse and continue to talk as if I was with you. Can you do that?'

Her mouth was so dry she couldn't speak so she nodded instead. 'Good girl. I'll be close by. It's me they're after and they won't reveal themselves until I'm close enough to shoot. The hedges on either side mean they can't use their rifles.'

She took the reins and prayed the horse wouldn't object to being led by a female. He removed his riding coat and draped it over the saddle, then he was gone. Her heart was hammering so loudly she could scarcely think.

'Come along, old fellow, we must do as we're told and continue as if nothing untoward is taking place.' The animal nudged her in the back as though encouraging her to resume her walk. She was supposed to keep talking as if Carshalton was still with her but she couldn't think of anything intelligent to say.

'I hope the carriage is not too far ahead. I have no intention of walking for miles, however scenic the route.' She waited a few moments and then continued as if he'd replied.

'I should like coffee and perhaps a piece of cake if there's any available...'

* * *

Grey kept to the shadow thrown by the hedge. He made his way stealthily towards the copse a hundred yards away in which his assailants were waiting to ambush him. Where the hell was Smith? A cold shiver slid down his back. Had he been ambushed already?

He was now equidistant between Madeline and the trees and he could hear her bravely carrying on a one-sided conversation as he'd asked. Thank God his grandmother was safe and wouldn't be subjected to anything that could cause her to have a fatal apoplexy.

He paused to remove his pistols from the deep pockets in his topcoat – he checked they were primed and loaded – and then continued to creep forwards. He was a crack shot with a rifle, but he would have to be no more than a few feet from his opponents to have any hope of killing them with a pistol.

He had been alerted to the presence of these men when he'd seen a flash of a white face amidst the leaves. An ex-veteran would know to wind a muffler around his face, so the men waiting to attack him might not be as skilled in warfare as himself. This gave him a decided advantage.

His breathing was steady, his mind clear. Skir-mishes and potential ambushes were something he was accustomed to. He was still a soldier despite having left the army six months ago.

'I think your horse would like to sample the lush grass before we move on, my lord, so shall we let him do so for a few minutes?'

Grey's mouth curved in appreciation. Madeline had done exactly the right thing – something he should have suggested before he left her. If the bastards hiding in the trees thought he was still fifty yards from them they would relax their guard and this could be his ideal opportunity. It was unlikely they would actually be able to hear her speaking from so great a distance, but he couldn't be sure there wasn't another assailant lurking unseen on the other side of the hedge.

6

Madeline let the horse graze whilst continuing to make inane remarks to herself in the hope that whoever was waiting in the woods ahead would be fooled by her play-acting. She pressed herself against the prickly hedge, grateful for the support it gave her.

Then the air was split by two gunshots. This noise was followed by the beat of wings as dozens of startled pigeons flew skywards. She clutched the pommel of the saddle and waited to hear further sounds of battle – but there were no more. It remained eerily silent. Then the yelling started and she didn't recognise the voices.

She couldn't lurk here. She must keep walking

until she was told she could stop. Who had fired the weapons? Was her companion injured or had it been he who had used his pistols? If he was injured she needed to get to him and do what she could. She pushed away the horrible thought that he might be dead.

'I don't care about showing my ankles, old fellow. You need to take me to the woods so I can see what's happened for myself.'

The horse was so high she couldn't mount unaided unless she found something to stand on. Even then she would have to pull up her skirts in order to swing her legs across the saddle. There was a milestone she could use as a mounting block. If she also lengthened the stirrup leather she thought she might be able to scramble aboard. That is, if the horse didn't object.

Fortunately the animal made no fuss about her being on his back. She clicked her tongue and squeezed. The stallion moved forward smoothly and her breath hissed through her teeth. She squeezed again and the beast accelerated into a smooth canter – slightly faster than she intended – but the sooner she was there the better.

Only as she approached the woods did it occur to her that she might be putting herself in deadly danger. If Carshalton had been the one who was shot then whoever had done this would not want any living witnesses.

Then several things happened at once. Smith arrived at a gallop from the opposite direction; two horsemen burst into the lane and disappeared through a gap in the hedge, and she lost control of her mount.

* * *

Grey fired and he was certain one bullet found its mark but the other missed completely. He dropped behind the shelter of the bushes and calmly reloaded his guns. As he stood up, the men made a run for it.

He hurtled after them and emerged in the lane as Smith arrived and two nondescript brown horses burst through a gap in the hedge on the far side of the lane and galloped away. Then Madeline, riding astride his horse, galloped after them. For a second he thought she was in pursuit, then his gut twisted in horror. Sampson had bolted and there was nothing he could do about it.

'Get after her, Smith; save Lady Madeline.'

He raced through the gap and to his astonishment and relief saw that Madeline had managed to stop Sampson and was now trotting back towards him. There was no sign of Smith or the two men who'd hoped to kill him.

'Smith has gone after the men.' She reined in and he reached up and lifted her from the saddle, holding her briefly against his chest before setting her on her feet. 'You must go after him. I'll be perfectly safe here.'

'If you're sure, I'll do that. There's a log over there you can sit on whilst you wait.' He scrambled into the saddle with more haste than dignity and Sampson was galloping before he got both feet in the stirrup irons.

The field was L-shaped, bordered by dense woodland, which made it impossible for a rider to enter, especially at speed. His horse negotiated the corner and immediately Grey saw Smith cantering towards him.

'I lost them, sir. By the time I'd stopped to make sure her ladyship was unhurt, they had too big a start on me. But I'm certain one of the buggers was hit. I don't reckon he'll survive.'

'I'll alert the militia on my return and have them search the area for a corpse. How the hell did they know I'd be travelling along this lane? Someone at

Heatherfield is in their employ – it can't be anything else.'

They cantered side by side back to the waiting girl. 'How far away is the carriage, Smith?'

'Damned if I know – that's why I came back in a hurry. There's no sign of it in the lane. They must have turned onto the toll road and will be waiting at the inn.'

'I'll take Lady Madeline up in front of me again as she can hardly walk all that way.'

Madeline overheard his comment and walked over to smile up at him. 'I think it might be easier if I sat behind you, sir, and if we still had your riding coat I could drape it over me so I don't show anything I shouldn't.'

He nodded to Smith and he grinned. 'I'll go back and find it, my lady. It won't take but a few minutes.'

Grey dismounted and pulled the reins over Sampson's head, allowing him to graze. He needed to make it clear to Madeline what he thought of her foolhardy behaviour but didn't wish to antagonise her.

'There's no need for you to scowl at me, I'm well aware you don't approve of me riding your horse. I'm not going to apologise. I thought you might be injured after I heard the gunshots and wanted to get to your side as quickly as I could.' She moved closer and stared earnestly at him. 'Your horse was startled but he didn't really bolt. As soon as I recovered my seat and pulled on the reins he slowed. I was perfectly safe; his temperament is not at all like that of my brother's horse.'

How could he reprimand her after that? 'This is getting to be a habit of yours, my dear. I sincerely hope you don't intend to steal another unsuitable mount in the near future.'

'Fiddlesticks to that! Please tell me at once what happened in the woods.'

'I shot at them, hit one and missed the other and they escaped. Good, Smith is back with my coat.' He gestured towards her pelisse. 'I fear your enchanting ensemble will not recover from today's experiences. When we find my grandmother I'll tell her we must abort the trip. I need to get back. You can't possibly continue as you are.'

He lifted her onto Sampson's back and then handed her his coat – between them they arranged it so her ankles were discreetly covered. There was something about her expression that gave him pause. She was trying to hide her amusement.

'I am safely mounted, sir, but how are you going

to get into the saddle without knocking me to the ground?'

He heard Smith sniggering behind him and this did nothing for his temper.

* * *

His eyes darkened and his lips thinned. She knew the danger signals. Before he could reach out and snatch her from the saddle she slid to the ground. Unfortunately the heavy coat left her shoulders and swirled into the air and Carshalton disappeared beneath the material.

His language made her blush. In fact she thought it might be best not to comment right at this moment. Smith extricated his master and stepped away with the offending object over his arm.

Once he was mounted his lordship leaned down and offered his arm. She had no option but to take it. 'Put your foot in the iron and then swing your other leg over.'

She managed this manoeuvre and Smith handed her the coat. Carshalton offered no assistance but stared ahead, leaving her to struggle with the voluminous folds. Eventually she had it correctly positioned and placed her arms around his waist.

'I'm ready. We can go.'

He didn't respond. His torso was rigid beneath her touch and she was aware he was barely hanging on to his temper. His horse moved away smoothly and this time she felt secure and in no danger of slipping sideways.

Were they going to travel the entire distance in stony silence? He must have made a formidable officer. As they cantered down the lane her thoughts turned to what might await her when she returned to Silchester Court. Beau would be furious with both of them for disregarding his instructions. This would probably mean the proposed supper party would be cancelled as a punishment. But what would he say to Carshalton?

'I do hope that my brother doesn't call you out...' She had spoken without thought and wished the words back no sooner were they out.

He glanced over his shoulder and his smile had a dangerous quality. 'Duelling is illegal. However, if he tries to draw my cork then he'll be in for a nasty surprise.'

For a second she was stumped, then she understood what he'd said. 'He's an expert pugilist, sir, but

I'm sure he wouldn't stoop to fisticuffs, however incensed he might be. I'm so relieved that duelling is no longer allowed.'

He laughed at her comment. 'You might well be, my girl, because I used to fight for my living and that makes me a deadly opponent.'

Shock made her react unwisely. She lashed out with her right foot and caught him in the calf. 'How dare you threaten to kill my brother? Put me down at once. I'm not travelling with you any longer.'

His arm came round and the next thing she knew she was sitting in a heap in the dust, surrounded by his coat, and he was cantering away into the distance. She scrambled to her feet, horrified he'd been so angry he was prepared to abandon her.

Then she realised Smith was still with her. 'Up you come, best to let him get over his ill humour. The major don't bear a grudge and will be all smiles and apologies when we catch up with him.'

This was indeed the case, but she detected a certain reserve in his demeanour. They located the carriage easily enough and Lady Carshalton was only too happy to return.

'I've sent my men ahead to find us somewhere pleasant in St Albans. No doubt they can make their own way home once they realise we are not coming.

I should never have suggested this outing, my dear boy, and shall be glad to return. I have no intention of venturing out again until I leave in a few weeks' time.'

The return journey was completed without mishap and Madeline was glad to bid the Carshaltons goodbye. His lordship rode away without a second glance, leaving her to go in alone and explain to her brother what had taken place.

* * *

'Smith, find the militia and let them know what happened.'

'Begging your pardon, major, but I reckon it might be better if we send someone else.'

Grey was about to snarl a reply when he reconsidered. 'Do you think I'm at risk in my own home?'

'I do, sir. Until we find the varmint what's sending out information, you've got to be vigilant.'

'I'm also concerned that we had no response from Horse Guards – surely it shouldn't have taken this long to identify the unusual crest on the weapon's handle?'

'I don't rightly recall who took the parcel, but I'll

find him and have a word when we get back and make sure he actually delivered it.'

'Whilst you're doing that, I'll write another letter to Horse Guards. Get someone to take it to the Red Lion as soon as it's done. I think it's time I introduced myself to your new recruits – have them assemble outside their temporary barracks.'

He rode ahead of the carriage and arrived some time before his grandmother. He hurried in to write his letter, leaving Smith to make his enquiries. Talking to Ned Bishop could wait until later.

When he arrived for his inspection, he was pleased to see the new recruits were clean and smartly clothed. He was introduced to each one and greeted them with enthusiasm. They were all thin and of middle years, but after a few days' good food in their bellies they would do.

He drew Smith to one side. 'Have you discovered the name of the man who took the parcel?'

'It were one of the gardeners, Sam Trotter, but nobody's seen him recently.'

'See if you can find him; someone will know where he is. I need to speak to him.'

An hour later his man appeared at the study door, his face etched with concern. 'Trotter never came back from the village. He was a journeyman so no one thought anything of it.'

Grey was on his feet before Smith had finished speaking. 'I've a bad feeling about this. Get the men together and we'll begin a search of the area.'

* * *

Madeline had no need to face her brother as he had been out all day and was unaware she'd even left the premises. Obviously she would have to tell him what took place, but that could wait until they met for dinner later.

The more she thought about what happened the more convinced she was that Carshalton must have the traitor in his employ. How else could the attackers have been waiting in that particular wood at exactly the right time?

They had parted on bad terms, but this didn't prevent her being concerned for his safety. She decided to send him a note explaining her concerns. Although she was sure he would have thought of this for himself, she didn't want to take the risk.

Once the letter was written she handed it to her maid. 'Lottie, I wish this to go to Heatherfield immediately. Don't give it to Peebles; take it out to the yard yourself.' The girl was walking out with a groom and would no doubt ask him to take the message.

'I'll do it at once. What do you wish me to do with the garments you wore for your outing?'

'Do what you can with them and then they are yours.' Lottie was a head shorter than her so the ruined hem could be snipped off and sewn again. 'Take the bonnet as well. I don't have anything else it will go with.'

'Thank you ever so much, my lady – as long as you're quite sure. I shall wear the gown and pelisse next time I walk into the village.'

* * *

Beau was shocked when she regaled him with her eventful morning. 'I hope you learned your lesson, Madeline, and will do as I bid in future.'

'I've no intention of going anywhere with that man – he's an objectionable gentleman.' She braced herself, waiting for a severe talking-to and the cancellation of the party, but he reached across the table and squeezed her hand affectionately.

'Sweetheart, don't look so worried. Your transgression was unintentional and I'll say no more about it.'

'Are you going to cancel the supper party?'

'No, it would be unfair to those who are looking forward to the event. However, I am tempted to stop the Carshaltons from attending.'

She was about to agree with his suggestion but said something entirely different, which wasn't quite true. 'He would have prevented me from getting in the coach if I hadn't forestalled him. He was as grumpy as a bear all day because of it.'

Beau chuckled. 'In which case the blame must be placed entirely at your feet, my dear. Perhaps the only person who should be excluded is you.'

7

Grey led the search party and his worst fears were realised when a shallow grave was discovered in a lonely place no more than a few yards from the lane.

'This is a bad business, Smith. To murder an innocent man in order to recover the knife means we're dealing with something far more dangerous than I thought.'

'The lad has a young wife and a baby in the village. I don't understand why she didn't send a message asking where her husband had got to.'

'I've sent one of the men back to get a cart so the body can be returned to his family. I want you to go with it and take my condolences and my word that

I'll look after her and her child. I'll give you a purse to take with you.'

'What do we tell her? She'll want to know how her man died.'

'Tell her the truth. He was murdered. The militia will be more motivated to help with the search after what's taken place today.'

'From now on, sir, you'd best be extra vigilant – especially as we haven't discovered which of the men here is working for the bastard.'

'It has to be someone who joined my household since I arrived. I took on everyone who was employed by the previous owner, so that will make your search a little easier. Make no accusations, just bring me the list of names and I'll decide how to proceed.'

His man touched his cap and nodded. 'I'll ride with you back to Heatherfield and return with the men and the cart to collect the cadaver.'

* * *

After several days of rigorous enquiries Grey was still no nearer to the truth. None of his employees, as far as he could ascertain, had any connection to the murderous attempts. Strangely, the militia hadn't located the villain he'd shot – the two of them must have gone to ground. This meant they had more resources than he'd anticipated. There was nothing further he could do until Jenkins returned from London with any information he gleaned from those in authority at Horse Guards.

He half-expected his invitation to attend the supper party at Silchester Court to be withdrawn, but he heard nothing from the duke so must assume he was still welcome there.

His grandmother had been indisposed for the past few days, but her unpleasant maid had assured him her mistress was in no need of a physician and would be well enough to attend the party that evening.

After taking particular care with his appearance, Grey descended to the drawing room still not quite sure if his ancient relative would be accompanying him.

'Grandmamma, I'm delighted to see you looking so well. Are you fully recovered?'

'I am, my dear boy, and more than ready to go out. I've heard so much about Silchester Court and cannot wait to see the splendours for myself. I hope you will forgive an old lady, but my maid is accompanying us in the carriage. I fear I cannot do without her, and especially as I've been unwell.'

The last thing he wanted was to be closeted with this woman but he smiled amiably. 'I'm sure she will remember her place and I will scarcely know she's there.'

His butler gestured to a footman and he opened the front door. The sun streamed in, making Grey feel a trifle overdressed in his evening rig. The carriage was waiting and he turned to offer his arm.

'Shall we go? I've no wish to be tardy.'

The journey was accomplished in silence as his grandmother immediately dozed. They arrived in good time but had to wait their turn as there were three other vehicles in front of them. He recognised most of the guests as he'd met them at Lord Sheldon's wedding a few weeks ago.

'Grandmamma, we are here. Do you need my assistance to get out of the carriage?'

'No, I can manage, thank you. But I like to take my time, so why don't you go ahead and I'll catch up with you inside?'

He was reluctant to do this as he thought it would look rather odd of him to abandon his grandmother to the ministrations of her maid. Then she rapped him painfully on the knuckles with her fan and he got the message.

He greeted several of the milling guests by name. Once inside, they were directed through the grand hall to the drawing room where the duke and his family waited to greet their guests.

His eyes were drawn to Madeline standing between one of her twin brothers and her younger sister. She looked *ravissante*.

* * *

'Lord Carshalton is looking at you in a most particular way, Madeline,' Giselle said softly. 'Do you have an understanding already?'

'That's fustian, sister; we hold each other in dislike as well you know. I expect he's admiring my new gown and wondering if it's the one he had made for me.'

Her sister snorted inelegantly. 'Of course he isn't. He might be a military man, but I'm quite sure he knows the difference between a promenade and an evening gown. Which reminds me, you've yet to show me this new gown. Is it truly hideous?'

Madeline couldn't answer as the new arrivals had reached her. She carefully avoided looking in his direction and feigned surprise when he eventually stood in front of her.

'Good evening, my lord, thank you for attending our informal gathering tonight.' She curtsied briefly and only then looked up to meet his eyes.

His eyes were glinting with amusement but his face was straight. He bowed. 'And thank you for inviting us. Lady Carshalton insisted that I come ahead of her, but she's somewhere in my wake and is equally delighted to be here.'

There was no time for further interaction as the next guests were waiting to be received. After an interminable time she was released from her duties as everyone had now arrived.

Giselle was bubbling with excitement. 'I'm so looking forward to this evening, Madeline. It's going to be such fun. It was an inspired decision of yours to have a musicale first and then dancing after supper. I do hope the gentlemen dance and don't disappear into the billiard room or go to play cards.'

'I am opening the proceedings on the pianoforte so had better go to the music room immediately.'

Although she tried not to, she couldn't help but gaze around looking for the gentleman who had made such an impression on her. He was taller than most, but so were her brothers, and it was hard to distinguish them from one another as they were dressed identically in black evening clothes.

Perry and Aubrey, the twins, were easily identified from the front as one was wearing a purple and green silk waistcoat and the other a red and gold. Beau, as always, was restrained in his attire with grey silk and a single diamond pin holding his cravat secure.

Lord Carshalton had been wearing a pale gold waistcoat and no jewellery of any sort. All of them had adopted the recent fashion of pantaloons and evening slippers instead of white silk stockings and knee breeches.

There were more than fifty guests attending this function, which made the house pleasantly full. Her sister had run across to join her bosom bow, Miss Lucinda Bagshot, and the two girls were giggling and taking stock of the single gentlemen who were there.

Her gaze followed Carshalton and she was pleased to see he was heading for the music room. She made her way in the same direction and took her place at the piano at the far end of the room. The chairs from the ballroom had been arranged in rows for the expected audience.

She had already placed her music on the stand

so had no need to search for it before she sat down. She was busy setting it out when he spoke from beside her.

'Allow me to turn the pages for you, Lady Madeline.' She was about to refuse but he leaned closer and whispered in her ear, 'I'm not going to perform myself so by helping you I'll seem to have participated in this event. I don't want to be seen as a curmudgeon.' His wicked smile when he said this reminded her he was a dangerous man in more ways than one. 'I'm hoping you will partner me in a game of cards when you have done here.'

'Very well, I should be delighted to have your assistance. My sister and her friend are going to sing after I've played so I'll be remaining here for that as well.'

He nodded amiably and took his position beside her. 'As long as you can escape immediately afterwards – I'll wait for you by the door.'

The noise in front of her slowly abated and she launched into a spirited rendering of the latest sonata by Pleyel. For a man averse to playing he appeared to be able to follow the music well enough. As the last notes died away the audience clapped loudly.

Lucinda and Giselle glided gracefully to the

space in front of the piano. They were singing two lively Irish airs for which she had no need of music. The girls had pretty voices and soon everyone was joining in the choruses.

All three of them curtsied and then made way for the next musician. To her astonishment the twins came forward. 'Don't look so shocked, sister, we've been practising a jolly song and intend to sing it without accompaniment.'

She dreaded to think what unsuitable ditty they were going to perform – it was bound to be extremely vulgar and shock the elderly tabbies to the core. She looked around desperately for her brother. He could put a stop to it but Beau was nowhere to be seen.

'If you intend to do something disgraceful, I'll never forgive you. I shall ask our brother to cut off your allowance this quarter,' she hissed.

They looked somewhat taken aback but quickly rallied. 'We thought the evening could do with something more lively,' Aubrey said.

'Lively is perfectly acceptable – vulgar is not.' She slipped through the chairs, determined to be as far away as possible from the music room before they started to sing.

In her hurry to escape she forgot a certain gentleman had said he would be waiting for her. He was forced to run after her.

'Is something wrong? Tell me, how can I help?'

'We must hide in the library as there's going to be the most frightful fuss any minute now and I've no desire to be involved in it. My brother can be the one to smooth the ruffled feathers for a change.'

She skidded to a halt, but as she reached out to turn the knob he did the same and their hands collided. The touch was fleeting but they had both been aware of the contact. Somewhat flustered, she tried to snatch her hand away but his closed over hers and he turned the knob.

'In you go; we can't dither about out here.' She was bundled unceremoniously into the library, but as he was about to close the door she prevented him.

'It must remain open. It would be unconscionable for us to be closeted alone together.'

He released his hold on the door. 'You don't wish me to compromise you? I thought that was the sole purpose of bringing me here.'

His expression was unreadable and her heart dropped to her slippers. What had she been thinking to invite him to accompany her? 'I beg your pardon...'

'I'm funning, my dear – don't look so horrified.'

'That's all very well, sir, but we shouldn't be in here together.' She was about to step around him when there were shrieks of protest and the noise of chairs being thrown aside. 'It's as I feared; my brothers have deliberately outraged my guests. I do hope they don't all decide to leave – we shall never live this down.'

'Your brother is the Duke of Silchester; this is his family seat. There's nothing any of you can do that would cause you to be disapproved of. However, it might be wise to linger here until the dust settles.'

Madeline moved closer to the doorway. 'The musical performances were supposed to continue for an hour. Now my careful planning is in disarray and people will be at a loss to know what they're supposed to be doing next.'

'Ladies will retire to the drawing room and twitter about such disgraceful behaviour and gentlemen will breathe a collective sigh of relief that they have been released so soon from such torture. They will then head for the billiard room or sit down for a hand of cards.' He spoke from the far side of the room and appeared more interested in the journal he'd picked up than continuing the conversation.

* * *

Grey had spoken in jest about the danger of them being compromised, but there was a grain of truth behind his words. Sufficient to keep him a respectable distance from her and make him feign disinterest. What he really wanted to do was take her into his arms and kiss her breathless.

The last thing he needed was a dalliance, however innocent, with the duke's sister. Silchester was a formidable man and wouldn't hesitate to ruin him if he harmed any of his family. His notion to make himself agreeable in order to get her to improve her opinion of him must be abandoned.

His knowledge of well-bred young ladies was negligible. His occasional liaisons had been with experienced women; he'd always avoided any contact with innocents even before he was eligible. If being close to Madeline made his pulse race, then it could be doing the same to her. As he had no intention of falling into parson's mousetrap, even with such a delectable girl, it would be ungallant of him to give her an erroneous opinion of his intentions.

'I shall return to the party; if I don't come back then you'll know it's safe to emerge as all the fuss has died down.' He put down the magazine and was amused to see he'd been holding a copy of *La Belle Assemblée*.

'That's kind of you, sir, but I think it best if I go out first and you remain here. Do you still wish me to partner you at a card table?'

'I doubt there will be any seats available as the occupants of the music room will have taken them in our absence.' He should have left it there. She didn't seem particularly upset by his comment, but something prompted him to continue. 'If we cannot be partners at a card table then will you partner me on the dance floor later?'

'Certainly, my lord, but I cannot promise as I must dance with whomever asks me first.' Her smile was no more than civil and she vanished through the door, leaving him puzzled by the encounter. Why had she all but refused him? Had he misread the signals?

He should be relieved she wasn't interested in him, that she didn't view him as a prospective husband, but her casual dismissal had made him think more deeply about the possibilities.

For a few moments he was lost in romantical thoughts and then sanity returned. Good God! The last thing he wanted was a wife who could well be made a widow if he couldn't find who was behind these assassination attempts. Time enough for setting up his nursery when matters were settled.

He strolled along the spacious passageways and moved smoothly into the drawing room where there were several groups in animated discussion, presumably about the disgraceful behaviour of the Sheldon brothers.

Lady Giselle saw him and beckoned him over. 'As the musical part of the evening has been abandoned, we have decided to set up a game of charades. Will you join us?' His look of total horror made her giggle. 'Please, it won't be as bad as you fear.'

'You mustn't pester his lordship, sister; being an older gentleman he will prefer to find himself a quiet spot where he can snooze until supper.' Madeline spoke from behind him and he was trapped. If he refused it was tantamount to admitting he was too staid to participate in silly games. If he agreed then he would be committed to an excruciatingly embarrassing hour – he would prefer to have his teeth pulled than participate in any sort of play-acting.

He turned and was about to phrase his friendly refusal but for some reason he said something else entirely. 'I should be delighted to join in. There's nothing I like more than indulging in pursuits best left to children.' He scowled down at her but she saw through this pretence. Her smile made him glad he'd agreed.

'It will be far more fun than playing billiards or a game of whist.'

'You will regret inviting me, my dear, as theatricals are something I abhor. However, I can never resist a challenge.'

He offered his arm and she placed her hand on it – he was ridiculously pleased that she did so. He escorted her to the music room where busy servants had already cleared away the chairs, leaving the space free for the group of a dozen ladies and gentlemen all apparently eager to begin this nightmare occupation.

8

Lord Carshalton had been quite right to say play-acting was not his forte – but as the game progressed his contributions became less stilted and he even looked as if he might be enjoying himself.

'It's time for supper, everyone, so I'm afraid you will have to abandon this pastime. Thank you for agreeing to play. It has been a pleasurable hour,' Madeline said.

Her brother, Aubrey, strolled over to join her. 'That was much more fun than listening to indifferent playing and less than tuneful singing. Have you forgiven us for ruining your musicale?'

'I have, but I doubt that our brother will have forgotten it. You will get a bear-garden jaw tomorrow morning, that's for sure. I can't imagine why you and Perry thought it appropriate to sing that particular song tonight.'

He laughed and threw his arm around her shoulders affectionately. 'You know us, sister, we like to cut up a lark.' His expression changed and became more serious. 'There's something we need to tell the family, but we've decided to wait until Bennett and Grace are back from their wedding trip.'

Aubrey waved to his brother, removed his arm and sauntered over to join his twin. Although they were three years her senior they still had a deal of growing up to do. Perhaps young ladies of almost twenty years were by nature more sensible.

It must be hard for them being younger sons and having no particular role to play in the family. They had a generous allowance from Beau and would inherit estates in the north when they were five and twenty, but were drifting from one scrape to another in the meantime.

Most girls of her age were already married, but the death of their mama five years ago, and then the demise of their father last year, had made it impossible for her to attend a London Season. Beau was determined that she and Giselle would make their official debut in March next year and she was dreading it. Her sister was actually looking forward to being crushed in overcrowded ballrooms and being compelled to be polite to the gentlemen on the lookout for a likely candidate to become their wife.

She pushed these thoughts aside and followed the others from the music room. Carshalton wandered up and fell in beside her.

'That was not nearly as appalling as I thought it would be. Thank you for insisting I join you. Will you allow me to take you into supper?'

'I shan't be going in immediately; I have to ensure that the musicians are set up and ready for the dancing, which will follow afterwards.'

His free hand rested briefly on hers. 'Nonsense, my dear, you have efficient staff to take care of that. No, don't poker up at me – you know that I'm right.'

'Very well, if you insist, but I doubt there'll be room at the buffet table at the moment.'

'In which case we shall stroll around the grand hall and make polite conversation.' He continued to converse about absolutely nothing of any importance until she was ready to scream.

She halted in the centre of the hall and removed her hand from his arm. 'My lord, desist. I've never been so bored in my life as I have in the past quarter of an hour. I'd not thought you a gentleman to indulge in idle chit-chat, but obviously I was mistaken.'

Instead of being annoyed at her less than civil comment he laughed out loud. 'Thank the good Lord for that, as I was running out of nonsense to talk about. I expected you to stop me a while ago.'

'I don't understand, sir, your purpose in talking to me as if I was a simpleton unable to hold an interesting discussion.'

'I'm sorry, but having been forced to play charades I thought I deserved a little fun at your expense, but now we shall talk of more sensible things.'

'In which case, tell me why you and your grandmother came in separately? Have you fallen out?'

He shook his head. 'She asked for a few moments to recover from the journey and insisted that I came in alone. I've been remiss in not discovering how she is. Forgive me, Lady Madeline, I must find her at once.'

'I expect she's already eating her supper in the dining room. Shall we check there first?'

Lady Carshalton wasn't with the others. 'I shall ask if anyone has seen her.'

'Thank you. I'm sure there's nothing to worry

about, as a member of your staff would have come and found me if she had been taken ill.'

Madeline enquired from several guests but nobody could recall having seen the dowager. Her older brother abandoned his meal and came over to speak to her.

'What's wrong, sweetheart? You've been in and out of here several times and look more worried each time you appear.'

'Lady Carshalton has vanished. His lordship has gone outside to check if his carriage has gone, as it's possible she decided to return home and didn't come in at all.'

'I remember greeting her myself, Madeline, and she looked perfectly spry then. She must be somewhere in the house. Where have you looked?'

She was about to answer when Carshalton appeared at the door and beckoned. He was looking more relaxed so must have discovered his errant relative. 'Don't worry, Beau, I believe she's been discovered.'

Her brother returned to his supper and she hurried over to hear what had happened. Once they were outside and away from eavesdroppers she spoke. 'You've found her? Where was she? Is she well?'

'She was playing Loo with three other ladies and they were reluctant to leave their game. They are coming into supper very shortly.'

'How strange – it's not often that ladies put cards over supper.'

His expression was worried. 'It would seem that my venerable relative might be addicted to gambling. They were playing for alarmingly high stakes.'

'I do hope you're wrong – my papa had a weakness for cards and managed to lose a large proportion of the family fortune.' She tried to lighten the mood with a jest. 'For one to have to pay the gambling debts for one's grandparent would be a novelty indeed.'

He didn't smile. 'She is all but a stranger to me and I know very little about her character. I wonder if her gambling is the reason she was so eager to visit with me when the remainder of the family hold me in extreme dislike.'

'Is it possible the dragon who acts as her personal maid is there to keep an eye on her? I can't think anyone would employ such a person if they had a choice in the matter.'

'You could be right – I've been perplexed by the fact that the woman is always in attendance when it would be usual to leave one's abigail behind.' He shrugged and nodded towards the laden table. 'Shall we join the end of the queue? I refuse to have my evening spoiled by worrying about my reprehensible relative.'

They strolled across together as if they were close friends and not merely acquaintances. She filled her plate with a variety of delicious items, remembering not to overfill it as she wished to leave room for the desserts for which their cook was famous.

He piled his plate with far more than she had. 'There's an empty table in the far corner of the chamber – shall we sit there or will you join your family?'

'They are about to launch themselves at the dessert table so I think it best if we sit elsewhere.' Only as she was settling did she become aware of several speculative glances being thrown in their direction. She had been absent from the party for some time and then returned with him.

Her insides lurched unpleasantly and she no longer wished to eat. She pushed aside her plate, not sure what to do. If she abandoned him abruptly that would give more cause for gossip than if she remained in his company.

'So you've noticed the tabbies adding two and

two and making five?' His smile did nothing to settle her nerves. 'Ignore them, my dear. I certainly intend to.'

She would have been better to have held her tongue but said what she thought of his casual comment. 'It's all very well for you as you don't have a reputation to lose...' Her hand flew to her mouth in horror. She had made a difficult situation so much worse.

Instead of being shocked by her suggestion that he'd compromised her he laughed and waved his fork in her direction. 'Do you wish me to go down on one knee before, or after I've eaten my supper? Or perhaps it would be better if I spoke to the duke first?'

She was tempted to pick up her plate and tip it in his lap, but something in his eyes made her think twice. The man was impossible – how dare he make fun of her.

After several calming breaths she picked up her napkin and draped it across her knees as if nothing untoward had taken place between them. 'I think your jest is in poor taste, sir, but that's hardly surprising as you've not been about in society for long.' Her eyes met his for the first time and he was no longer amused. 'I suppose,' she continued pleasantly, 'that having been a soldier most of your life you are unaccustomed to rubbing shoulders with the *ton* and have yet to master the refinement necessary...'

Her sentence remained unfinished as he leaned across and placed his hand on hers. To a casual observer it would seem a romantic gesture, but his grip was hard and she bitterly regretted her spiteful comments. When Beau was angry he was not to be trifled with – but this gentleman was terrifying.

'You are impertinent. Do you think you can speak to me as you like because you have your brothers close at hand? I promise you, my girl, you are going to regret your intemperate outburst.' He stood up and half-bowed. 'Pray excuse me, but I must speak at once to the duke and get his permission to make you an offer.'

She could scarcely take in what he'd just said. 'Have you run mad? He will have you ejected from the house for your insolence. Do you think to embarrass me by doing so?'

He smiled but there was no humour in it. His eyes were hard, and he nodded in acknowledgement. 'By the time I've explained what took place between us in the library he will have no option but to give his permission to our betrothal.'

Then he was gone, leaving her stunned by his words. He didn't want to marry her any more than she did him – so why in heaven's name was he doing this? Did he think to punish her for her incivility by forcing her into a loveless union?

The fact that nothing improper had taken place made no difference – they had been alone together and that would be enough to add fuel to the fire their tête-à-tête had started.

* * *

Grey's fury carried him across the room but sanity returned before he arrived at the duke's side. It would do her no harm to believe he was actually asking permission to address her. He bowed to Silchester, who looked up with a friendly smile.

He leaned down and spoke quietly so no one could overhear. 'Your grace, Lady Carshalton has been playing Loo for exorbitantly high stakes and I fear the ladies she has inveigled into this game are likely to come out of it owing her hundreds of guineas. Do you wish me to take her home?'

'I hope that won't be necessary. Thank you for warning me – shall we see if we can take care of the situation before anyone else is involved?' He smiled at his sister and brothers. 'Excuse me, I must attend to some business. Don't eat my dessert, Aubrey. I'll be back shortly.'

Although Grey had said the first thing that came into his head, he now realised his grandmother had yet to appear despite saying she was coming forthwith. God knows how much she'd won from the other participants. He hoped between them they could get any gambling debts cancelled.

By the time he and the duke left the dining room he'd forgotten that Madeline believed he was asking permission to make her an offer.

* * *

Madeline could hardly remain sitting by herself at the table, as she would be too conspicuous. Her appetite had gone and the food no longer looked appealing. Joining her brothers and sister was not an option. Beau hadn't seemed perturbed by Carshalton's request – in fact they'd strolled off together in good spirits.

She held her hand to her mouth as if feeling nauseous and then rushed to the exit hoping her pretence sufficient to stop any further tittle-tattle. Once she was away from prying eyes she relaxed and hesitated for a moment. She wasn't sure whether to return to her apartment as if she was indeed unwell, or search out her brother and the obnoxious gentleman who was attempting to trick her into marriage.

Where would the two of them go in order to discuss such a weighty matter? The study was the most likely place and she decided to go there and make her views on the subject quite clear to both of them. She was about to head in that direction when Peebles approached her.

'My lady, the musicians haven't arrived. Do you wish me to announce that the dancing has been cancelled?'

'No, my sister and I can play, but I must find the appropriate music immediately.' Her confrontation could wait until she'd completed this task. The plan had been for the dancing to start at nine o'clock, which meant no one would be expecting to start for another hour at least. This gave her ample opportunity to sort out the necessary sheets and also go to the study.

A while later she was satisfied she had all she and Giselle would need to provide the necessary accompaniment for the various dances. In a way she was relieved she would be unable to dance herself as now she didn't have to take the floor with a certain gentleman.

The ballroom wasn't being used tonight as there were too few couples to make it necessary, instead the carpets had been removed from the far end of the drawing room and the pianoforte had been rolled in from the music room.

The majority of the guests were still enjoying their supper and wouldn't be drifting through for some time yet. The study was on the other side of the house and she picked up her skirts and hurried in that direction. If she dawdled she would change her mind and might find herself obligated to become betrothed to a most disagreeable person.

A murmur of male voices came from inside the half-open door. Without pausing to knock she burst straight in. Her brother was sitting behind his desk with his slippered feet on the surface – he was holding a full glass in his hand. His lordship was sprawled across the leather-covered sofa with an equally full glass.

Her sudden appearance caused him to shoot upright and slop the amber liquid down his immaculate waistcoat. Beau attempted to get his feet to the floor but instead tumbled backwards and disappeared in a flurry of arms and legs behind his desk. He used words quite unsuitable for a lady's ears.

Whilst they were gathering their wits she made her announcement. 'I don't care what he's said to you, Beau, nothing improper took place between us at any time. Even if you give your permission for us to become engaged I shall refuse his offer.'

Her brother's head and shoulders appeared and he was staring at her as if she were an escapee from Bedlam. Carshalton was mopping ineffectually at his ruined waistcoat and giving her dagger looks.

'I've no idea of what you speak, Madeline. Carshalton hasn't spoken to me on this matter and even if he had I would refuse my permission.' He rose to his full height. The look he directed towards his lordship was arctic.

'This is entirely my fault, your grace. Your sister and I had a slight difference of opinion and I believe I might have misled her somewhat about my reason for speaking to you.' Carshalton didn't seem particularly bothered about having upset both her brother and herself. He had the temerity to wink at her. 'I beg your pardon if you thought I was actually intending to ask for your hand. I was speaking in jest.'

She should have been pleased that she wasn't going to be required marry him, but his casual assumption that he could play fast and loose with her emotions so incensed her she spoke without thinking. 'Your grace, this gentleman made me an offer and he cannot now retract.' The fact that this totally contradicted her previous statement didn't prevent her from continuing. 'Are you going to stand there and allow him to toss me aside as if I'm of no account?'

Beau smacked his forehead with his hand. 'Good grief! Make up your mind. Either you wish to marry him or you don't – did he or did he not make you a formal offer?'

Common sense reasserted itself and she was about to apologise for her statement when his lordship appeared in front of her. To her absolute horror he dropped to one knee and took her hand in his. His grip was so tight she couldn't remove it.

'Lady Madeline, would you do me the honour of becoming my wife? I'll not take no for an answer.'

9

Madeline wasn't sure if Carshalton's offer was intended to be taken seriously or was another ill-judged jest. Whatever it was, she had brought it upon herself by her nonsensical behaviour.

'No, thank you, I've changed my mind. Please get off your knees and stop making a cake of yourself.' This was hardly a conciliatory statement but she was beyond behaving sensibly and just wanted this nightmare to be over.

He sprung to his feet but didn't release his firm grip on her fingers. 'You're as contrary as a windmill, my dear.' He nodded at her brother who was watching with bemusement.

'I'm seldom at a loss for words, but now find myself all but speechless. Whatever's going on between you, it must be settled now. I shall leave you alone for a short while and then return in the hope that you can offer me a sensible explanation.'

The last thing she wanted was to be abandoned by her brother, but before she could protest he strode from the room and closed the door firmly behind him.

'Shall we sit down?' Her intended husband gestured towards the leather-covered sofa and reluctantly she allowed herself to be led towards it.

Now that her hands were free she found it easier to regain her equilibrium. He was a rather alarming gentleman and she had no idea how this conversation was going to end.

Fortunately the sofa was more than two yards wide. She positioned herself in one corner, spreading her skirt out in the hope that he would take the hint and sit as far away from her as was possible.

'I'm not going to talk to you, sir. What was the duke thinking leaving us alone together like this?'

He folded his arms and crossed his legs, the epitome of elegance, and as far as she was aware in no way discommoded by what had transpired between them.

'Madeline – no don't poker up, sweetheart – I refuse to address you formally. From now on you shall be Madeline and I shall be Grey.' He ignored her muttered protest and continued. 'This situation is entirely my fault. I should not have allowed myself to rise to your bait and respond as I did. I'm afraid that by the time I walked across to the duke's table I'd already forgotten the exchange.'

'Forgotten? You're quite impossible, sir. I don't believe there's another gentleman in the kingdom who could have done so.' She hesitated. She supposed she should also apologise for being impertinent, but – in her opinion – her sins paled into insignificance beside his. 'We spent so much time closeted alone I'm sure the entire company is now of the opinion we are about to make an announcement.'

'I take it you don't want to be betrothed to me?'

'Of course I don't. We are at daggers drawn every time we meet. I've spent my entire life living with gentlemen like you and I've no intention of continuing the experience when I leave here as a married woman.'

'I see. You have a fancy to marry a milksop, a gentleman who will allow you free rein and indulge your every whim.' She was about to agree when he frowned and she held her tongue. 'Such a partner would bore you within a month or two. No, my dear girl, you need a man like me. Someone...'

'Someone dictatorial and irascible? I think not. I've no wish to be married at all at the moment. However, I'm sure I'll meet someone suitable when I have my Season next year.'

'That's as may be, but if you want your good name to remain intact you would do well to consider my offer.'

This was the outside of enough. 'Your offer wasn't serious, sir. Admit it, you're as opposed to this match as I am.'

'Marriage to you would certainly not be dull. Shall I suggest a compromise? We'll announce our engagement tonight, which will stop any unpleasant gossip, but you're free to end the betrothal as soon as you go to London in March. I give you my word I'll not take advantage of this temporary arrangement.'

'Our engagement would not be genuine?'

'No, it certainly would. Until you go to London next year and then you may send me a polite letter saying you've reconsidered and are terminating the agreement.'

She stood up and began to pace the carpet, her thoughts in turmoil. Their behaviour this evening would definitely give rise to speculation, but would it be serious enough to warrant such a step? Surely as the daughter of a duke, society would accept her eccentric behaviour and such a drastic move wouldn't be necessary?

'Do you dislike me so much, Madeline, that even to save your reputation you're unprepared to link your name to mine?'

She turned to face him and was surprised at his expression. His eyes were watchful and he looked almost sad.

'I shall agree to your suggestion but only if my brother thinks it wise. Before I do so, however, I must make some stipulations.' She had his full attention now; he sat up straight and watched her through narrowed eyes. 'During the next few weeks I'm prepared to attend functions with you, will remain at your side as if I was your genuine affianced, but if ever we're forced to spend time together in private then there's no need for us to converse at all.'

'I'm sorry, Madeline, but I can't agree. As far as the rest of your family are concerned this must seem real. Think about it – such behaviour would soon be talked about by your servants and before you know it you will be subject to more unpleasant speculation.'

She wasn't absolutely sure she was subject to any speculation – after all the only people who were aware that she'd been spending time alone with him were members of her family or close friends. Surely they wouldn't draw unnecessary conclusions?

'Are you suggesting we dissemble? After your pitiful performance in the charades earlier this evening I doubt that anyone will be convinced.'

'I can assure you, sweetheart, that no one will question my commitment. After all, I'm elevating my status by marrying into one of the most prestigious families in the country.' He smiled and this time she didn't make the error of believing he was serious.

'And I, sir, will become fabulously wealthy. This will be considered a perfect match.' She couldn't stop a gurgle of laughter from escaping. 'The fact that we cordially dislike each other is a mere bagatelle when balanced against the advantages of our marriage.'

He joined in her laughter and the atmosphere between them changed. 'In which case, Madeline, are we agreed? You will become my betrothed until you cancel the arrangement next March.'

* * *

Grey watched the play of emotions across her lovely face and bitterly regretted being compelled to force her into this uncomfortable situation. She deserved better than him. He was – as she had pointed out – little more than a rough soldier unused to mixing with the *ton*.

He prayed he wasn't putting her life in danger by linking her name to his. He would do his damnedest to keep her safe until she could get rid of him next year.

'Very well, but I want your word that if my brother or your grandmother asks when we intend to tie the knot, you tell them it won't be until next summer at the earliest as we are going to get to know each other better.'

'Agreed. I want your word that you will allow me to take care of you.'

Her eyes flashed. 'I have brothers who can do that. I've no need for any other protectors.'

He had no time to explain as the door opened and the duke walked in. 'Well, am I to congratulate you both?'

She looked at him and he held his breath – then she moved to his side and her smile was radiant. 'Yes, Beau, you are. I'm surprised you've agreed but naturally I'm delighted that you have.'

'The pair of you have left me little choice in the matter. I don't understand how two members of my family can have become besotted in so short a time. First Bennett, and now you.' He turned and his eyes were no longer friendly. 'Carshalton, we need to talk but that will have to wait until tomorrow. Be here at ten o'clock.'

Grey nodded briefly. He refused to be intimidated by this formidable aristocrat. 'Unfortunately I have a business meeting with my factor first thing tomorrow, your grace, but I'll come as soon as that's done.'

'Are we going to tell everybody tonight or leave it until tomorrow, Beau?'

'I shall announce your engagement after I've spoken to the others – perhaps before the dancing begins would be an ideal moment.'

'I forgot to say, the musicians I engaged have failed to arrive and Giselle and I will be required to provide the accompaniment.'

The duke raised an eyebrow. 'You'll do no such thing. Unless you can find someone else, there'll be no dancing tonight.'

Grey knew Madeline was going to argue. 'Don't worry, my love, I'm sure there's someone amongst your guests who will be delighted to step in. I intend to dance with you and couldn't do that if you were playing.'

He slid his arm around her waist and drew her close. Her brother's lips thinned. For all he'd given his permission Grey was pretty sure the duke had no intention of allowing his sister to actually marry someone as unsuitable as himself.

'I'll leave you to arrange matters, Madeline, whilst I go and speak to the twins and your sister. No doubt they will be as... as delighted as I am by your unexpected news.' The duke strolled away, leaving an uncomfortable silence in his wake.

'Don't be upset, sweetheart – it's not you he's angry with. It's his duty to take care of his family. Before we return to join the throng, shall we sit down and talk about what's likely to happen over the next few weeks?'

He guided her to the daybed and joined her, ensuring there was a respectful distance between them. 'Being engaged to me would give you more freedom to enjoy yourself without fear of offending the tabbies. You might even consider remaining attached when you go to London – it will allow you to ignore the attentions of other gentlemen.'

'And if I meet someone I don't want to ignore?

What then? I can hardly spend time with another gentleman whilst still engaged to you.'

'If that happens you must cry off immediately – I'm sure you can think of a suitable excuse for breaking the engagement.'

'In which case... in which case, Grey, I'll no longer cavil. I'm not exactly sure how these things work. I seem to remember Bennett believed that once he was betrothed to Grace he should take over the role of her father and that she was then answerable to him.' She fluttered her eyelashes outrageously and simpered. 'I do hope, my lord, that you don't expect to assume my brother's position?'

She was enchanting when she chose to be, and he rather thought he was going to enjoy this masquerade. 'Much as I would like to take you in hand, my girl, the duke is more than capable of continuing in that position.'

He offered his arm and after a moment's hesitation she took it. 'Of course, I'll expect you to hang on my every word when in public.' He pulled her gently to her feet and had an irresistible urge to kiss her, but refrained. He had no intention of taking unfair advantage of this innocent – he rather envied the lucky man who would eventually have that privilege.

'I forgot to mention that my grandmother was none too pleased at being made to return her winnings. I'll be in her bad books for a while.'

'I am sure that you will soon charm her into a better humour. Far more importantly, I wonder if our supper remains on the table after all this time.' She shook her head sadly. 'I doubt that it does, but there are probably a few things left on the buffet table and I cannot go another minute without sustenance.'

* * *

Madeline was relieved that her sister and brothers received their extraordinary news with equanimity. There had been no difficulty finding willing matrons to take turns at the piano and the remainder of the evening was quite delightful.

When Grey, for he would be that to her in future, appeared to lead her onto the floor for a third dance she shook her head. 'We've already danced twice and this is a waltz.'

His smile made her toes curl and when he took her hand she allowed herself to be led forward. 'I am your future husband, sweetheart, and if I say we can dance as often as we like – including the waltz – then there's no one here to gainsay this.'

'Fortunately for you, the duke's in the card room so can raise no objection. Anyway, after our scandalous behaviour this evening I hardly think matters could be any worse.' The comment was intended to be light-hearted but his smile faded.

'I've no wish to cause you any further embarrassment, Madeline...'

'Fiddlesticks to that! I intend to waltz with you and care not for the opinion of anyone else. If you are satisfied I'm not behaving immodestly, then that's enough for me.'

His eyes blazed. He needed no further encouragement and, as the first bars of the tune echoed down the room, he swept her away. He was an expert and within a few turns of the floor she was confident of her own steps and began to enjoy the dance.

Being held so close to a gentleman was a heady experience and when the final chords died away, she was giddy with excitement. 'I can see from your expression, my love, that you enjoyed the waltz. Shall we join in the country dance or stroll around the grand hall and catch our breath?'

'I'm not dancing with you a fourth time, sir; even

Beau would be incensed at that. I'd be delighted to promenade with you. I can't believe it's already past midnight and no one has yet departed.'

'You can consider your evening a resounding success. That reminds me, I'd better see if Lady Carshalton is ready to return. I've not seen her since she went into supper in high dudgeon some time ago.'

As before there was no sign of his elderly relative, even in the card room. After a fruitless search they came to the conclusion that the garrulous old lady had taken herself back to Heatherfield.

'I've sent a footman to the stables to see if my carriage is still there. If it isn't then I fear I'm going to have to stay here tonight.'

'We have plenty of spare rooms. I'll speak to Peebles and he'll arrange for a temporary valet and find everything you will need.'

The tea tray had been taken into the drawing room and she could hardly leave her younger sister to oversee this ritual. 'What about your meeting tomorrow morning? I doubt your carriage will be back in time to return you.'

He grinned, making him look years younger. 'There is no meeting; I invented it in order to annoy your brother.'

'Then you may have your appointment before

you leave. I expect he wishes to discuss the settlement – I suppose you must go through with that as if we intended to be married next year.'

'I'll answer as I would if this was genuine. I've no need of extra funds. I'll tell him your money will remain yours to spend or save as you wish.'

He said this with such sincerity she was quite taken aback. 'Then he will be satisfied. I'm at a loss to know why he acquiesced so easily. Although we spent time together this evening I can't believe it was reason enough for my reputation to have been in tatters.'

'I'll ask him when we meet tomorrow but I think I know the answer. Someone must have overheard me when I said I was going to ask for permission to address you. Word would have been all over the county tomorrow, so he was left with little choice in the matter.'

Madeline could recall exactly what had taken place at the supper table. 'I'm sure you're correct. I can only apologise again for provoking you, for being so uncivil...'

'The fault is mine; I lay no blame on you for the situation we find ourselves in.' He turned her so she was facing him and raised both her hands until they were resting on his waistcoat. She could feel his heart pounding beneath her fingers. 'This won't be so bad, sweetheart; we can ride together and I'm hoping to persuade you to come up with me on my phaeton.'

'I'll do no such thing – but I'll be happy to ride with you. Look, the footman is returning.'

He moved over to talk quietly to the servant and then returned to her. 'It's as we thought – she left some time ago. He's conveying the information to your butler so we can return to the drawing room and enjoy the remainder of the evening.'

When Madeline eventually retired, she was almost beginning to believe she was really engaged. The congratulations and toasts in their honour made it seem real. Would it be so very bad to marry him? He was the handsomest gentleman she'd ever seen, was wealthy and titled and, if she was honest, he did make her heart beat a little faster.

10

Grey stretched out on top of the bed in the guest chamber he'd been allocated and reviewed the extraordinary events of the evening. He'd discovered that his grandmother was a hardened gambler and then become engaged to the delectable Madeline.

He should be unhappy, angry at finding himself in this situation, but instead he was surprisingly sanguine. Spending time with her would be no hardship.

He was eight and twenty, a wealthy man, perhaps the time had come for him to step into parson's mousetrap. She wasn't, perhaps, the sort of girl he'd have chosen but she was intelligent, kind, resourceful and undeniably lovely.

Whatever his feelings on the matter he wouldn't take liberties, wouldn't make it impossible for her to retract if she wanted to. It was going to be dammed difficult being in close proximity and not be able to make love to her.

He was drifting off to sleep in a happy daze of good wine and cognac when he jack-knifed. His stomach roiled and for a moment he thought he'd cast up his accounts. A few months of civilian life and his military brain had deserted him.

He said he would protect Madeline but she would need protecting from him as things stood. There was someone in his employ working with those who sought to murder him and he'd yet to discover their identity. Once word of his engagement circulated, she would be in the line of fire – what better way to bring him to his knees than to threaten the woman he was supposedly in love with?

This was an unmitigated disaster and of his own making. Tomorrow, when he had his meeting with the duke, he'd explain his concerns and give his word that he would keep his distance. Perhaps it would be better if he removed himself from the neighbourhood – he could escort his relative to his ancestral home and finally meet his uncle and cousin.

He flopped back into the pillows happy that he'd come to a sensible solution that would keep Madeline safe, but he slept fitfully despite his decision.

* * *

He was woken from his restless slumber the next morning by the rattle of curtains and the banging of the shutters as they were opened. Peebles had finally sent him the valet he'd been promised.

'Good morning, my lord, I beg your pardon for disturbing your slumber, but his grace wishes to speak to you immediately.'

As Grey hadn't bothered to undress the night before, he was heading for the dressing room before the man had finished speaking. A quick glance at the overmantel clock told him it was not yet eight o'clock. To be summoned so early didn't bode well.

In a short time he was shaved. He was a trifle conspicuous in his crumpled evening rig but he had nothing else to wear. He had no idea where he was to attend this meeting, but no doubt there would be a footman hovering about eager to give him the information he required.

To his surprise the duke was pacing the grand

hall. 'Excellent, come with me. We must talk in private.'

His grace strode off and Grey took the last few stairs in one bound and hurried after him. The room they entered was a small, private chamber with only a table and a couple of armchairs in it. The fire had been lit and took the early morning chill from the space.

'Close the door. I don't wish us to be overheard.'

Grey did as instructed and waited to hear what had disturbed his host. 'Something is wrong – tell me why I've been summoned here.'

'I've had disturbing news from London – it arrived by express two hours ago. I took the liberty of making enquiries of my own after my sister was almost killed at your house. I've just received the answer.' He paused and then continued. 'Someone influential is orchestrating these attempts on your life.'

'How the hell do you know that? How did you gain access to such information?'

'My brother was a serving soldier; I used his contacts to elicit this news. You cannot remain here – your life is in grave danger; I've been reliably informed that there will be more attempts. Even with the militia patrolling the neighbourhood, it will be impossible to prevent such men infiltrating the area.'

Grey hesitated and then decided to tell the duke about the murder of the man who had been given the task of delivering the letter and knife to Horse Guards. When he'd finished his tale the duke shook his head. 'I wish I'd known this yesterday, for I would never have announced your engagement if I had. You must both go away from here – leave in secret – and whilst you're residing somewhere safe I'll lead the hunt for the perpetrators.'

'I can only apologise for involving your sister in my problems. I'd come to the same conclusion myself and have the ideal solution. I'll escort Lady Carshalton back to my ancestral home and Madeline can accompany us. This way she will be chaperoned and, when news of our visit eventually becomes common knowledge, no one will think it odd that I took my future wife to meet my family.'

'We think alike. However, nobody must know of your departure. I shall announce to the world that Madeline has contracted the measles and will be confined to her apartment for the next few weeks.'

'My grandmother had already told me she's intending to return home in November so nobody will think it strange if she decides to leave earlier. Madeline can travel with her. I'll ride and leave at night. My staff can announce that I too have contracted the measles and am also confined to my quarters.

'I'll not travel alone; I'll take two men with me but leave the rest patrolling my grounds as if I'm still in residence. I'm certain the informant is an outside man and... Dammit! I've not thought this through. If I take any of my horses, or men, they will be missed from the stables and my absence will immediately be discovered.'

'In which case, Carshalton, you must take mounts and men from here. I think it might be more plausible if we say you've both contracted influenza.'

'We have to organise how Madeline is to join my grandmother. On reflection, your grace, I think it might be simpler if I remained here and didn't return to my home. I'll send for my valet and he can bring what I'll need. I'll also send a note to my grandmother and suggest that she sets off for Blakely Hall immediately. Your sister and I will meet her and then Madeline can transfer to the coach.'

The duke frowned. 'Are you suggesting she travels on horseback with you? What about her luggage and her maid?'

'If the girl can ride, then she can accompany us. We can take what we need on a packhorse. Once we're safely established, it will be a small matter to have our trunks sent on to us.'

'I'm not happy about this, but can see no alternative.' The duke gestured towards his desk upon which were the necessary writing materials. 'I'll leave you to compose your letters. There'll someone waiting outside to deliver them for you.'

He headed for the door and turned as he reached it. 'I'm not sure that you're the right man for my sister, but matters have moved on too fast for me to intervene. Let me make one thing clear, Carshalton, if you make her unhappy then you'll have me to answer to.'

Grey nodded. 'I give you my word, sir, that I'll keep Madeline safe. I also can assure you that if your sister wishes to end the engagement anytime I'll not stand in her way.'

'Then I'll have to be content with that. I'll go and speak to her myself.'

The letter to his grandmother was brief and to the point and required little reflection. However, the missive to his factor was more complicated as he wished him to act in his stead. When the militia arrived to begin the investigation into the murder of the journeyman the man needed to be in charge. He also wished him to be wary and not reveal the whereabouts of his master to anyone, even the men employed to patrol the grounds.

It was quite possible one of the new men was the informant and he'd no wish for his location to be known. Jenkins should be back from London soon and Grey was eager to know what he'd discovered about the traitor's family.

When all three notes were sanded and sealed with a blob of wax, he strode to the door, but as he was about to fling it open something occurred to him. There were over one hundred staff employed here and the fact that he was wandering about apparently fighting fit might well be common knowledge and thus defeat their intention.

The duke should have thought of this – indeed, they both should have. Madeline mustn't come down as she was supposed to be indisposed.

He ruffled his hair and loosened his stock before pulling open the door. 'Here, these must be taken to Heatherfield at once.' He staggered and grabbed for the door frame as if feeling faint. 'I don't feel at all well – I'm sending for my man to take care of me.'

His performance must have been believable as the young man stepped forward, his face anxious. 'Allow me to assist you to your chamber, my lord, and I'll let Mr Peebles know you're taken poorly.'

'Thank you. The way I feel at the moment I doubt I could ascend the stairs unaided.'

He leaned his weight on the unfortunate footman and allowed himself to be half-carried back to the apartment he'd so recently left. As he flopped onto the bed he asked that the duke attend him at his convenience.

As soon as the man had gone he hooked off his boots, removed his topcoat and flung himself onto the comforter. Better to behave as if he was indeed struck down. He left the bedroom door ajar and was relieved to see his host appear ten minutes later.

'We almost gave the game away, Carshalton. Thank God you thought of it in time. I've spoken to Madeline and she too has retired to bed as if struck down by a sudden illness. You must both remain incommunicado until after dark tonight.'

'Influenza is highly contagious, your grace. It would be best if I received no visitors and both Madeline and I are considered in quarantine. I'm not sure what you do about the doctor – is he reliable and can be taken into our confidence?'

'I've no idea, I hardly know the man. Far better to keep him away – the fewer people who know about your departure the better. By the by, my sister's maid cannot ride; it would have been a miracle if she could. She will have to accompany the luggage next week.'

'Lady Carshalton must overnight twice but we will only do so once – hopefully by then your sister will be in the carriage. It wouldn't do for Madeline to be seen to be travelling alone with me.'

The duke's eyes were hard. 'I'm well aware of that, but am assuming you will successfully liaise with your grandmother somewhere *en route* before you arrive at the second stop.'

Grey understood the warning but chose not to comment on it. 'My knowledge of the route is non-existent so I'm relying on her to supply me with the information I need. I've suggested that my grand-mother departs this afternoon. We shall make far better time on horseback and should be able to catch up with her during the morning.'

'I shall keep up the pretence for a week. Hope-fully, by then this matter will have been settled. I take it you've still not heard from Horse Guards?'

'My man was expected back yesterday – he'll come after dark to join me.'

The duke seemed satisfied with this. 'I cannot visit you again as I'll be expected to stay away from the invalids. It wouldn't do for the Duke of Silch-ester to be struck down with influenza.' Unexpectedly he grinned. 'Until my brother Bennett met Grace this summer, my life had been remarkably staid. Now it seems to be one drama after another and I'm beginning to enjoy the excitement.'

'When I left the army I'd hoped my life would be more settled, that I'd no longer be in any danger, but it appears to have followed me into my civilian life. I sincerely wish I'd not involved your sister in this.'

'I'm relying on that. I wish you Godspeed and safe passage to your ancestral home, my friend, and must hope that next time we meet this matter will have been put to bed.'

The door closed softly behind him, leaving Grey alone with his thoughts. There would be no rest tonight so he might as well sleep whilst he could.

* * *

Madeline prowled around her apartment becoming more agitated as the hours passed. It was the outside of enough to be forced to sneak away in the middle of the night – but not to be able to take her abigail with her was too much.

The more she thought about it the more annoyed she became. She understood the need to remain in her apartment, to not be seen around the house if she was supposed to be unwell. If she took the servants' stairs she could creep unnoticed to the guest wing and speak to the gentleman who had caused this upset.

Her maid was equally distressed, as she would be required to remain in this apartment, ostensibly looking after her mistress, in order to maintain the deception.

'His grace has explained to you, Lottie, that you'll be unable to join me. You can spend the time catching up on the mending and when that's completed you have my permission to do whatever you like – as long as you keep my secret.'

'I do wish I could come with you. I don't like to think of you managing on your own.'

'I'll be joining Lady Carshalton tomorrow morning and we should be at our destination that evening. I'm sure I'll be supplied with someone suitable until you can come.'

'I'll go down to the kitchens and tell them how poorly you are. No doubt Cook will send you up something suitable for an invalid.'

Madeline shuddered. 'I well remember the last occasion I was confined to bed and sincerely hope I don't get bowls of gruel this time. I must resign myself to being hungry. We can hardly pack up a picnic to take with us and won't be able to stop until we meet Lady Carshalton.'

Discussing such things with her maid would be considered highly improper – but they didn't stand on ceremony at Silchester Court. Lottie had been with her for three years and was completely loyal and discreet.

'There's no need to come back until noon when you bring up my tray. I shall curl up in a chair and read until you return.'

No sooner had the girl departed than Madeline collected a candlestick, pushed the end into the fire to ignite it, and followed her. She and her sister had often played hide-and-go-seek along these passages and she was confident she could find her way without getting lost. She must pray she met no other servant about their duties.

Beau had told her Grey was occupying the principal guest apartment and she knew exactly where that was. There was no danger of encountering his valet, as this gentleman's gentleman would still be at Heatherfield.

She counted the doors and arrived at her destination. She could hardly knock, as he was unlikely to hear her. He would be in his sitting room; this would mean walking through his bedchamber, which would be a most scandalous thing to do.

Should she go back without speaking to him? No – it was imperative that they settled matters between them before they left on their clandestine ride. She dithered outside the door into his dressing room, not quite sure if she should continue or return to her apartment.

After a few moments she made her decision and burst into the room. She dropped the candlestick and couldn't prevent her squeak of horror. He was stripped to the waist and was about to remove his nether garments too.

She turned and fled. His hateful laughter following her down the passageway. She'd never been so embarrassed in her life and it served her right for her immodest behaviour.

11

Grey was tempted to go after his unexpected visitor but thought she'd had enough shocks for one morning. He would never forget her expression when she had seen him unclothed. She would know better than to creep into a gentleman's dressing room in future.

What the devil was she doing down here anyway? He could think of nothing pertinent she might have to say to him that would cause her to ignore the rules and venture where she shouldn't.

He removed the remainder of his garments and continued with his ablutions. He didn't want to get between the clean sheets as he was, and the valet had left him with a nightgown so he might as well make use of it.

This time he slept soundly and his manservant had to shake his shoulder in order to wake him. He was relieved that Slater had arrived from Heatherfield.

'Funny time to be abed, sir, but I reckon it's time to rise and shine.'

His valet – like Bishop, Jenkins and Smith – was an ex-soldier. But Slater had been his orderly and knew him better than anyone else. He'd been given an honourable discharge when Grey had resigned his commission and so had been able to accompany him into civilian life.

'I'm not getting up unless I've got something to wear.' He yawned and stretched, feeling well rested and ready for whatever lay ahead.

'I've brought what you asked for, sir.'

'Thank you. Have you arranged for my baggage to be sent with Lady Carshalton?'

'I made sure it was loaded before I left. Jenkins is anxious to speak to you – shall I bring him up the back way?'

'Yes, do that. I'm glad he's back from London – I want my best men with me on this journey.'

He prowled around his sitting room, waiting for

the arrival of his minion. Jenkins shuffled in looking highly uncomfortable at being brought upstairs.

'Well, what did you learn?'

'Captain Rogers, the traitor who was shot, has an older brother but I don't reckon he's behind this. He's a man of the cloth. But his younger brother is a rakehell and could well be the instigator of these attacks.'

'Have you any idea where he is?'

'No, he's not been seen for a while. Gone to ground more like – I've got a couple of good men looking into it.'

'Did you tell the others at Heatherfield that you were going in search of him? I don't want anyone there to know what's actually happening.'

He nodded. 'All right and tight, sir – no one will suspect a thing. What time are we leaving tonight?'

'As soon as it's dark – we don't want anyone seeing us depart. It's fortunate the duke keeps such a large stable and the three horses we need won't be missed immediately.'

Grey dismissed Jenkins and tried to settle with a journal. The afternoon dragged by and Grey welcomed the arrival of a second tray; although he wasn't particularly hungry it broke the monotony.

* * *

Madeline was mortified. She doubted she would be able to look his lordship in the eye again after the embarrassing incident that morning.

On her return to her chamber she attempted to calm her nerves by immersing herself into the novel that had arrived from Hatchards last week. The day dragged interminably and she was relieved to have an excuse to retire to bed for the afternoon.

'Lottie, you must wake me in time to get dressed and eat my supper. I shall be leaving as soon as it gets dark. I do wish you could come with me, but you must see it's impossible.'

'I'm sure whoever you have to assist you, my lady, will be adequate. Is his grace not coming to say goodbye?'

'No, I'm supposed to be infectious and we thought it better to maintain the fiction. If I were really ill nobody would visit.'

* * *

When her sister entered via the dressing room at six o'clock Madeline was delighted to see her. 'I'm so glad you've come. I don't know when we'll be to-gether again.' They embraced fondly.

'Beau assures me you'll be home in good time for the festive season. I promise you I'll arrange everything as you planned so when you return all will be as you'd hoped.'

'Thank you, sister – I'm sure you'll do an excellent job.' She glanced at the clock. 'I must go now. Word from his lordship arrived to tell me to be down by a quarter past six.'

Giselle stepped back. 'With that hooded cloak on, no one will recognise you even if you are seen. Imagine! Such excitement – to be creeping out of the house in the dead of night in order to ride away with one's lover.'

'Don't talk fustian. You make it sound like something from a romantical novel...'

'That's because it is, Madeline. I've always wanted to write a book and I'm going to use this as my plot.'

'I don't want to star in your tale, Giselle. I can assure you that I don't feel at all like the heroine in a romance and Lord Carshalton is certainly no hero.'

She hugged her sister and then left her apartment for the second time that day using the servants' route. Her bag was already downstairs as it needed to be secured to the horse they were using to transport their belongings.

The curtains and shutters were drawn so her departure would not be observed. There was a sickle moon, just enough light to see her way around to one of the home paddocks where she was to rendezvous with his lordship.

The sound of horses just ahead was enough to lead her safely to her destination. A large, caped figure emerged from the darkness. 'I'm glad you're not tardy, Madeline. We need to set off immediately whilst the outside staff are eating their supper.'

He made no enquiries as to her well-being and for that she was grateful. Far better to keep things formal as this removed the necessity of her having to apologise.

'My sister thinks this escapade's romantic and is intending to use it as the starting point for her novel.'

His teeth flashed white in the darkness. 'It's certainly unusual, sweetheart, but riding through the night's hardly romantic. Come along, allow me to help you mount.'

Once she was settled in the saddle she had time

to look around and see who was accompanying them on this journey. There were three other men and one of them was holding the lead rein of the packhorse.

'How far do we have to travel before we catch up with Lady Carshalton? Although I'm a competent horsewoman, I've never ridden for more than an hour or two.'

He moved his massive gelding alongside. 'We should reach the inn by first light. You'll be able to continue the journey in her carriage, which will be a deal more comfortable.'

None of his men had lanterns; they were obviously to progress by the light of the moon alone. She must suppose they were used to night-time manoeuvres as they were all ex-soldiers.

The only sound in the darkness was the soft pad of hoofs on the path and the occasional clink of a bit. The night had a crisp, autumn nip to it and she was grateful for her warm gloves, muffler and hooded cloak. This would have been a nightmare journey if it had been raining.

Whoever was leading this small group of travellers obviously knew his way through the woods and along the back lanes, as they didn't venture onto the more frequented routes at all. After riding in si-

lence for an hour or so, she thought it safe to converse with her companion who had remained close
beside her.

'I wish to apologise for...'

'There's absolutely no need, sweetheart. I've forgotten the incident already. I hope you got some rest
this afternoon, otherwise I might be obliged to pick
you up from the ground when you fall asleep later.'

This bracing comment had the desired effect.
'Thank you for your concern, sir, but I can assure
you I've absolutely no intention of either falling
asleep or falling from this horse.'

'I'm relieved to hear you say so, Madeline. My
man has reconnoitred the route. We're going to stop
in another hour at a charcoal burner's hut where we
can eat and rest the horses until dawn.'

'I shall be in complete disarray by the time I step
into Lady Carshalton's carriage. I'm not looking forward to the supercilious looks I shall receive from
her bracket-faced abigail.'

He chuckled, the sound loud in the silence. 'You
won't have to endure that for long as we'll arrive at
Blakely Hall by mid-morning.' He stopped as if un-
sure how to continue. Was there something unpleasant he wished to tell her?

'Although my grandmother and I are the best of

friends, she told me that my uncle and his son are still holding on to the feud that separated my father from the family thirty years ago. They don't know we're descending on them and I'm not sure what sort of reception we'll receive.'

No wonder he'd been reluctant to impart this news. 'And you didn't think to tell me this until now? We could have gone to one of my brother's estates in the north. We would have been just as safe and sure of getting a friendly welcome.'

'That's correct, my love, but it's high time I repaired the rift. I've no notion why my father cut himself off from the family, and my grandmother has refused to enlighten me. My uncle's the next in line, so ostensibly my heir, so it behoves me to make his acquaintance.' He cleared his throat noisily and then continued. 'Remember, Madeline, we're travelling in this ridiculous fashion because there have been several attempts on my life. This is the only way we can remain safe.'

Her stomach clenched and inadvertently she jerked the reins. Her mount surged forward, almost unseating her. Unfortunately the sudden movement caused a collision between her horse and the one in front.

This animal took objection to being barged in the hindquarters and lashed out with his back legs. She was still struggling to regain her seat when her mare shied in order to avoid the flashing hoofs. With a despairing cry she toppled sideways, expecting to land with a painful thud in the dirt.

Grey reacted in time and managed to catch a handful of her cloak and prevent her from hitting the ground. 'Keep still, you'll have me out of the saddle too if you continue to struggle.'

His words came too late and both he and she plummeted downwards. She landed painfully on her side and his bulk arrived on top of her, compounding her injuries.

From the cursing and commotion coming from just ahead the two loose horses were causing chaos. Were they about to be trampled by the animals that had been travelling behind them?

* * *

'Slater, for God's sake hold hard or you'll be on top of us. Jenkins, Smith, shut the racket and get yourselves sorted out. You're making enough noise to wake the dead.' Grey rolled away from the ominously silent girl beneath him, but remained on his knees beside her.

'Madeline, speak to me. Are you hurt?' He began to methodically run his hands down her limbs and this instantly elicited a response.

'Desist that at once. I don't want to be mauled by you, or anyone else. I'm not seriously injured, but I think I was bruised by my fall and things weren't improved by you crushing me.'

His breath steadied – for a horrible moment he'd thought her unconscious, or worse. 'I apologise, my dear, but I did warn you to keep still and you chose to ignore me.' He sprung to his feet and leaned down to take her hands, intending to pull her up beside him, but as he did so she couldn't hold back a sharp intake of breath.

'Stay where you are, sweetheart. You must allow me to examine you. If you've broken anything it would be foolish for you to stand up.'

'I landed on my hip, but I'm sure it's not broken, merely painfully bruised. I can stand up if I do it slowly.'

'Before you attempt to do so, Madeline, I insist I check for myself. It's too late for being missish – we're already so far beyond the pale as to be invisible from those safely within the confines of society.'

This time she didn't protest when he put his hands on her. 'Can you move your leg?'

'I can, but I get a shooting pain from my knee to my waist when I do so.'

This wasn't good – he didn't like the sound of it at all. If she'd fractured her hip joint it would be the very devil to heal and might well leave her with a permanent limp. During his experience with the army he'd noticed that soldiers with broken limbs who were dragged from the field of battle before they'd been splinted rarely recovered completely – if at all.

'You won't be able to ride any further.' He removed his riding coat and folded it carefully. 'I'm going to put you on this. If you remain on the damp ground you'll become dangerously chilled.' When he gently moved her, she winced but didn't complain. 'Stay here, little one. I must talk to my men before deciding how to proceed.'

His valet had dismounted and tethered his horse, and the horse he was leading, to a nearby tree and was hovering a yard away. 'Put a blanket around Lady Madeline and talk to her until I come back.'

He strode into the darkness. His night vision was excellent and he could see well enough. Jenkins and

Smith had caught the loose horses and were waiting for him to speak to them.

'How far away are we from the charcoal burner's cottage, Smith?'

'Another hour if we were riding as before – too far to be of any use to us at the moment. Jenkins reckons there's a dwelling just across the field – no more than half a mile from here.'

'Then one of you go there and raise the alarm. We need a vehicle of some sort to transport Lady Madeline – I daren't risk carrying her myself in case she has sustained a serious injury.'

Smith touched his cap and gestured to his companion as he rode up. 'Jenkins, you go to the house and ask for assistance.' The man kicked his horse into a gallop and vanished into the night. God willing he wouldn't come to grief travelling at that speed.

'Smith, I want you to continue to the inn that Lady Carshalton is staying at and tell her not to wait for us – that we'll join her at Blakely Hall as soon as we're able to.'

His valet came across to join him. 'Slater, what the hell am I going to tell these people? I can hardly reveal our identities – but I can't think of any re-

spectable reasons as to why we should be gallivanting around the countryside unchaperoned in the
middle of the night.' He'd spoken more loudly than
he'd intended and the injured girl overheard him.

'I'm not going to shout at you; could I ask that
you come to my side so I can participate in this conversation? I believe I've a solution for you.'

He returned to her and dropped down so he was
crouching beside her. 'Well, sweetheart, what pertinent contribution do you have to make to this impossible situation?'

'I think we should say we're eloping. We must
give false identities and make much of the fact that
my wicked stepfather intended to marry me to an
elderly friend of his in return for his gambling debts
being settled.'

He was about to laugh at her nonsense but then
reconsidered. 'Your suggestion has merit, but we
must be very clear on our facts so we don't give ourselves away.'

She reached out and clasped his arm. 'Your men
can keep their own identities – but you must be
someone else entirely. I shan't be a member of the
aristocracy but the daughter of a nabob whose father perished when I was still in leading strings. My

mama remarried but she died in childbirth, leaving me in the clutches of this monster.'

This time he couldn't keep back his amusement. 'Sounds like something from one of your romances, Madeline. As you have worked this out so splendidly, what part do I take? It might be wise to make me a captain – perfectly respectable but not wealthy.'

She clapped her hands. 'Perfect. Now all we have to do is think of our names and, of course, from where we've come and what our destination is.'

He joined her on the comfortable cushion of his coat, rather enjoying this game of make-believe. 'You must be Miss Charlotte Devenish, and I shall be Captain Robert Clark. I think we can refuse to reveal from whence we've come, and the name of your supposed stepfather, on the grounds that we don't wish news of our whereabouts to reach him.

'I'll say that I've a special licence in my pocket and we intend to be wed when we reach the coast. I've permission from my commanding officer to marry and bring my wife with me when I return to my regiment.'

'After you've told your men our new identities we'll be ready to begin.' She managed a weak smile and he admired her bravery. 'How fortuitous that you joined in the charades the other night and are now quite adept at play-acting.'

'You'll soon be warm and comfortable, my love, and I'll find you the best doctor in the vicinity.'

'Grey, do you really think I've fractured my hip? If I have done so I'll be laid up for weeks. We'll have to inform my brother and everything will become unravelled.'

12

'I sincerely hope not, but I'm not taking any chances.' Grey regained his feet in one bound. 'Pray excuse me, Miss Devenish, I must speak to my retainers.' His hand dropped slightly on top of her head and then he was gone.

Madeline could hear him talking quietly to his men. He was a kind man underneath his brusque exterior. Slater spoke to her from the darkness.

'Never you mind, miss, his lordship will get things sorted for you. No one under his command is left to fend for themselves.'

'Do you think I'll be obligated to sit here for much longer? Can you see the house he was sent to?'

'I don't reckon it'll be much longer. I'm sure I can hear a carriage of some sort approaching from behind us.'

Grey must have heard it too, although sound couldn't penetrate through the thick folds of her hood, as he returned to her side leading his horse.

'Here they come, sweetheart. I'll ride out to meet them and explain the circumstances. I think it might be better if you remained quiet and kept your face hidden as much as possible. It's just possible they might recognise you.'

'We must be miles away from Silchester Court; we'd been riding for hours before I had my tumble.'

'I prefer to keep the risks to a minimum. I'll be back directly.' He vaulted into the saddle and vanished into the night. She still couldn't hear a carriage even when she lowered her hood for a moment. A full fifteen minutes passed before she too heard the welcome sound of jangling harness and carriage wheels and there was the flicker of lanterns in the distance.

The pain in her hip was still acute and any inadvertent movement of her right leg sent shafts of agony from her toes to her shoulder. She sent up a fervent prayer to the Almighty that her injury might prove to be far less serious than she feared.

Grey dismounted and tossed his reins to his valet crouched beside her. 'This is going to be both painful and undignified, my love, but you must be stoic. I suggest that you pretend to be in a swoon.'

She nodded and allowed him to support her so she was prone, and then she closed her eyes as instructed. A male voice, well-modulated and articulate, was talking quietly to Grey about the correct procedure for transporting her.

'The trestle is the best way to carry Miss Devenish to the cart, sir, but it's essential we put no pressure on her injury and keep her horizontal at all times.'

'I agree, which is why I didn't attempt to carry her to your house.'

There was scuffling and bumping and then she held her breath as the trestle was gently pushed beneath her. Even so the experience was unpleasant and she had to bite her lip to avoid crying out and revealing that she was fully conscious.

Several excruciating minutes later she was safely lying flat in the back of a cart. From the pungent smell she guessed it to be a farm vehicle of some sort and if the situation were not so dire she would have smiled at her predicament.

The unknown voice spoke again. 'Captain Clark,

it's going to take a while to transport Miss Devenish back to my house. With your permission I'll administer some laudanum. It would be better if she's completely comatose.'

'I'll do it, Dr Faulkner; she'll rouse enough to swallow it.'

Then the vehicle rocked and he was beside her. 'I know you don't want to take this, my love, but it will spare you from the pain of being jolted and bounced.' Reluctantly she swallowed the noxious fluid and he cradled her in his arms until she drifted off into a drug-induced sleep.

* * *

Grey gently placed her head on the pillow made from a saddlebag, checked that Madeline was securely tucked inside the blankets the doctor had provided, and carefully slithered from the cart.

'I'll ride alongside, Faulkner, but my men can go on ahead and get our baggage inside.' He remounted and edged his horse close to the side of the cart so he could watch her and be ready to assist if she got into difficulties. Although laudanum was a boon for such times it could also have a deleterious effect on the patient taking it. If she were to cast up her accounts he wanted to be able to take care of things himself.

Dr Faulkner stretched across and placed his fingers at the juncture of her neck and chin. From the light of the lanterns Grey saw him nod. 'I'm satisfied with her condition, Captain, but will be more sanguine once I have been able to examine her.'

'I'll be forever in your debt, sir, for offering to take us in. I can't believe our luck that it was your house my man came to.'

'What's even more fortuitous is the fact that I'd just returned from a difficult delivery and was fully dressed and wide awake.'

The cart trundled on and Grey rode in silence, reviewing his options. His lie about the special licence might well prove to be the undoing of this escapade. If they were forced to remain for more than a night or two with the doctor he might well expect them to make use of this certificate and summon the local curate to perform a marriage ceremony.

When they eventually reached the house he was unsurprised to find it fully illuminated and half a dozen servants were waiting to greet them. He also saw Smith lurking in the shadows. He beckoned the man across.

'Her ladyship weren't there, sir. I spoke to an

ostler and he says no one has stopped there recently.'

This was another disaster, but not one he could concern himself with at the moment. 'At least that's one thing we don't have to worry about. I must go in – but the doctor has arranged for all of you to be accommodated above the stables. I'll talk to you tomorrow when I know more about Miss Devenish's injury.'

This establishment was substantial, no comparison to Heatherfield, but demonstrated that the doctor was a man of means. He was directed to the rear of the house where he was compelled to kick his heels in a sitting room whilst the housekeeper and the doctor took care of Madeline.

After a while he marched to the room in which the patient was situated. He banged on the door and a maid appeared. She didn't open it wide enough for him to see into the room. He raised his voice to parade-ground level. 'Dr Faulkner, I'm going to my room and will return here later.'

The poor girl recoiled at his noise but it served the purpose. An equally loud response came from inside. 'I'll speak to you then, Captain.'

Grey, despite the circumstances, smiled. He

doubted this house had ever heard two gentlemen yelling at each other in this way.

His chamber was commodious, but had no adjoining sitting room. Slater was there before him and had laid out fresh raiment. 'There's hot water in the dressing room, sir, for your ablutions.' His valet didn't comment on the fact that it was the middle of the night and these clothes would only be worn for an hour before being removed again.

Soon Grey was dressed in clean clothes and his top boots had been restored to their customary shine. He strode through the house and returned to the rooms in which Madeline was resting.

He was greeted by the doctor when he stepped into the sitting room. 'Captain Clark, I'm delighted to tell you that Miss Devenish hasn't sustained any serious damage. Her hip is severely bruised but she will be able to continue in a day or two.'

'Thank you, sir, I'm relieved to hear you say so. As you can imagine it's imperative that we get on our way as soon as possible.'

The doctor was of average height, a similar age to him, and he was no fool. 'I must assume that you've already travelled a considerable distance as I've never heard of a Miss Devenish, or her family, and I know everyone within twenty miles of here. As you cannot leave immediately I'll arrange for a curate to come so that you can be married at once.'

'An excellent idea – once the knot's tied there will be nothing her stepfather can do. However, can I ask you to refrain from contacting the reverend gentleman until I've seen my beloved?' He was thinking fast as he spoke, trying to come up with a believable reason for delaying matters. 'We were compelled to leave her wardrobe behind when we eloped. I promised Miss Devenish that I would supply her with her bride clothes so she could be married in style.' He shrugged as if puzzled by this requirement. 'I'll do my best to persuade her, but I can't promise she'll agree. I have family in Kent and we were to be married there, with them as witnesses.'

'Surely that is the first place the search will go?'

'There's no reason to suppose the whereabouts of my family home is known to him.' He wasn't enjoying this conversation one jot – he prided himself on being a truthful man and was drowning in his own falsehoods. 'I wish to see Miss Devenish before I retire. Thank you again for your assistance – but don't let me keep you up any longer. You must be desperate for your bed.'

The man nodded. 'Indeed I am. I'll take myself

off and see you in a few hours. Miss Devenish is asleep and won't be aware of your presence. I'm leaving a girl with her in case she wakes and requires anything.' Faulkner pushed open the door so Grey could look inside.

From the light of the many candles he could see Madeline was sleeping peacefully and there was no need for him to go inside the chamber. 'In which case, I too will go up. Goodnight, Dr Faulkner.'

* * *

Madeline opened her eyes and looked around with interest. The curtains were still closed but there was sufficient light filtering in to tell her it must be late morning. She hesitated before attempting to push herself upright, knowing how painful every movement had been last night.

'Good morning, miss, how are you feeling? Dr Faulkner said you must stay in bed today but can get up tomorrow.'

'I'm feeling perfectly well and whatever the good doctor said, I must get up immediately.'

The maid smiled and flicked back the covers. 'I'll help you to the commode, miss, and then will fetch your breakfast.'

Putting weight on her injured hip was painful but not impossible; she managed to hobble in both directions without too much trouble. Once she was safely reinstalled in bed, the maid left to fetch a tray.

Where was Grey? She needed to speak to him and discover exactly what he'd said about their outrageous excursion. Was Lady Carshalton still waiting for them at the rendezvous point?

There was a soft tap on the door, but before she could respond it swung open and he strolled in. His smile made her cheeks glow. 'Good morning, my love, I'm delighted to see you looking so much better.' He raised an eyebrow towards the dressing room.

'The girl has gone to fetch my breakfast so we are alone.'

He pulled up a chair and sat next to her – far too close for her composure.

'Dr Faulkner says you should be well enough to ride tomorrow but we have to leave before that. My grandmother didn't stop at the hostelry as planned – God knows where she is. And I had to tell our host I carried a special licence in my pocket and he's determined to fetch the curate so we can be married before we leave here.'

She wasn't sure which piece of news was the

more worrying. 'If we were who we said we are then his suggestion would be sensible. What did you tell him?'

'I said we'd intended to marry at my family home in Kent, and that you would be devastated to be required to marry without your bride clothes being ready.'

'How ingenious! I cannot think how a rough soldier was able to think of something so sensible – I wouldn't have expected you to even know about bride clothes.'

'I've heard talk of such nonsense in the mess. Refusing to marry me because you don't have the correct ensembles won't work as a reason, sweetheart. Any young lady who was prepared to ride through the night with her betrothed would be eager to marry as soon as the opportunity presented itself.'

'Does that mean we have to creep away like burglars in the night? It seems a poor way to return his hospitality. Once this matter is settled I shall get my brother to visit him and explain...' She stammered to a halt as the enormity of her situation registered. If she was to appear in public again, she had no alternative but to make this betrothal genuine and marry Grey.

He had already come to this conclusion and took her hands in his. 'Don't look so stricken, little one. Being married to me won't be so bad. I'll make you a good husband.'

'I wanted to marry for love not because I had no choice.'

His smile was sad. 'A lot of unions begin without strong feelings on either side, but I see no reason why this should be an impediment to a satisfactory marriage.' He raised her hands to his mouth and a shiver of something she didn't recognise flickered down her spine.

'There are other things involved between a man and a woman, sweetheart. Do you understand of what I speak?'

His eyes burned into hers and she was transfixed. Slowly he kissed each knuckle in turn and her breath caught in her throat. She wanted to tell him to stop but for some reason the words wouldn't come.

Slowly he stood up and without releasing her hands leaned down. His lips brushed across hers. Something strange was happening to her. She couldn't think straight. Her heart was racing and she couldn't stop herself from responding.

Her hands were free and of their own volition

they reached out and encircled his neck, drawing him down. His kiss deepened and one hand pulled her closer whilst the other cupped her face. She was lost to all sense of propriety, wanted something more from him but didn't know what this was.

'Captain Clark, have you taken leave of your senses?' Dr Faulkner said loudly from right behind them.

Grey slowly raised his head as if nothing untoward had taken place. He winked at her and then turned to face his accuser. 'Good morning, sir, one would have expected a gentleman to knock before entering a lady's room.'

'I am a physician, and this is my home. Your behaviour is disgraceful and I must ask you to leave immediately.'

'We shall be happy to do so as soon as Miss Devenish has broken her fast and got herself ready.'

Madeline knew this wasn't what the doctor had meant and felt sorry for the man being put in this invidious position.

'That wasn't my intention – I've no desire to evict you from my house, merely from this chamber.'

'In which case, I'll do as you request and apologise if kissing my bride-to-be does not meet with your approval.'

The two men were talking as if she was invisible and now that her initial embarrassment had faded she was ready to take part in the conversation. She pushed herself upright and drew breath but Grey, who was still holding her hand, squeezed it sharply.

Obviously he didn't want her to participate and she must be careful not to exacerbate the situation. 'I shall come and see you again, my love, but only if you're in a position to receive me.' With a casual wave he strolled out. She wasn't sure if she was pleased or sorry to see him depart.

'Miss Devenish, have you walked on your injury this morning?'

Her cheeks flushed anew as there was only one reason she could have left her bed. 'I have, and it was not as bad as I feared.'

'Excellent news. I suggest you remain where you are until this afternoon and then move into your sitting room and see how you feel.'

'Do you think that when I can walk about easily I will also be able to ride?'

'Absolutely not – if you are set on leaving here so precipitously then I suggest you borrow my carriage to convey you to your destination.' He gave her a direct stare. 'From Captain Clark's prevarication, am I to assume that you don't actually have the required document that would allow you to get married today?'

She coloured under his scrutiny and couldn't deny his accusation. 'We didn't anticipate having to spend the night anywhere, sir, and thought we could call the banns as soon as we were with his family in Kent.'

'Then I shall suggest to your future husband that he sends one of his men to London to obtain the special licence. If he travels post he can be there and back in twenty-four hours. This should be no obstacle as you will be unable to continue your journey on horseback for several days.'

She could do nothing but acquiesce to his suggestion. 'Could I ask you to inform the captain?' She twisted her fingers in the sheets before risking a glance in his direction. To her surprise he was looking sympathetic. 'This was not how I anticipated my marriage, but we must do what is right. I apologise if our behaviour offended you.'

To her astonishment he chuckled. 'I might be a bachelor, Miss Devenish, but I'm well aware how things are when a couple is as much in love as you two are.'

13

Grey received the news that he was to send Jenkins to London for a second time with resignation. He also sent Smith with a message to the duke informing him of what had taken place. He was still mystified by the fact that his grandmother had chosen not to stay where they'd agreed or, he must assume, be there to take up Madeline.

The only explanation he could think of was that she decided she wished to have no active part in his arrival at his ancestral home. He hadn't expected his uncle or cousin to be overjoyed to see him and Madeline, but he hadn't thought things might be so bad that his elderly relative felt the need to distance herself from the event.

This escapade was a mistake – what had he been thinking of to embark on such a scheme? Had he known all along that he would be obliged to marry Madeline because of it? He hoped that he'd demonstrated how passion was enough to make their union successful, and that the romantic love she'd thought essential to happiness could be dispensed with.

Mutual respect and affection, coupled with desire, was more than most couples had when they embarked on matrimony. Being forced into a hasty marriage wasn't ideal for either of them, but he was determined to make a success of it. He would do his damnedest to be a good husband. He was sure once the nursery began to fill she would forget her dreams and be content with what she had.

His trunk was with his grandmother and he only had the overnight essentials with him. If he was to be married tomorrow, then he wished to do so in smart togs and not the ones he had on.

The doctor went on his rounds, leaving Grey to his own devices. He was loath to return to speak to Madeline until he had been sent word she was fully clothed and in her sitting room. His valet must act as his messenger as his two men had already set off on different errands.

He found Slater staring morosely out of the window in his temporary abode. 'I've a task for you. I wish you to go after Lady Carshalton so that you may bring me my baggage. Hopefully you'll catch up with her before she reaches Blakely Hall.'

His valet looked dubious. 'That's all very well, sir, but what am I expected to do with your trunk once I have it? I can hardly bring it back on the packhorse.'

'Of course you can't – I'm not a simpleton. Her ladyship must return with you – I'd like her to be here when I exchange my vows. I'm sure she'll be only too happy to come – but if she is already at her destination, don't go after her.'

Half an hour later Slater was on his way riding the gelding Grey had borrowed. If his valet cut across country he might well be lucky and reach the carriage before it turned onto his uncle's property. He refused to remain apart from Madeline a moment longer – there were things they needed to talk about before tomorrow.

* * *

The girl who'd been allocated to Madeline was inclined to gossip. However, being able to hear what was taking place elsewhere in this establishment made her incarceration less boring. Although her instructions had been to remain where she was until this afternoon, she refused to remain in bed a moment longer.

'I intend to get up now. I believe you've already pressed the one gown I have with me so I shall wear that. Do you have the experience to dress my hair?'

The girl dipped briefly. 'I do, miss. I've acted as a lady's maid for other guests.'

A tedious and painful twenty minutes passed before Madeline was clothed and able to sit at the dressing table to have her hair arranged. She was pleased with the result. 'Thank you, that looks splendid. Would you be kind enough to assist me into the sitting room? I'll sit on the *chaise longue* so that I can put my feet up.'

This time she was able to hobble quicker than before but the thought of riding in the near future filled her with horror. Molly, the maid, had already informed her that Jenkins, Smith and Slater had ridden off, which meant that only she and Grey remained of their small party.

She was about to ask the girl to find him when he knocked and put his head around the open door. 'Excellent, sweetheart. I'm glad you're dressed because now I'll cause no further offence to our charming host by visiting you in here.'

'No doubt you would have done so regardless of his disapproval. Come in, Grey; please tell me what's going on and where you've sent your men.'

'I shall do so but first I have to tell you we are to be married tomorrow afternoon – in fact as soon as Jenkins returns with the special licence.'

She should have been horrified by his announcement but she'd already resigned herself to this fact. After the way they'd behaved earlier there was no alternative. 'Actually I'm relieved to hear your news. I'm sorry you've been pushed into this union, but I give you my word I'll be the best wife I can in the circumstances.' Her heart was heavy as she spoke again. 'I wish there were stronger feelings on both sides, but we respect and like each other and after this morning I know that becoming your wife will not be too unpleasant.'

He bent down, carefully picked up her legs and then slid in beneath them. 'I'll make you happy, sweetheart, and unlike many brides you will still be close to your family home. Lord Sheldon and his wife will be back in a week or two and will reside no more than two miles from Heatherfield.'

'In that case, Grey, we must discuss what's to

happen next. Are we to continue to Blakely Hall as planned or return to Heatherfield after the ceremony? Which reminds me, what happened with Lady Carshalton?'

'For some reason she didn't stay at the hostelry as expected, but I've sent Slater after her. Hopefully he will return before dark with my grandmother. I've also sent a letter to the duke – so it's possible he will turn up here as well.'

He announced that both his family and hers were about to descend upon this establishment as if it was perfectly normal to foist one's relatives on a complete stranger. 'I sincerely hope you asked Dr Faulkner if he was prepared to accommodate these extra guests before you sent the letter?'

He grinned, quite unrepentant. 'Of course I didn't, my love; he might have refused and then where would we be?'

'In which case I suggest you do so forthwith. How big is this house? Are there sufficient guest rooms to accommodate those you invited so cavalierly?' She almost tumbled from the *chaise longue* as she recalled something else they'd quite forgotten. 'You must tell the doctor who we are – we can hardly keep up the pretence now.'

His expression was comical. 'Good grief! My wits

are wandering. Of course I must do that when I tell him he's to expect further uninvited guests.' He smiled and stroked her leg, sending ripples of pleasure to a most unusual place.

'To answer your previous question about this place, sweetheart, it's not as big as Heatherfield but still substantial. I'm sure there are at least another two guest rooms available – if there aren't then your brother and I will have to share.' He said this with a commendably straight face but she didn't rise to his teasing.

'And I suppose that your grandmother must come in with me? I quake in my boots at the thought of being required to share with that redoubtable lady.'

'Nobody will have to share, Madeline, so don't look so perturbed.' His expression became more serious and he picked up the hand that was lying on the coverlet closest to him. 'Did your mother explain to you what happens in the marriage bed?'

She snatched her hand back and stared at him open-mouthed. Until he mentioned it she hadn't even considered he might consummate the union immediately. 'I scarcely know you. Surely you don't expect me to become your true wife so soon?'

His eyes blazed and then the darkness was gone.

'I don't expect you to, sweetheart, but I would like you to. You are the most desirable and loveliest young woman I've ever met and it's only natural that I should want to make love to you.'

This conversation was totally unsuitable and she was scarlet from top to toe. 'Please go away – this discussion is over. I want your word this will remain a marriage in name only until I'm ready.'

'You have my word – you shall remain inviolate until you invite me into your bed.'

His wicked smile made her hot all over again and he showed no sign of doing as she asked. If her hip were not so sore she would attempt to kick him from the daybed.

He leaned back apparently unconcerned by her agitation. 'I've been thinking about what you said earlier – I think it wise not to go back to my home until we have the man behind the attacks in custody. If you're agreeable, sweetheart, I'd like to continue to Blakely Hall and introduce you to my estranged relatives.'

'Actually, I should like to do that, especially as we will be married. I wasn't looking forward to the visit before, although I understood the necessity for leaving our homes. I shall be more sanguine meeting your estranged relatives when I am your wife.'

'I'm relieved to hear you say so. The duke's making further enquiries in London on my behalf and I should have news before long.' He lifted her feet a little so he could stand up. 'I'll go and speak to the doctor now. I hope he isn't too dismayed to discover he might have the Duke of Silchester arriving on his doorstep at any minute.'

'I should be overjoyed if Beau came – I'd really like there to be a member from either side of our family to stand as witnesses to our nuptials tomorrow.' She couldn't restrain her giggle. 'I don't envy you your conversation and wish I could be a fly on the wall when our host discovers our deception.'

'I don't think he'll be unduly surprised that we're not who we say we are – he's an astute gentleman and must already be puzzled by our strange story.' He bent down and before she could protest his mouth closed over hers in a gentle kiss. 'I'll come back later and tell you how he received the news.'

After he'd gone, Madeline closed her eyes and let her thoughts drift. Would Beau bring Lottie and her luggage with him? She would prefer to have something elegant to wear at the makeshift ceremony tomorrow – after all she wouldn't be a bride again – at least she hoped she wouldn't.

* * *

Grey finished his explanation and waited for Dr Faulkner's reaction.

'I wondered how long it would be before you were forced to tell me the truth. I can understand your reasons for the masquerade, but I'm relieved that your adventure was not in fact an elopement.'

'I can only apologise, sir, but we cobbled together the story without considering the consequences. I'm hoping that whoever has been orchestrating these attempts on my life won't decide to follow the duke. I don't want to visit further disruption on your home.'

'I have half a dozen stout outside men who all know how to use a firearm. They are at your disposal.'

'Thank you. With your permission I'll reconnoitre your boundaries and speak to your men.'

'Go ahead; as a military gentleman I'm sure you know best how to arrange matters. Now, if you will excuse me, I've paperwork to attend to. I'll speak to my staff and you can be sure everything will be ready, if and when Lady Carshalton and the duke arrive. Dinner will be delayed until five o'clock – hopefully they will be here by then.'

This was the first opportunity Grey had had to examine the property from the outside. As expected the usual offices were below stairs, and directly behind the kitchen was a cobbled courtyard. To the left was the laundry and to the right the dairy. The far side of the yard had an archway that led to the stables and coach house. No doubt the various doors either side of the arch were storerooms of some sort.

This was indeed a grand establishment for a country doctor – the man must have deep pockets. The stables were, like the house, of modern construction and the animals had comfortable stalls with plenty of room to lie down if they so desired.

After speaking to the coachman and the two grooms, he was satisfied they could handle a musket if necessary and actually seemed excited at the prospect of being involved in something dangerous. He was then directed to the gardens where he found the other three men busy about their tasks.

By the time he returned to the house, everything was in place. The six men would be on the lookout for strangers and all had access to weaponry if needs be.

The housekeeper greeted him with far more enthusiasm than she had done the previous night. She curtsied deeply. 'My lord, everything is ready for when Lady Carshalton and his grace arrive. I've also made arrangements for rooms for their personal staff. It would be of great assistance to me if I was to be given some information about how many there might be accompanying his grace and her ladyship.'

'My grandmother is accompanied by her maid and has four men travelling with the carriage. The duke will no doubt bring Lady Madeline's personal maid and his own valet. He will probably have outriders as well.'

She curtsied again in a rustle of blue bombazine. 'Thank you, my lord, I'll speak to the butler immediately and make sure there is sufficient accommodation for everyone.'

He nodded and made his way through the house to the apartment in which his future wife was staying. Madeline was no longer on the daybed and the sitting room was deserted. His stomach lurched. Had she been obliged to return to bed?

He strode across the carpet and hammered on

the door. There were running footsteps and the door flew open. A maid, her cap askew, bobbed. 'My lord, Lady Madeline is unavailable at present. She asks that you return later.'

Grey was tempted to barge in but restrained himself. 'Is she unwell?'

The girl beamed. 'Oh no, the master found her some gowns and she's selecting something suitable.'

He could hardly interrogate the maid as to the provenance of these items and he wasn't pleased that a complete stranger had been required to provide his future wife with clothing. 'Tell her ladyship I intend to remain here and don't wish to be kept waiting any longer than necessary.'

The maid's sunny smile vanished. 'Yes, my lord, I'll do that.' The door closed, leaving him to his own devices. He flipped out his pocket watch and saw that the hour was approaching three. His men had set out at dawn, so it was possible his grandmother and future brother-in-law could arrive at any time.

He stared out of the window at the handsome grounds and the peaceful panorama soothed his agitation. He had resigned his commission in order to take up his inheritance and had expected to lead a quiet life. How was it possible he now found his very existence in danger from unknown assassins? And that he was about to embark on matrimony to a young lady he scarcely knew?

14

Madeline stepped away from the full-length mirror in order to admire her gown. Grey was lounging on a chair, a sour expression on his face. He shouldn't have been in here, but he'd refused to remain next door. They decided to ignore convention as they were to be married the next day.

'I can't believe that Dr Faulkner was able to find me such an elegant ensemble. Don't you like it?'

'You look lovely as always, sweetheart, but I'm not comfortable with you wearing garments given to you by another man...'

'Good gracious! He didn't purchase them for me, you ninny, they were already in a closet. His sister prefers to leave things here for her visits.'

His mouth thinned and she wished she'd not called him a ninny. She was about to apologise when his expression changed and he smiled his heart-stopping smile.

'You're quite right to reprimand me – I was being curmudgeonly. The good doctor has been nothing but hospitable and I've no right to criticise his kindness.'

She returned his smile. 'That's all right then. I thought you were objecting to what I said.'

'I've been called far worse and deserved it too. Now, shall we repair to the sitting room and play a game of Piquet until dinner time?'

Her hip ached abominably but she wasn't going to complain, as he might refuse to let her come down for dinner. She viewed the distance to the door and prayed she could get that far without collapsing.

Before she could take her first step he was beside her. 'Idiot girl, you've been standing for too long. I'll carry you next door and if you intend to join us later then I'll do so again.'

Obediently she turned towards him and slipped her arm around his neck. He hoisted her into the air and strode into the sitting room. She was in his arms when she saw Beau's carriage turn into the drive.

'My brother's here. As I can't go down to greet him, could I ask you to do so in my stead?'

He dumped her unceremoniously on the daybed. 'Your wish is my command, my love.' He swept her a deep bow and she almost believed him – but then he winked and quite spoilt the effect.

'Go away, sir, and make sure that you don't annoy the duke.'

'I wouldn't dream of doing so, sweetheart; it's only you I love to tease. Do you wish me to bring him to you immediately?'

She was tempted to tell him to explain the whole debacle before he brought Beau up to see her. However, she decided it would be unfair to ask him to bear the brunt of the duke's anger on his own.

'No, I'd like to tell him what's transpired myself.'

A further half an hour went by before she heard Grey returning with her brother. She checked her skirt was smooth, her hair tidy and then slowly swung her legs to the floor. She wished to be able to stand up to greet him.

They weren't talking – was this a good sign? She would hate Grey and her brother to be at daggers drawn on her account.

Beau stepped through the doorway first. 'Madeline, how badly are you hurt? You shouldn't be standing up, silly girl. Sit down at once.' He was beside her in two strides and she was enveloped in his loving arms. She inhaled his familiar scent – quite different from that of her future husband.

'I'm so glad to see you, Beau, and I'm recovering fast. I'll be perfectly fine in a day or two.' There was the welcome sound of a trunk being delivered next door. 'Did you bring Lottie with you?'

He gently pushed her down onto the daybed before answering. 'Of course I did. I know how much store you ladies put on your appearance.'

Grey joined her on the *chaise longue* and she was glad of his comforting presence beside her. Her brother found himself a seat on the other side of the fireplace and sat down. He looked from one to the other of them and then raised an aristocratic eyebrow expectantly.

'I understand from the urgency of your message, Carshalton, that there's more to this accident than I might have supposed.'

Grey squeezed her hand and then gave Beau a succinct explanation. She held her breath waiting for her brother to say something, not sure if he was scandalised, relieved, or amused by their tale.

'I guessed that might be the case, Madeline. At least you will have one of your family present at your nuptials. I'll hold a celebration for you both when you get back from your visit to Blakely Hall.' He looked at Grey as he spoke. 'I take it you still intend to go there? That you've heard nothing from your lawyers that tells you the danger's over?'

'I wish I had, your grace. I was rather hoping that your enquiries around Town might have brought news of Captain Rogers' brother.'

'Nothing so far – but I'm hopeful the information will arrive in the next day or so. I'll send whatever I hear by express to you at Blakely Hall.'

'Do you think this will be settled before Christmas? I should much prefer to be home by then.'

'I'm sure it will, sweetheart; we are only just into October now.' Grey was still holding her hand, but if her brother had noticed this breach of etiquette he made no comment. 'Perhaps we could spend the Christmas period at Silchester? I should like to get to know your siblings better.'

'I was about to suggest that myself, Carshalton. A New Year ball would be an excellent way to celebrate your marriage.'

Whilst they were chatting about the state of the roads, the likelihood of rain in the next few days and various other banalities, there was a polite knock on the door. She was about to invite whoever was outside to come in, when in a flurry of calico, Lottie dashed past and opened the door.

Nobody came in and her maid turned and curtsied. 'My lord, Lady Carshalton's carriage is coming down the drive.'

Grey stood up. 'Then I'd better go down and speak to her myself. I doubt that she's going to be overly impressed by the situation.' He nodded at Beau and smiled at her. 'I'm sure you don't want to see my grandmamma until I've smoothed the path.'

'I hope she's not too cross with us. With hindsight I think it might have been better not to have dragged her back – after all she's a vulnerable old lady and being bounced about in a carriage for several days cannot be good for her health.'

'The good doctor has suggested that we remain here for another few days to allow my grandmother and yourself to fully recover.'

* * *

Grey walked smartly through the house and positioned himself at a window in the entrance hall where he could see the arrival of the carriage. He was relieved to see his valet leading the way. His attention turned to the outriders and there was something about them that caught his attention.

There was no time to dwell on this, as Dr Faulkner joined him. 'From your demeanour I take it you're not looking forward to this meeting.'

'You're correct, sir, but not for the reasons you might suppose. Lady Carshalton is ancient and I should never have insisted that she travelled here. I'm hoping her health hasn't suffered from this added stress.'

His companion raised his hand as if intending to slap him on the back and then wisely reconsidered. 'Then she has come to the right house. I'll take care of her – don't you worry about it. My housekeeper will escort her ladyship straight to her apartment and I will be sent for if there's any need.'

'I must thank you again for your hospitality. Without your assistance we should have been in difficulty indeed.' He hesitated, not sure how he could make this next remark without possibly causing offence. 'I'd like to contribute to the costs of our unexpected and uninvited visit.'

'There's no need, but if you would feel more comfortable doing so then I'll have my man of business speak to you before you leave.'

The sound of carriage wheels crunching to a

halt outside meant that his grandmother had arrived. His mouth curved as he headed for the front door. He'd rather face a cavalry charge than his formidable relative.

As he hurried down the steps he looked around, but the outriders had already vanished into the stable yard. He arrived at the carriage before the footman had opened the door and pulled down the steps.

'Well, my boy, I hope you've a good reason for this inconvenience. I'm not accustomed to being summoned in this way.'

He half-bowed and held out his hand to assist his grandmother from the carriage. 'I most humbly beg your pardon, Grandmamma, but I wished you to be at my wedding tomorrow.'

She almost pitched head first onto the ground and only his fast reaction prevented a nasty tumble. Once he'd righted her he apologised again. 'That was badly done of me, madam. I should have waited until we were safely inside before giving you my unexpected news.'

The woman who accompanied his grandmother everywhere arrived at her side, and was about to step between them when his icy stare gave her pause.

'Come along, I'll introduce you to our host and explain how this extraordinary situation has come about.'

'I've no need for any further conversation with you, Carshalton, you've said more than enough.'

Fortunately Dr Faulkner was an instant success and his grandmother allowed herself to be escorted to her rooms by him. Grey was dismissed without further comment and he hoped that by dinner time she would be in a better frame of mind. He had no wish for Madeline to be subjected to a similar display of ill humour.

He'd expected his grandmother to be angry at having her journey diverted, but her reaction had surprised him. She'd glared as if she hated him – not something he was accustomed to seeing – as in the short time he'd known her she had been pleasant and good-natured.

Slater would be in his apartment and unpacking his trunk. He would speak to him and see if he could throw any light on the matter. As expected his valet was busy in the dressing room, but dropped the top-coat he was unfolding and came across to speak to him.

'I'm glad to see you, sir. There's something rum going on.'

'Tell me. I suspected as much – Lady Carshalton's reaction was excessive.'

'Them outriders, they're not your usual sort of servant. Shifty like, won't meet your eyes and say naught. Another thing, I am almost sure one of them's different – not the same cove what was with her ladyship originally.'

'Devil take it! I knew there was something about those two. They were both dark-haired and now I'm pretty certain one of them is fair. He had his cap pulled down low so not much of his hair was visible.'

'I reckon the one that's gone missing was the one working for the traitor's family, sir, and he sloped off when you left Heatherfield.'

'I'll speak to Lady Carshalton, but not until after the ceremony tomorrow. I'll not worry her at the moment.'

There was little point in replacing his garments with something fresh, as he would have to change in an hour or so for dinner. 'I'm going to find Smith. He must be around somewhere as he came with the duke. Jenkins should return from London tonight. I need to warn both of them to be vigilant as it's possible the missing man followed Lady Carshalton's carriage.'

He must suppose that his grace was with Madeline and wasn't going to disturb their privacy – for tomorrow she would become his responsibility and the duke would no longer be entitled to spend time with his sister whenever he wished.

The poor man must be bewildered by the speed with which Lord Sheldon, and then Madeline, had found their respective partners and got married. Four months ago he had five unmarried siblings residing at his home – after tomorrow there would only be three.

Lady Giselle was to be presented at court next year and no doubt her twin brothers, a few years her senior he thought, would join her in Town. Perhaps he too would rent a smart house, as he would enjoy escorting his beautiful wife to the soirées, routs and balls that would be going on from March until May.

There was plenty of time before he needed to change – more than enough to go outside and find Smith.

* * *

Madeline had grown bored with her book. 'Beau, I've been thinking about next year and have decided I'd like to chaperone Giselle. There's no need to send for Aunt Prunella – Grace and I, as married women, will be perfectly capable of organising everything as it should be.'

He'd been perusing a journal and with a sigh he put it down. 'Don't you think you'd better discuss it with Carshalton first? He might not want to be in Town for the Season.'

'I'm sure he will indulge me – after all doesn't every husband spoil his new wife?'

'I've no idea. However, I can assure you that in the unlikely event I become leg-shackled I'll expect my wife to do as I wish, and have no intention of being led by the nose.'

She was about to protest, but then saw his lips twitch and knew she was being roundly teased. 'You're a confirmed bachelor. I'm sure you'll never find anyone to live up to your high standards. You don't like children and have more than enough heirs, so what possible reason could you have for giving up your freedom?'

'Exactly so, sweetheart, you know me too well. I'm sure Bennett and Grace will soon have their nursery full – and if they don't produce any boys then there's still Perry and Aubrey. There's no danger of my line or title falling into abeyance.'

She was about to ask if he got lonely. Then she

recalled Perry telling her that Beau had a *chere amie* in Town whom he visited whenever he felt the need for feminine company. Before she'd met Grey she'd wondered why her brother wasn't content to spend time with his sisters. Now she knew a little more about what took place between a man and a woman in the privacy of their bed, she understood why he visited London so frequently.

'I'll gladly open up the house in Grosvenor Square for you and Grace. As long as I'm not expected to dance attendance on any of you, you may do as you wish.'

He glanced at the clock. 'I'd better find my accommodation and leave you to prepare for this evening.'

The evening gown Lottie had selected for her was in pale green silk with a silver gauze overskirt. She thought she looked well enough considering the circumstances. Grey tapped on the door and strolled in at the appointed time, looking even more handsome in his evening rig.

'You look enchanting, sweetheart, far too elegant for a country dinner. Is your hip better than this afternoon?'

'It is – thank you for enquiring. I'm intending to walk to the dining room – if I lean on your arm I believe I can manage perfectly well. Have you spoken to Lady Carshalton yet?'

'I attempted to but the dragon refused to let me in, saying that my grandmother was sleeping. I hope she is more amenable this evening, otherwise we could be in for an unpleasant time.'

'I'm sure you're worrying unnecessarily; she was probably just out of sorts because of travelling.'

'I sincerely hope you're correct, my love. Now, shall we go?'

Instead of offering his arm he put it around her waist so he was taking most of her weight. In this manner they set off on the short distance to the dining room and she was glad she hadn't had to negotiate more than one flight of stairs in order to get there.

'The voices are coming from the drawing room. Are you able to walk that far?'

'With your assistance, of course I can.'

He had the good sense to pause outside the double doors and remove his arm from around her waist so they could go in without upsetting his grandmother any further with another breach of etiquette.

Her brother was standing beside Lady Carshalton and they appeared to be on the best of terms. There was no sign of their host; she must suppose he'd been called away on a medical emergency. Beau looked up at her entrance and smiled warmly. 'You look lovely as usual, my dear, and walking almost unaided too.'

Madeline braced herself as Lady Carshalton also turned. She couldn't curtsy, her damaged hip wouldn't allow that, but she bowed instead. To her astonishment the old lady bustled over, her wrinkled face wreathed in smiles.

'Lady Madeline, I cannot tell you how delighted I am to hear from my grandson that you are about to join our family. I would have preferred a more conventional occasion, but needs must. I've sent one of my men with a letter to my son informing him of the good news. I'm sure he will extend a cordial invitation to you and old animosities will be forgotten.'

Madeline released Grey's arm in order to embrace her future grandmother. 'Thank you, ma'am. I'm glad you are happy that Grey and I are to be married so precipitously.'

15

The sound of rain hammering against the windowpane woke Madeline the next morning. Not an auspicious start to her wedding day – that's if Jenkins had managed to return with the necessary certificate. The ceremony was to take place at midday and the local rector was coming to perform the service.

Beau had agreed to send the announcement to *The Times* on his return to Silchester Court. Giselle and the twins would be bitterly disappointed to have been excluded from her wedding, but there was nothing that could be done about it.

Lottie would bring in her morning chocolate at seven o'clock as usual, so there was no need to get up before then. She had slept surprisingly well considering this was her last night as a spinster. This was because unlike all other young brides she didn't have to concern herself about what would take place in the marriage bed that night.

A ripple of excitement ran through her. Grey was the handsomest man she'd ever met, even more attractive than her brothers, and they were all considered to be well-set-up gentlemen. She wasn't ready to become his true wife at the moment. When the time came she thought she might rather enjoy the experience. Although she wasn't exactly sure what this would involve.

If Grace had returned from her wedding trip she could have asked her what to expect, but her new sister-in-law was still away and wouldn't return until December. Mama had died before this conversation could take place and she could hardly discuss such a matter with her brother.

Lady Carshalton had been in good spirits and had congratulated both of them on their forthcoming nuptials. She was a delightful old lady and obviously very fond of her grandson.

The dressing room door opened and her maid appeared with her tray. 'Good morning, my lady; it's a good thing you don't have to go anywhere today.

The roads will be knee-deep in mud after all this rain.'

Madeline sat up. 'Did Jenkins get back from London during the night?'

'He did, my lady. I've asked for hot water to be sent up so you may take a bath and I can wash your hair. There'll be ample time for it to dry before you have to get ready.'

'I don't think I could get in and out of the bath so will make do with a wash.'

'Very well, my lady. I can still do your hair if you'd like me to.'

* * *

The hours flew past and Madeline had no time to be anxious about marrying a man she barely knew. Her hair was freshly washed and had been dressed in a becoming style. The ensemble she'd selected suited her to perfection – the green cambric and matching spencer complemented her colouring.

'There, you look pretty as a picture. It's a shame you've decided not to wear the bonnet.'

'It would be inappropriate as I'm not going out-side – and I don't need the gloves either.'

She took a final look in the long glass and, satisfied with her appearance, she went into the sitting room to await the arrival of her brother. Beau was going to escort her to the drawing room where the wedding would take place.

A few minutes later he arrived looking every inch the Duke of Silchester in his smart blue top-coat, buff inexpressibles and highly polished hessians.

'You look beautiful, sweetheart, exactly as a bride should.' He took her hand and threaded it through his arm. 'If you're unhappy with this match, my dear, it's not too late to say so. I'll take you to India and by the time we return everyone will have forgotten what took place.'

'Thank you for making that offer, Beau, but I'm happy for the wedding to go ahead. Grey and I are well suited. It's not a love match like Bennett's, but I sincerely believe we can have a happy union.'

'I'm glad to hear you say so, as I've no desire to travel abroad. I'm still concerned about the risks involved with you becoming Carshalton's wife, but he's assured me he'll keep you out of danger.'

They made their way downstairs and she was too nervous to say anything else. As she reached the open double doors to the drawing room, she was greeted by a flurry of piano music.

The furniture had been pushed to one side and a very short row of upright chairs had been placed in front of a lectern. Behind this stood a small, rotund gentleman with a bald pate and a disapproving expression. Presumably this was the man of the cloth come to marry her to Grey.

Her husband-to-be was standing to the right but he wasn't facing the rector, he was turned towards her. His eyes blazed with something she didn't recognise and she almost tripped over her feet.

Lady Carshalton was sitting facing forwards and didn't turn round or stand up – for some reason her unpleasant dresser had taken the seat next to her mistress. Why was this servant present at her wedding ceremony?

Dr Faulkner had the place next to Bates and he got to his feet immediately the music started. A mousy young woman was seated at the pianoforte and playing remarkably well.

Beau guided her the length of the room and then placed her hand on Grey's arm. 'Take care of my sister, Carshalton, or you will have me to answer to.' This comment was spoken quietly; only she and Grey heard it.

Her brother moved aside, leaving her standing next to the man who was about to become her husband. Her mouth was so dry her tongue appeared to have stuck to the roof of her mouth. She doubted she would be able to speak her vows when asked.

'You look beautiful, darling. I can't tell you how happy I am to be marrying you today. I don't deserve such luck.'

The weight on her chest lifted at his words, and she smiled at him but was too overcome to respond. The service progressed and somehow she managed to mumble her first response. Grey spoke so loudly the rector recoiled and then he winked at her.

Her next vow was spoken clearly and within a short space of time he was pushing a plain gold band over her knuckle and they were pronounced man and wife.

'I promise you'll never regret this, sweetheart. I know I'm not the ideal husband – you could have done so much better.'

He sounded so wretched, so sure he'd got the best of the bargain, that she closed the gap between them and stretched up on tiptoes to place her lips on his. He drew her tight so her breasts were pressing against his shirt front. She forgot every-thing apart from the touch of his mouth on hers as he kissed her with such tenderness her knees might have buckled without his strong support.

* * *

Grey was reluctant to release his new bride but he couldn't help but be aware of the rector positively quivering with rage at their display.

'Well, Lady Madeline Carshalton, the deed is done. The duke and my grandmother just have to witness the ceremony and everything's legal.'

His young wife gazed at him, her beautiful green eyes wide and her lips parted invitingly. He was about to kiss her a second time when she spoke. 'I wish the rest of my family could have been here to see me married and that it could have been in our own chapel.'

'And so do I, sweetheart, but events conspired against us. We have our celebration ball to look forward to.'

The duke appeared at his side. 'Dr Faulkner has arranged for a wedding breakfast to be served in the dining room. Lady Carshalton and I will join you as soon as we've signed the certificate.'

Instead of turning to him, Madeline flung herself into her brother's arms. Grey stepped away, allowing them to be alone. She was so young, scarcely out of the schoolroom, and now he'd snatched her away from the loving care of her brother and dragged her into God knows what.

The duke stroked her hair, kissed the top of her head and gently spun her round. He pushed her in his direction. She looked lost and her eyes were tear-filled when, if this had been a love match, she would have been glowing with happiness.

He put his arm around her waist and drew her close. 'Don't look so sad, darling girl. I promise things will not be as bad as you fear. Once you're well enough to travel we'll continue our journey to Blakely Hall. I know nothing about my ancestral home, so it will be a new experience for both of us.'

She leaned trustingly against him. 'I'm not unhappy about marrying you, I just wish that it could have been next summer as we'd planned. I'd always dreamed of a June wedding and that it would take place at Silchester.'

'That would have been perfect, my love, but we must be satisfied with what we've got. Are you able to walk to the dining room or do you wish me to carry you?'

'I can walk quite well as long as I have your arm around me. I've been thinking, Grey, are you expecting my maid and I to sit with Lady Carshalton? I really don't want to spend time closeted with her and Bates.'

'I don't blame you. Your brother has kindly agreed to lend us his carriage for the journey. He will ride the horse I borrowed from him back to Silchester. I've yet to decide how your maid and my valet are to travel.'

They'd arrived at the dining room, which had been transformed. Every available surface was covered in flowers and a sumptuous buffet awaited them on the sideboard. Bottles of champagne stood ready to be poured for the toast.

Madeline was delighted. 'This is everything it should be. How kind our host has been to us. I cannot imagine why such a charming and wealthy gentleman is not already married.'

'I don't suggest that you ask him, sweetheart. He might purport to be a country doctor, but there's far more to him than that. I've invited him to visit us when we return to Heatherfield. I like him and intend to get to know him better.'

A slight frown marred the elegance of her brow. 'Should I not have been consulted about this proposed visit?'

'I beg your pardon, of course I should have told you of my plans...'

She giggled endearingly. 'Told – not asked for my views? I see how things are to be in future, sir. I'm to be a downtrodden and subservient wife allowed no opinions of my own.'

He couldn't stop himself. He lifted her from her feet and kissed her soundly before restoring her to the carpet not a moment too soon. 'You're as likely to be downtrodden as I am to sprout wings and fly.'

The remainder of the day passed pleasantly and he was well satisfied. The duke was to leave at first light and he bid his sister a fond farewell before they all retired. It was purgatory kissing his wife at the door and not being allowed to go in with her.

As he turned to go she called him back. 'Thank you for allowing me time to adjust to my married state. I don't believe there are many husbands who would be so kind.'

'You may have as much as you need, my darling, but I'm praying it won't be too long before you send for me.'

If he took her in his arms again, he doubted he would have the resolve not to persuade her into bed. He stepped away and bowed from a safe distance. 'Goodnight, Madeline, we shall breakfast tomorrow at eight o'clock.'

'I'm hoping we can depart for Blakely Hall tomorrow. I'm sure I'll be perfectly comfortable in a carriage and Lady Carshalton told me that she's leaving after breakfast.'

'I didn't know that – I thought she was waiting until she had a reply from my uncle. We discussed the matter and we decided it would be best not to go if we're still not welcome.'

This wasn't strictly true as his grandmother had been most insistent that they go regardless of the reception they might receive. She seemed determined to reconcile the two sides of the family, however unpleasant it might be for himself and Madeline.

Before he could stop her, his wife left the sanctuary of her sitting room and hurried up to him. 'I'm so glad you said that. I was really not looking forward to being an unwelcome guest. Do you think Dr Faulkner could be persuaded to accommodate us for a few weeks?' She was so close the faint scent of rosewater filled his nostrils.

'I'll talk to him tomorrow. He's rattling around in this large establishment and might well enjoy the company.' If she didn't go he was in danger of forgetting his promise and taking shameful advantage of her.

Then she stretched out and placed her hand on

his chest. 'I can feel your heart pounding. Mine is doing the same.'

'Sweetheart, please go away. I want to make love to you and if you remain where you are I won't be able to stop myself.'

He'd expected her to scamper away but she did something quite remarkable. She moved closer and put her arms around his neck. 'I've decided I want to be your true wife. This is our wedding night and we should spend it together.'

'Are you sure?' His control was slipping, but he held himself back. He'd do nothing to upset her.

Her answer was to pull his head down so she could place her lips on his. He swung her up into his arms and shouldered his way into her apartment and didn't stop until he reached the bedroom.

Gently he set her down and cupped her face in his hands. 'There's still time for you to change your mind, darling. I'll understand.' He could feel her trembling beneath his fingers. 'I'll take things slowly and you can tell me to stop whenever you want.'

Her smile was radiant. 'I'm a little nervous because I don't know exactly what's going to happen between us. Mama passed away before she could explain the intimacies of the marriage bed to me.'

'You don't need to know the details, my love. What we are about to do is as natural as breathing.'

* * *

Madeline woke in the arms of her husband and apart from a slight soreness in her nether regions she'd never felt so wonderful in her whole life. If Mama had told her what took place between a husband and wife involved being entirely without clothes she might not have been so quick to suggest she became a real wife.

She didn't want to wake him, so slowly turned her head and it was to find he was propped on one elbow watching her. 'Good morning, my love, how are you today?'

'I didn't know anything could be so... so enjoyable. I'm so glad I decided not to wait.'

His eyes darkened and she recognised his intent. 'Not nearly as glad as I am.' His hand began to stoke the contours of her body and she forgot everything else apart from what was happening between them.

A considerable time later they decided it was high time they got up. 'I hope we will still be able to break our fast – it's disastrously late. I expect Lady

Carshalton has already gone and I wished to bid her farewell.'

He rolled away from her and threw back the covers to stand, completely unabashed, as naked as the day he was born. She gazed at him in wonderment. The male form was quite stunning when unclothed – at least it was from the rear.

He wandered across to his discarded clothes and pulled them on unhurriedly. 'I must return to my rooms before breakfast. I'll collect you in half an hour.' He looked over his shoulder and grinned. 'That's if you can be ready in time.'

He was waiting for her to leap out of bed as she was, but that wasn't going to happen. 'The sooner you go, sir, the sooner I can get up.'

He slung his evening jacket over one shoulder and strolled from the room. She tumbled out of bed and raced for the screen, behind which was the necessary receptacle. If he hadn't gone, there might have been an embarrassing accident.

Lottie must have been waiting to hear her moving about and came through to tell her there was hot water waiting in the dressing room. 'I thought you might like to wear the russet gown, as it's perfect for your colouring.'

The last pin was just being pushed into her hair

when Grey reappeared. He hadn't knocked before entering her private domain.

'Good, you're ready. I've spoken to our host and he'd be delighted for us to stay for as long as necessary. He's having your belongings moved up to my apartment today.'

Surely he should have consulted her about this? Did this mean that now the relationship was consummated she would no longer be allowed a say, even on matters that concerned her?

16

'Come along, sweetheart, don't dawdle. I'm ravenous and I expect you are too.' He said this with a wicked smile and she flushed from her toes to her crown.

'I take it that my brother and your grandmother have long since departed.'

'Indeed they have, and even the good doctor's abroad somewhere so we'll have the breakfast parlour to ourselves.'

She had no option but to place her hand on his arm and accompany him down the spacious passageway. She glanced at him through her eyelashes and was struck again by how attractive he was. How was it possible she could wish to be intimate with him when she didn't love him and wasn't even sure that she liked him very much?

There was nothing she could do about it; she supposed she was fortunate that this side of the marriage was going to be so enjoyable. 'If we do go to Blakely Hall, your valet can ride but Lottie will have to sit inside with us.'

'Of course she will. I hardly expected her to sit on the box with the coachman. She's a perfectly pleasant girl, unlike the woman my grandmother employs to take care of her.'

Over a substantial breakfast he regaled her with amusing anecdotes about his life as a soldier and she told him about the exploits of Bennett and Grace during their tempestuous courtship.

As the weather was clement, and her hip no longer painful, they decided to take a stroll around the garden. They were enjoying the late roses when a footman hurried out with a letter on a silver salver.

Grey snapped open the wax seal and unfolded the paper. 'My word, this is a prompt response. My uncle cordially invites us to make a prolonged stay with him and is eagerly anticipating our arrival as soon as we can manage it.' He didn't offer to show her the letter but tucked it in his waistcoat pocket.

'I'm so glad we can meet your estranged relatives

after all. I'll consider it my wedding trip. Shall we be leaving tomorrow?'

'Yes, at first light. I don't think it advisable for us to complete the journey in one day, so we'll overnight somewhere and then arrive at mid-morning the next day.' He stretched down and plucked a creamy-white rosebud and handed it to her with a smile that made her pulse race. 'For you, my love – you are my perfect rose.'

In some confusion she accepted his gift but was at a loss to know what to do with it. He gently removed it from her hand and pushed it into her hair. 'That looks exquisite. Which reminds me, do you have sufficient garments for a long stay?'

'More than enough, but when we return I'll replenish my wardrobe. You didn't know that a bride is expected to prepare her bride clothes before the wedding day.'

'Actually I did know that. I'm so sorry, my love, this is yet another thing I've failed to provide. I'll ensure that you have everything you could possibly want as soon as we're back at Heatherfield.'

He looked so contrite she took pity on him. 'I was teasing you. I've no need of anything else at the moment. However, no doubt Grace and I will peruse the latest fashion plates and have new ensembles made up before we attend our first Season next year.'

As they stepped onto the terrace, Dr Faulkner joined them. He half-bowed. 'I was just informed you received a letter by express. From your demeanour I assume it was good news.'

'My uncle has invited us to stay and we will be leaving here first thing tomorrow. Although we have to cut short our stay we shall renew our acquaintance when you join us at Silchester Court for the Christmas house party.'

Madeline frowned. Silchester was her ancestral home, not his. She should have been the one to renew the invitation. Neither of the gentlemen seemed to think that Grey's comment was out of place, so perhaps she was being too proud.

After all, since yesterday her husband had the legal right to do as he pleased with her person and her property – no doubt this included extending an invitation to all and sundry to visit Silchester.

'I'll certainly attend if I can find someone to take over my duties here. I've no intention of leaving this neighbourhood without a physician in attendance.'

She was surprised that the doctor didn't seem unduly bothered or indeed especially honoured to be included in the house party. Her opinion of the gentleman went up. There were more than enough toadies and sycophants around, all desperate to be noticed by her family. It was refreshing to meet someone who was not impressed by their elevated position in society.

'If there is anyone particular you would like to bring with you, Dr Faulkner, then please do so.'

He smiled, making his face look less austere. 'If you're angling to know if I'm romantically involved with anyone, my lady, then I'm happy to inform you I'm not.' For a moment he looked unbearably sad but then he was himself again. 'I'm far too busy to look for a partner – perhaps I'll find someone at your party.'

This was said with a laugh and she knew he didn't intend for his comment to be taken seriously. She would, however, make sure there were several suitable young ladies included in the guest list and then leave things to chance.

* * *

On his arrival at his apartment, Grey stripped off his garments and put on his bedrobe. All this was accomplished without the assistance of his valet. Madeline would be waiting in the adjoining room

and he was eager to resume introducing her to bedroom sport.

There was a slight noise behind him. 'I beg your
pardon for not being here to help, sir. I didn't realise
you'd already retired.' Slater looked decidedly
shifty.

'Out with it, man – what aren't you telling me?'

'Lady Madeline decided it would put the staff to
too much trouble if she moved in here for just one
night.'

'My wife isn't next door?'

'She is not, my lord.'

Grey muttered imprecations under his breath.
He had two choices – either he got dressed again
or paraded through the house as he was. No –
there was a third option and reluctantly he took
this one.

'In which case, I'll remain here. Make sure you
wake me at dawn.'

He wasn't sure if he was more angry at Madeline's defiance or frustrated that he wouldn't be able
to make love to his beautiful wife. He flung back the
covers and rolled into bed without bothering to find
his nightshirt.

When he saw her tomorrow he would make it
very clear he expected his instructions to be fol-

lowed to the letter. He hoped she was regretting her decision as much as he was.

* * *

The following morning he was up before his valet appeared with his shaving water. He headed for the stable yard as soon as he was dressed, confident he'd forgotten nothing – that he'd arranged their departure with military precision. Fortunately neither he nor Madeline had brought a second trunk and there was ample space at the rear of the vehicle for all their trappings.

Jenkins, Smith and Slater were well mounted but this still left two spare animals – the one that had been used as a pack animal and the mare Madeline had ridden.

He spoke to Faulkner's head groom. 'Will it be a problem if I leave these two here?'

'No, sir, as you can see we've plenty of spare stalls.'

'Perhaps your master could return them when he comes for his Christmas visit in a few weeks?' He dipped into his pocket and tossed the man a couple of coins.

He turned to Smith. 'We shall be leaving in an

hour. Make sure you are ready and that the coachman has the carriage waiting outside.'

His man touched his cap. 'We'll be there. I've sent Jenkins ahead to arrange for overnight accommodation – he'll rejoin us on the journey so you'll know where we're stopping.'

Grey nodded and returned to the house to find his wife calmly eating her breakfast as if nothing untoward had taken place last night. 'Good morning, I trust you slept well. I certainly did and I'm eager to set out on this adventure.'

He'd fully intended to severely reprimand her but her sweet smile dissuaded him. 'Good morning to you, my love. I'm delighted you are here in good time.'

He joined her at the table with a laden plate and neither of them spoke until they'd finished. She dropped her cutlery and her napkin with a sigh of contentment.

'That was truly delicious. I've just to run upstairs and put on my bonnet and collect my gloves and reticule and then I'll be ready to depart. Dr Faulkner was called out an hour ago, so will be unable to say goodbye in person.'

'I'm at a loss to understand why a man of his substance devotes his time to doctoring the poor of the neighbourhood.' He gestured around at the expensive fittings. 'Usually becoming a physician is the lot of a younger son, someone without a substantial income, and this obviously isn't the case with him.'

She stood gracefully before answering. 'I believe he's immersing himself in good works in order to forget a broken heart. He is a handsome man and as you pointed out, obviously wealthy – why else would he not be married?'

'You've been reading too many novels, sweetheart. It's far more likely he's a confirmed bachelor like the duke.'

'We shall see when he comes to stay. I'll join you outside in ten minutes.'

True to her word she appeared on the top step looking, as always, quite beautiful. If he had his way all her garments would be made in that particular shade of green, as it set off her hair and eyes to perfection.

His mouth curved at his thoughts. He was an ex-soldier, not a simpering poltroon with a head full of romantic nonsense.

He handed her into the carriage and her maid scuttled around to the far side and scrambled in under her own volition. He was about to join her when he decided he would rather ride than spend hours cooped up inside a stuffy carriage, unable to speak freely because there was a servant present.

'I'm going to ride after all, my dear – far too clement a day to be inside.' He slammed the door and the under-coachman put away the steps before climbing nimbly to take his position on the box.

The coachman released the brake, snapped his whip and the vehicle moved away smoothly. 'Smith, you follow and, Slater, you wait for me. We'll catch you soon enough.'

In less than ten minutes he was astride the erstwhile packhorse, a handsome bay gelding well up to his weight.

* * *

Madeline was glad he'd decided not to sit with her inside the carriage – not because she didn't enjoy spending time with him, but now she could put her feet up on the squabs and travel in comfort.

'Lottie, I'm not sure how long we'll be travelling before we stop for refreshments, but knowing his lordship he will expect to complete a goodly part of the journey. I'm going to sleep if I can. I had little rest last night.'

'Very good, my lady, I'll keep an eye on things out of the window and rouse you in good time.'

The Silchester travelling carriage was extremely luxurious. No expense had been spared when her father had had it built the year he passed away. Despite the poor quality of the lane they were travelling along, the excellent springs softened the discomfort.

She'd expected Grey to give her a frosty reception this morning after her refusal to follow his instructions, but he'd been his usual friendly self. Was his sudden decision to ride a direct result of her refusing to sleep in his bed last night?

Being married to a man with a tendency to think he was still commanding his brigade was going to be more difficult than she'd anticipated. If only they had been able to spend more time together, get to know each other and maybe fall in love, then things might be easier between them. Tears seeped from the corners of her eyes and she turned her face away so her maid wouldn't see.

Mama had told all of them to marry for love and not for any other reason. Her brother Bennett had done so, but circumstances had pushed her into this situation and she wished with all her heart she'd not been obliged to marry so hastily and to a man she barely liked, let alone loved.

The fact that what took place in the marriage bed was very much to her liking would make things bearable for both of them. He had promised to be a good husband to her, to make her happy, and she must believe what he said.

Once she was with child things would be different – they would have a shared interest. She was confident whatever his failings as a husband he would be an excellent father. Her hand moved surreptitiously to her middle. Was it possible she was already carrying his baby?

She must have dozed because she was jolted awake by a sharp tap on the window. She looked round and saw her husband peering in at her.

'Lottie, let down the window – his lordship wishes to speak to me.'

When the window was open he leaned in. 'We're about to turn onto the toll road and will be travelling more speedily. I've arranged for us to halt for midday refreshments but we can stop before then – just let the coachman know.'

'Thank you for informing me. I'm perfectly comfortable and sure I can wait until noon to...' She stopped, horrified she'd been about to mention something so indelicate.

His wicked smile made her blush the more. 'How is your hip?'

'It hardly hurts at all, thank you. Being able to put my feet up makes all the difference.'

He straightened and cantered away. She decided she would prefer to have the window left down and be covered with dust rather than travel without fresh air.

'We've been going a good while so I reckon it must be ten o'clock by now. There's a picnic basket under the seat – do you want me to find you something?'

'No, I'm content to wait until we stop. I'm now wide awake and intend to take more interest in the journey.' She sat up and put her feet on the floor so she could look through the window.

The carriage halted and then lurched to the left. Immediately the ride became smoother and the pace picked up. The sun was shining and the hedges and trees were glorious in their autumn finery. They had been travelling at a spanking pace for some time when the under-coachman blew his horn, indicating there was another vehicle approaching.

Their carriage slowed and the horses were guided towards the far side of the road and, as often happened in these situations, the inside rear wheel of the carriage dropped into a pothole. She clutched at the strap to stop herself being tipped from the seat but was too late and her world turned upside down.

* * *

Grey watched in horror as the rear wheel of the carriage came away from the back axle and the vehicle lurched. For a moment it teetered and he held his breath, praying it wouldn't tip into the deep ditch that ran alongside the road.

Then it pitched sideways. The horses were dragged backwards kicking and screaming in protest. The two coachmen were thrown from the box and the cries from inside the coach turned his blood to ice.

'Slater – see to the horses. Smith, with me. You drag the men from the ditch before they drown. I'll try and get into the coach.'

He vaulted from his horse and jumped into the ditch, disregarding the water that came over the tops of his boots. Why was there no sound from inside the vehicle? If anything had happened to Madeline he would be devastated. She was already dear to his heart.

17

Madeline was crushed beneath her maid and the various boxes and baskets that had been stored under the squabs. 'Lottie, are you injured?'

'A bit bruised, my lady, but I reckon I'm fine. I'll try and move from on top of you.'

'No – stay still. I fear the carriage might slip further into the ditch if we rock it.'

Then she realised Grey was shouting at her. 'We are unhurt, but there's water seeping in through the roof and already our gowns are sodden.'

'Thank God! I feared the worst when you didn't answer immediately. Don't try and move. Assistance is coming from other vehicles and we'll soon have the carriage righted and be able to get you out.'

The horses were now quiet and she prayed this meant none of them had been seriously injured in the accident. The carriage rocked and more cold water gushed in through the split seams of the roof. From what she could make out there were several gentlemen outside and Grey was organising them into a rescue party.

Suddenly his face appeared at a door and he smiled encouragingly. 'It won't be long now, sweetheart. I'm tying a rope to the carriage and then we can pull it upright. You must brace yourselves as best you can but it will be uncomfortable, I fear.'

'It can't be worse than things are at the moment.' He vanished and immediately the carriage started to shift. 'Jam your feet into the window, Lottie; that should keep us steady long enough to avoid further damage.'

There was barely time to do as she suggested before the vehicle began to move more quickly. Unfortunately the substantial quantity of ditch water in which they had been lying poured over their heads, adding to their discomfort.

As the coach crashed back to its correct position both she and her maid fell into the well of the carriage. She couldn't hold back a yelp of pain as her injured hip hit the floor.

Both doors were prised open and he was beside her. 'Sweetheart, let me lift you out and then I can put my riding cape around you.'

She was about to protest, to ask him to remove Lottie first, but there was no need as he'd already arranged for her maid to be taken care of. 'Has anyone been hurt in the accident? Are the horses all right?'

He gently lifted her and placed her on her feet, then his warm coat was around her shoulders and immediately she felt warmer.

'The coachmen are wet and bruised but otherwise unhurt and the horses took no harm.'

She then became aware the road was blocked by two carriages and it was to one of these that he was striding. A plump matron was peering anxiously through the open door and greeted her with a cry of distress.

'My lady, what a dreadful business. I thank God that no one has been mortally wounded. Put her in here with me. As soon as the way is clear I shall take your wife to Chorley Manor. If you take the next turning to the right it leads directly to my home. It's no more than a mile from here. As soon as I get there, I'll send sufficient men with a diligence and ropes to assist you in recovering your carriage and also a cart to collect your luggage.'

Madeline was bundled into the warm interior and Lottie joined her. She had no idea who this kind person was and Grey had not thought to introduce them.

'I'll follow as soon as I can, sweetheart. We need to clear the road so the traffic can continue.'

He slammed the door and she barely had time to settle before the vehicle moved off. Her sodden garments were going to soak through the thick cloth of Grey's coat and would damage the smart squabs.

'Madam, I fear my maid and I are going to cause irreparable damage to your carriage...'

'I care not for that – your well-being and comfort is paramount. I should have given you my name – I am Mrs Belinda Chorley. My husband is Squire Chorley.' She said this as if Madeline should recognise the name so she nodded and smiled.

'I'm so glad you were there to offer your assistance, Mrs Chorley. I apologise for any inconvenience we might cause to your household by our unexpected arrival.'

'I'm delighted to help, Lady Madeline. I find myself with little to do now my children have left home.

Having you and his lordship to stay, even if it is only for a night or two, will brighten my days.'

A few minutes later the carriage turned down a leafy lane and Mrs Chorley was happy to tell her they were now travelling on her husband's land and would soon be at the manor.

'My lady, I can find you and your maid something to wear until your luggage arrives. My youngest daughter only recently got married and has left some of her wardrobe behind. You are a similar size, so one of her gowns should be ideal.'

'Thank you, ma'am, I much appreciate your kindness. I can't understand how a wheel can have come off our carriage. It was purchased only a year or two ago and it's of the highest quality.'

'No doubt your husband will be able to ascertain the reason for the accident once he has the carriage in our coach house. We employ our own smith and cartwright so the repairs can be undertaken immediately.'

'We are on our way to visit Lord Carshalton's relatives and they will be expecting us tomorrow morning. I expect my husband has already sent one of the grooms to Blakely Hall with a message.'

The carriage rocked to a halt outside an imposing manor house. A footman emerged from the front door immediately to let down the steps and assist them from the vehicle.

'Come along, my dear, the sooner we have you in clean, dry clothes the better.'

Madeline was conducted by the housekeeper, a Mrs Reynolds, a woman of middle years and pleasant countenance, to a suite of rooms at the rear of the building. 'My lady, someone will be along immediately to light the fires. A bath will be drawn for you and a maid will come to assist in your ablutions until your own abigail can join you.'

'Lord Carshalton will also require a bath, but as he will have his valet and luggage with him that should present less of a problem.'

The housekeeper curtsied. 'My lady, nothing you and his lordship require is any trouble at all. There's a large staff here and they are underemployed. Having house guests is a rarity and I can tell you that Cook is beside herself with excitement.'

'Good heavens! Why is that?'

The housekeeper beamed. 'The master and mistress prefer to eat plain food and she has little opportunity to prepare anything that demonstrates her culinary talents. You will have nothing to complain about when you sit down to dinner, I assure you. There will be three courses and several removes as fine as anything one could eat at the grandest tables in the land.'

This garrulous lady was nodding so vigorously several pins flew from her hair.

'In which case I'll forego any refreshments at the moment, Reynolds, and save my appetite for later.'

'Not at all, my lady, a tray will be along directly. Dinner isn't served until five o'clock, so there'll be plenty of time before you are required to eat again.'

As they'd been conversing the sound of buckets clattering and various other noises had been coming from the far door, which presumably led from the sitting room into the bedchamber. Madeline glanced down and was horrified to see a spreading pool of muddy water had seeped from her saturated garments onto the pristine carpet.

'I need to change out of my wet clothes. I'm ruining the carpet.'

'I apologise – I shouldn't have kept you talking. My tongue runs away with me. If you would care to come with me I'm sure everything's ready next door.'

* * *

As soon as the carriage had departed with Madeline the two other vehicles that had been delayed were able to continue on their journey, leaving him alone in the road with his men and the damaged coach.

He joined Smith who was helping the coachmen unharness the team. As the horses were released, Grey inspected each one in turn for any injury and was pleased they were unharmed by their unpleasant experience. Two more carriages trundled past and the occupants of each stopped to offer assistance. He was able to thank them and send them on their way.

'You'll need to let Blakely Hall know what's transpired here. Tell Mr Carshalton we'll be with them as soon as we can. God knows how long it will take to repair the carriage and we can't travel until it's done.'

His man touched his cap. 'I'll get off directly, sir. I reckon Jenkins should be back anytime soon. I'll call in at the hostelry and tell them not to expect us for a day or two.'

'Do that, thank you.' The sound of a cart approaching interrupted their conversation. 'Excellent, I believe the first of the rescue vehicles has arrived.'

He supervised the transfer of the baggage. He told the driver to get the trunks taken to whatever apartment they'd been allocated immediately he returned to Chorley Manor. By the time these were on their way a lumbering diligence arrived, pulled by two massive farm horses. He was pleased to see there were half a dozen men travelling on the cart. This should be more than enough to manoeuvre his carriage aboard.

After a deal of swearing, shoving and pulling, his objective was achieved. The carriage was safely roped to the diligence. The vehicle would have to travel another half a mile before it could turn safely.

The six outdoor men cheerfully trotted off alongside the cart in order to ensure it didn't topple from its precarious position.

As soon as they were out of earshot, his coachman indicated he wished to speak. 'My lord, it weren't no accident. Someone tampered with the wheel and that's why it came off.'

'How in hell's name did the bastards get to the carriage without being seen? More to the point – how did they know where we were?'

Slater, his valet, looked grave. 'They must have followed the duke, my lord; there's no other explanation.' He looked around as if expecting they would be ambushed at any moment.

'We need to get away from here. The coachmen

can ride one horse and lead another. I think it highly unlikely they are still in the locality – they'll just wait to hear if their interference managed to kill me.'

His hands clenched and a white-hot rage took hold of him. His beloved could have perished in the accident so the perpetrators would die. No one could attack his wife and live. He would get Madeline settled at Blakely Hall under the protection of his estranged family and then hunt down those behind the attacks and dispose of them.

The distance was no more than a mile, which was fortunate as the weather worsened and it began to rain heavily as he turned into the drive. He kicked his mount into a canter and led his troop around to the rear of the house straight to the stables.

The cart that had transported the luggage had arrived ahead of them and he was pleased to see all but one of the trunks had gone upstairs already.

He dismounted and tossed the reins to a waiting stable boy. There was no need to give further instructions to his men; they knew what they were about. He followed the brick pathway to the side door and it opened as he approached.

The male servant conducted him to the chambers he was to share with Madeline until his coach was repaired – God knew how long that would be. Replacing the wheel was a simple matter, but it would be more difficult to repair the coachwork and the squabs, which had suffered from being immersed in the ditch.

His wife was curled up in front of a substantial fire. She sprung to her feet and rushed across to greet him.

'Dearest Grey, you're soaked through. There's a bath waiting for you next door and your valet is there putting out fresh garments.'

He held out his hand and she took it without hesitation. He drew her closer and then held her hard against his chest for a moment. 'I'll join you here shortly. How is your hip? Did it suffer further damage from your experience?'

'It's no stiffer or more painful than it was before. Go – get out of your wet clothes. We can talk when you're comfortable.'

* * *

Madeline picked up her discarded book and resumed her place by the fire. Her maid and his valet were going to have to come to an arrangement as she and Grey were sharing one room. Her lips curved at the thought of Lottie's reaction if she blundered in whilst he was taking his bath. She thought that her husband would not be amused either.

A sudden gust of wind hurled rain against the window, making her jump, the panes rattle and the curtains move. Would someone come in and close the shutters or should she do it? The draught was unpleasant so she might as well do the job herself.

Although it was early afternoon she could scarcely see across the park. Heavy, black clouds had blotted out the sun and she was relieved they had not been caught out in the storm. The wooden shutters unhooked easily and she pulled the first one across without any difficulty. She was moving the second when she was certain she saw a shadowy figure lurking in the woodland that bordered the grass.

She blinked, screwed up her eyes and took another look, but this time there was nothing untoward to see. Her imagination was playing tricks with her – there'd been too many accidents and ambushes and she was seeing danger where none existed. Hastily she fastened the shutters, pulled the curtains and moved on to the second window.

The candles were already lit and with the cheerful fire the room was warm and welcoming. A soft tap at the door heralded the arrival of the promised refreshments. By the time the two maids had arranged matters to their satisfaction the appetising aromas were making her mouth water.

Once they had departed she knocked on the bedroom door. 'Grey, there's food here. Soup, meat pasties, bread and cheese, and a selection of pies and pastries.'

'I'll be there in a moment. Start without me.'

She didn't need to be told a second time and quickly filled a bowl with the delicious-looking vegetable soup. After adding a chunk of bread she took a seat at the second table that had been laid for them.

'I'm ravenous, sweetheart. Is the soup as tasty as it sounds?' Grey dropped a kiss on the top of her head as he walked past to help himself.

'Was I slurping? I do beg your pardon, my love, I hadn't realised my enjoyment was so noisy.'

There was far too much food but, despite knowing they would have to sit down to an elaborate dinner in less than four hours, they devoured a good part of it.

When they were comfortably settled on the *chaise longue* Madeline told him about her wild imaginings. Instead of laughing he looked grim.

'I hadn't intended to tell you this, but the carriage had been tampered with. Whoever is trying to murder me is out there watching us.'

Her recently eaten meal threatened to return. 'What are you going to do?'

'I have matters in hand, sweetheart; there's no need for you to worry. We'll set out for my uncle's house as soon as the carriage is repaired and you will be safe there. My men and I will then take care of matters.'

There was no necessity for her to ask what he meant – he was a soldier and wouldn't hesitate to dispatch the miserable cowards who were trying to injure him. 'I won't be happy until the man behind these attacks has been apprehended. Are you any closer to discovering who this might be?'

'Your brother's making enquiries on my behalf in London and will send word to me when he gets a definitive reply.' He stretched out and plucked her from the seat and placed her in his lap. 'Enough of this gloomy discussion, darling – there are far more enjoyable ways of passing the afternoon.'

18

The following morning when Madeline awoke Grey had already left. She was astonished that he'd managed to get dressed without awakening her. She stretched luxuriously and came to the conclusion that married life suited her very well despite the disadvantages of having a husband with a short temper and a tendency to treat her like one of his junior officers.

She stretched out and rang the little brass bell on the bedside table and immediately Lottie rushed in. 'Good morning, my lady. I've got your hot chocolate keeping warm in front of the fire in the dressing room. His lordship has been gone this age.' The girl dashed across the room and pulled back the curtains and then folded back the wooden shutters.

'Oh dear! It's as gloomy as it was yesterday afternoon. I hope the weather improves by the time the carriage is repaired.'

'From what I've heard downstairs it should be ready by tomorrow. The damage wasn't nearly as bad as was thought.' Her maid vanished to return with the tray immediately.

'Lottie, how have you and Slater arranged things so you don't clash?'

The girl grinned. 'It's working ever so well and he's very accommodating and quite happy to share the dressing room with me. What do you want me to put out for you this morning?'

As she was speaking she retrieved the discarded nightgown and draped a bedrobe over the end of the bed. Only then did Madeline remember she was totally naked beneath the sheets – something she was quite certain her abigail would be shocked by.

'I'll wear whatever you like. As long as it has long sleeves and a spencer I'll be satisfied with your choice.'

Breakfast was served at ten o'clock and she was on her way to the breakfast room in good time. She had expected Grey to join her there but he failed to appear, so she ate a lonely meal as Mrs Chorley also failed to appear.

After eating, Madeline wandered along to the drawing room where she found her hostess sitting by the fire lost in thought. Mrs Chorley was some-what subdued this morning. 'Madam, are you un-well? Is there anything I can do for you?'

'No, Lady Madeline, I'm never at my best until midday. Lord Carshalton has gone out riding with two of his men – I cannot imagine what possessed him to do so when the weather is so dreary.'

Madeline felt a flicker of unease – Grey must be searching for the intruders she'd seen last night. She prayed he wouldn't come to any harm at their hands. She pinned on a bright smile. 'I expect he's gone to check if anything was left behind yesterday at the accident site. He was a soldier for many years, you know, and a little rain is nothing to him after what he endured.'

'Gentlemen are strange creatures. I've yet to fathom out the workings of my husband's mind even though we've been together for more than thirty years.'

'I have four brothers, Mrs Chorley, so I could consider myself an expert on the subject. However, apart from knowing that they prefer to be outside rather than indoors, and have no interest in novels, I'm as much in the dark as you are.' She smiled. 'No doubt I'll learn more about my husband as the months pass.' An image of Grey beside her in bed, his eyes dark with passion, caused her cheeks to colour.

'You are newly wed, my dear, and Lord Carshalton is still besotted with you. Make the most of it, as I can assure you once the gloss has worn away life will be quite different.' Mrs Chorley sighed heavily. 'My children were my life and I am bereft without them. I wish they hadn't grown up and left me and could have remained at home with their mama.'

This was hardly encouraging news. Mr Chorley had seemed a cordial gentleman when she met him the previous night and although not especially affectionate with his wife they seemed to rub along together well enough.

'Of course, my dear, yours is a love match whereas Mr Chorley and I barely knew each other when we were conjoined. Pray don't misunderstand me, we both entered the union willingly. He offered for me because I was very pretty when I was a girl and had a substantial dowry – I accepted because he was wealthy and reasonably attractive.'

'Didn't you know anything about him before agreeing to marry? Surely you must have been aware of his habits and interests?'

'My father made the usual enquiries. He wouldn't have allowed the wedding to go ahead if Mr Chorley had been a gambler or philanderer. He was neither and I'm sure I have nothing to complain about. He's never raised his hand to me, took a reasonable interest in our children and has always given me a generous allowance.'

'In which case, ma'am, why don't you visit your children? I'm sure they'll be delighted to see you. Do you have any grandchildren?'

'I have two – a girl of one year and a boy of few months. Of course I went to see them when they were born but I've not been since.' She smiled sadly. 'I wasn't warmly welcomed by either son-in-law, and it was made plain to me that I must limit my visits to a few days a year.'

Small wonder Mrs Chorley was so low in spirits. 'What about holding a Christmas and New Year house party? This is a vast establishment and you could invite all the family including your grandchildren. There are few gentlemen who would refuse such a generous invitation.'

'That's a splendid notion. Mr Chorley will not

travel but would be happy to have a house full of gentlemen that he can play billiards, hunt, ride and play cards with.' She jumped nimbly from her seat her previous ill humour quite forgotten. 'Forgive me, I must leave you and find him at once and get his approval for this scheme.'

She dashed away, leaving Madeline to her own devices. She glanced at the mantel clock and saw she had an hour at least to fill before she could expect Grey to return.

* * *

'That was a monumental waste of time, Jenkins. Although I'm sure my wife wasn't mistaken when she said she saw men lurking in the trees last night, there's no sign of them now. I'm sure they were just investigating our current whereabouts and no doubt planning further attacks.'

'None of the varmints has been near the stables or coach house, my lord. They'll not get the opportunity to tamper with your carriage a second time. I reckon we should be safe enough whilst we're here.'

Grey dismounted in the yard and tossed his reins to a waiting boy before heading to the coach house to see how the repairs were progressing. He was delighted to find the carriage looked as good as new. As soon as the interior was dry, they could continue their journey.

'I've decided to take Mr Chorley into my confidence, Jenkins. He's the magistrate and I'm sure will look unfavourably on what transpired. I'm hoping he'll be prepared to lend me half a dozen men so we can complete the distance to Blakely Hall confident no one would be foolish enough to attack us.'

His man nodded. 'That should do it, sir, but I'm not sure he'll have that many men and horses to spare.'

'I'll speak to him immediately. If he hasn't got what I need then he must tell me where I can find the extra men and horses. I also think it would be wise to complete the journey in one day and not overnight somewhere. If we leave before light and take it steady it can be done. We must make sure we halt a couple of times to allow the horses to recuperate.'

Grey strode off to the house and tossed his dripping coat, gloves and hat to a waiting footman. 'Direct me to your master.'

'Mr Chorley is in his study, my lord. If you walk into the main hall and take the passageway on your right, you will find the room at the far end.'

His boots were leaving muddy imprints on the spotless boards but that was no concern of his. There were more than ample staff here to deal with such minor problems. He knocked loudly and was bid to enter.

'I apologise for disturbing you, sir, but there are things I need to talk to you about.'

Chorley was horrified by his account and agreed to help him in any way he could. 'There's no need for you to go in search of men, my lord. I'll organise matters for you. This is a damnable business – the sooner these villains are apprehended the better.'

'Thank you for your assistance. My carriage is ready and we will leave just before dawn tomorrow. Can the necessary men and horses be found by then?'

'Indeed they can, my lord. I must now apologise in turn. Mrs Chorley has taken it upon herself to invite half the neighbourhood to dine tonight in honour of your unexpected visit. Although short notice, I expect a full quota to attend as it's not often we have such toplofty folk in our neighbourhood.'

'Lady Carshalton and I will be honoured to attend your dinner party, sir, but I'm sure you and your guests will understand if we retire early so that we can be up in time to leave.'

Jenkins was already aware they were leaving at dawn, so there was no need to go back to the stables and update him. What he must do instead was get Slater to spruce him up so he could join Madeline wherever she was.

He went in search of her and found her stretched out on a daybed reading a periodical. Her smile when she saw him made him feel ten foot tall.

'Grey, I'm so pleased to see you. Mrs Chorley has abandoned me to set in motion invitations for her Christmas house party.'

He leaned down and kissed her. 'That's not the only thing she is organising, sweetheart. We are to be the guests of honour at a formal dinner party this evening. Your maid is searching out a suitable evening gown and my valet is taking care of my evening rig.'

'Sit down, my love – you're far too tall to be looming over me. It's quite intimidating.' Her feet were already on the floor and she patted the space beside her.

'It's not my intention to intimidate. I cannot help my unusual size.' He folded himself down and turned sideways to face her. After he'd explained his plans for the next day she agreed this was the right decision.

'Your relatives will be heartily sick of us before we even arrive, for we've been nothing but trouble so far. We've changed our travel arrangements three times, which is hardly civil.'

'I'm sure they'll just be happy to have us arrive in one piece.'

'I've been thinking, what about Smith? Did you tell him to remain at Blakely Hall or ride back to join us only to repeat the process? The poor man and his horse will be quite exhausted.'

'I told him to remain at the inn where we originally intended to stay overnight. Instead, we'll stop for refreshments and allow the horses to recover from their exertions.'

The rain continued to lash the windows and the fire spattered as water found its way down the chimney. 'It's going to be heavy going with the roads so wet. Wouldn't it be better to stay here until it's more clement?'

It had not been his intention to discuss the matter with her, but now he had no choice. 'Sweetheart, I need to have you somewhere safe so my men and I can root out these villains and their master. Obviously, I cannot leave you here whilst I do so.'

'In which case, why don't I return to Silchester?

My brothers are perfectly capable of taking care of me in your absence.'

This was a valid point and he could hardly tell her why he didn't want to do this. The duke exerted undue influence over his wife and he wished to weaken this link. Madeline was his concern and what better place to leave her than with his family?

'We can hardly renege on our promise to visit, my love, and it's considerably further to Silchester Court than it is to Blakely Hall.'

She frowned for a second and then relaxed back into his embrace. 'How silly of me, I should have realised. Won't we be more vulnerable travelling so slowly tomorrow?'

'It doesn't matter how slowly we travel, with six extra men to escort us, an ambush or attack is highly unlikely.'

* * *

After luncheon Madeline retired to their shared chamber for an afternoon rest, although why she was so tired when she'd done absolutely nothing was a mystery to her. Grey joined Mr Chorley in the billiard room.

The dinner party passed without incident but

she was relieved she had the excuse of the early departure, which allowed her to escape from the drawing room before tea was served.

She wasn't left alone in the huge tester bed for long and the house was silent before she eventually fell into a deep and contented sleep.

She was awake in good time but Grey had already gone down. Warmly dressed in a dark green travelling gown and cloak, she joined him outside. The carriage was waiting, the team stamping and snorting in their eagerness to depart. The fact that it was still dark seemed not to bother them one jot.

This time her husband was to travel inside with them, which pleased her but not her maid.

'At least it's no longer raining, which should mean that our journey will be less hazardous.' He handed her into the carriage and her maid scrambled in behind her.

The door was left open whilst he went to have a final word with the mounted escort. 'It's going to be a long day, Lottie. You can't huddle in the corner with a rug over your head for the entire time – you will suffocate.'

'My lady, I find his lordship ever so fierce. I'm all of a tremble when he looks in my direction.'

'I'm not suggesting that you join in our conversation – that would be unsuitable. However, you can look out of the window on your side of the carriage and I promise we'll pretend you're not there.'

The girl smiled and appeared more comfortable in her seat. The vehicle rocked alarmingly as Grey climbed in and took the window seat next to her. The door was closed and the steps put away, then the coachman cracked his whip and they were moving.

Grey nodded towards Lottie, who was studiously staring out of the window, the brim of her chip straw bonnet making her face invisible. He lowered his head and spoke quietly directly into Madeline's ear. His breath was warm and caused heat to pool in her nether regions.

'Do you think your maid would prefer to travel on the box when it's light?'

'I've no idea, but if it's not raining she might be happy to do so. I'll ask her later on.'

Neither of them had had much sleep the previous night as it had been spent in far more enjoyable activities, so with her head resting on his shoulder, and his arm firmly around her waist, her eyes were slowly becoming heavy. He was already asleep – no doubt his military life had given him the

facility to take rest when it presented itself, regardless of the circumstances.

19

Madeline didn't rouse until Grey gently squeezed her shoulder. The carriage was stationary and the door open. She looked around with surprise. 'Good heavens! It's sunny outside and I do believe I must have slept for hours.'

'We both have, sweetheart, and now we've arrived at our first stop. We will remain here for a couple of hours to allow the horses to rest.'

'I've no idea what the time is, but it seems an age since I ate last – I am hungry.'

He chuckled. 'As am I. A substantial meal has been prepared for us all and it will be served in a private parlour. There's also a chamber put aside for you to refresh yourself.'

He leaned in and swung her from the vehicle. She blinked at the brightness after being so long in the gloom of the carriage. The hostelry he'd selected for their first break was an old, rambling building but looked in good repair. The cobbled yard in which they were standing was substantial and even with two other vehicles there was still ample room for a mail coach or stagecoach to trundle in and disgorge its passengers.

The sky was blue and cloudless, a great improvement on earlier. 'This appears to be a respectable place, Grey. I hope the food lives up to my expectations.'

Their escort had already dismounted and led their horses round to the stables. The coachmen were busy unharnessing the team and Slater and Lottie were waiting to accompany them inside.

The meal was everything she'd hoped and when she was replete she headed for the chamber allocated to them. Refreshed and comfortable, she returned to her husband who was outside talking to Jenkins.

He beckoned her over. 'We can't leave for another hour, my love, and in the circumstances I don't think it would be wise to wander about the countryside. There's a pleasant flower garden at the rear of the premises – do you care to take a stroll around it with me?'

* * *

Their final stop was in a village no more than a mile or two from their destination. Madeline was heartily sick of the journey, as being cooped up in a stuffy coach for hours had been decidedly unpleasant. Her maid had opted to travel on the box and she envied her the fresh air.

Although they'd had the carriage to themselves neither of them were inclined to repeat the pleasures of the night-time. If they had drawn the curtains it would have been obvious to those who rode alongside what was going on inside.

Grey had bespoken a chamber with a plentiful supply of hot water. Lottie produced a fresh gown and packed away her heavy cloak. 'Do you want the spencer, my lady? The sun will be down soon and it will be a mite chilly.'

'Yes, thank you.' She stepped away from the dressing table and tried to see her reflection in the window. This pale green dimity gown was a favourite of hers and she thought it perfect for her introduction to her new family. The emerald sash and the matching ribbons on her bonnet were a trifle flamboyant, but suited her to perfection.

This time Grey had been given a room of his own and he too had changed his raiment. Was he as nervous about meeting his estranged family as she was?

There was a soft tap on the door and her maid ran to open it. He stepped in, looking devastating in his dark green jacket, spotless white shirt and cravat and pale green waistcoat. His smile made her toes curl.

'You look enchanting as always, sweetheart.' He gestured to Lottie and she scuffled from the chamber. 'There's something I've still not told you and I really should have talked about it before this.'

'Is it why your family became divided?'

He nodded. 'I don't know the full story, as my grandmother was reluctant to talk about it. My father married against his parents' wishes – they had a bride picked out for him but he rejected their choice and married for love.'

'Was your mama considered unsuitable as my brother's wife, Grace, was initially?'

'Exactly so – she was the daughter of the local curate – perfectly respectable but had no inheritance either.'

'So did they leave voluntarily or were they sent away?'

'My father severed all connection to his family and moved to another part of the country. He sold the smaller estates he'd inherited and with the money bought himself something less grand. He invested wisely and we lived comfortably on the income.' His eyes were sad as he continued. 'My mother died in childbirth when I was scarcely out of leading strings and I'm afraid I don't remember her. My father never remarried but he always seemed content as he was.'

'Did you never ask him about his family?'

'It didn't occur to me to do so. I received a good education, had a happy, if somewhat lonely, childhood and he bought me my colours on my seventeenth birthday. We remained close and exchanged regular correspondence until he perished from a congestion of the lungs four years ago. I remained in ignorance of my elevation to the aristocracy until the letter caught up with me in Portugal last year.'

'I'm glad that finally you will be reunited with your uncle and cousin. I'm just surprised they didn't contact you sooner – eight and twenty years is a long time to carry a feud.'

'My grandmother said they didn't know of my

existence until my grandfather died and the lawyers discovered my whereabouts.'

He gathered her close and cupped her face in his hand. 'I can't believe I'm married to you – I must be the luckiest man in England.' His eyes blazed, and then he kissed her hard and she forgot everything else for a few blissful minutes.

He raised his head. 'Come along, darling, we must arrive in time for supper. I would prefer to see Blakely Hall before it gets dark.'

The horses looked remarkably fresh considering the great distance they'd covered that day. Lottie resumed her place on the box with such enthusiasm Madeline wondered if the girl had developed a tendre for one of the coachmen. They were both handsome young men and she could do a lot worse than pin her hopes to one of them.

'How much land does your uncle possess?'

'Blakely Hall is set in around three hundred acres and contains several productive farms as well as the village of Blakely. We are already travelling on Carshalton land.'

She looked around with interest. 'Does that mean the inn we just stopped at belongs to Mr Carshalton?'

'They will be his tenants, yes. Everywhere looks

well cared for, the cottages in good repair and the village folk seem happy enough.'

'Why would you think otherwise? The fact that your grandfather was a hard man doesn't mean he was a bad landlord. Look, I can see a magnificent house on the hill to the right of us. Is that Blakely Hall?'

'It must be – it's far bigger than I anticipated. Small wonder I inherited such a vast fortune.'

He sat back against the squabs and for the first time since she'd met him she saw he was apprehensive. She pressed her hand against his cheek. 'You mustn't worry about your reception, my love. These people might be related to you but they are strangers. I'm your family now and so are my brothers and sister. If they are not to your liking we can leave and return to Silchester Court next week.'

He turned his face and kissed her palm. The touch of his lips on her skin made her catch her breath. Instinctively she leaned towards him and was rewarded by the touch of his lips on her mouth.

'Enough, young lady, your wanton ways will lead me astray.' His voice was playful and she sighed theatrically, enjoying his teasing.

'La, sir, how can you say such things? I'm an innocent country girl and you are a society gentleman well versed in the art of seduction.'

What might have taken place next she could only imagine, if the cheerful face of one of their escorts hadn't appeared at the open window. 'My lord, I reckon we'll be turning onto the drive in a moment. Do you want one of us to ride ahead?'

'Is that necessary? Can they not see us approaching?'

'The hall's on the hill, my lord, and trees border the edges of the drive making it impossible to see any vehicles until they're almost there.'

'In which case, send Jenkins.' Grey relaxed into the corner with her hand still clasped in his. 'I expect you will want to retire early, sweetheart, after such an arduous journey.' His wicked smile made her blush.

'Indeed I will. However, I expect you might like to stay up until the small hours becoming acquainted with your family.'

'I might be an ex-soldier, my love, and well used to managing on little sleep, but not even the prospect of spending time with my uncle, cousin and grandmother will keep me long from your bed. This is our honeymoon. We should be spending it alone in some romantic spot, not gallivanting

around the countryside pursued by murderous attackers.'

'Blakely Hall is so huge I'm sure we'll have
ample opportunity to be private.' Then she recalled
what he'd said about abandoning her whilst he
hunted for the perpetrators and her smile slipped.

The carriage turned onto the drive. On the right
was a gatehouse but there was no sign of a gate-
keeper. Immediately they moved into the shadow of
the trees and she shivered. No sunlight filtered
through the dense foliage and the carriage was
plunged into darkness.

He released her hand and put his arm around
her waist, drawing her closer. 'If this were mine I'd
thin out these trees and let some light in.'

A full twenty minutes later they emerged into
the evening sunlight and immediately her spirits
lifted. 'How beautiful! I understand why they keep
the drive as it is – it makes one's first view of Blakely
Hall such an amazing contrast. Although the edifice
is far older than my ancestral home, I consider it
almost as lovely. It has obviously been extended and
modernised over time.'

'An attractive building – but far too large for
comfortable living. It would take an hour to walk
from one end to the other.'

She giggled at his exaggeration. Then she noticed something that gave her pause. 'There are footmen waiting on the steps but I can't see your relatives or even the butler.'

'I expect they consider themselves far too grand to greet us in public, sweetheart.'

'I am the daughter of a duke; you hold the title and are the head of the family – this is not a good start. Wherever I've visited, the host and hostess always come out to meet me – unless it's unpleasant weather or late evening.'

The impressive front door remained closed even as they rolled to a halt in front of it. The footmen sprang into action and the steps were let down and the carriage door opened with a flourish. Only as Grey handed her from the vehicle did anyone appear.

The servants were already busy unloading the trunks under the watchful supervision of Lottie and Slater.

A tall, thin man in black stood on the steps. He was obviously the butler and didn't look at all pleased to see them. He didn't bow and he didn't make a move towards them as he should have done.

'As you say, my love, not an auspicious beginning to our visit. Despite having a cordial invitation from my uncle, I'm not sure that his feelings are shared by his staff. No doubt the fact that his master didn't receive the title as expected has not gone down well.'

'Grey, it's not a servant's place to have an opinion on such matters. The butler's behaviour is unacceptable. The only explanation is that we're not welcome and Mr Carshalton was compelled to invite us because your grandmother insisted.'

He frowned. 'I bow to your superior knowledge on such matters, Madeline. I think we've spent long enough dawdling here; we shall go in and see for ourselves how the land lies.'

He offered his arm and she placed her now gloved hand on it. Neither of them enjoyed wearing gloves but it was *de rigueur* and so they had no option if they wished to make a good impression.

She risked a glance in his direction. She didn't know if his icy expression was for her or the butler and prayed it was the latter.

He ignored the servant sent out to greet them and she was whisked into the vast hall. She couldn't hold back her shiver. 'It's like an icehouse – how can that be when it's quite mild outside?'

'No fires lit and no curtains and little furniture. Decidedly unwelcoming for any visitors.' He reached across and squeezed her hand. 'Do we remain here like nincompoops or go in search of our missing host?'

For a moment she thought this to be a rhetorical question then realised he was genuinely puzzled. This remark had been made so quietly only she could have heard him. 'The wretched butler should come in and escort us. I would have expected the housekeeper to have been here to introduce herself as well.'

Grey turned and fixed the sullen butler with a basilisk stare. 'You, direct us to Lady Carshalton immediately.'

The man recoiled but then recovered his composure. 'My lord, I fear you've arrived at a time of crisis in the house. Lady Carshalton was taken dangerously ill when she returned and Mr Carshalton and Mr Frederick are at her bedside. They are unaware of your arrival. I thought it best—'

Grey stepped forward, towering over the speaker. 'It's not your place to think about anything that takes place here. Summon the housekeeper and see that Lady Madeline is taken to her apartment immediately. Have a supper tray sent up.' The butler didn't respond. 'Do I make myself clear? Get on with it. Now.'

'I beg your pardon, my lord. My name is Cornwall – at your service.' Finally he bowed deeply and Madeline unclenched her fists.

Moments later an elderly woman, with her hair scraped back into an unbecoming bun, almost ran across the floor. She curtsied. 'Matthews, house-keeper here. If you would care to come with me, my lady, your apartment is ready and your dresser is waiting.'

Madeline ignored her. 'I'm so sorry to hear that your grandmother is so desperately ill. It explains why things are as they are.'

'Go up, sweetheart. As soon as I know how things stand, I'll come and tell you.'

She turned to Matthews. 'Conduct me to my chambers.'

He strode off behind Cornwall – obviously Lady Carshalton was situated downstairs. He prayed the news would be better than he feared.

* * *

Grey waved the butler aside and knocked softly on the door. He was about to knock again when it opened and a maid stared at him in astonishment.

'I'm Lord Carshalton. Lady Madeline and I have just arrived for our expected visit.' He stepped around the girl into the spacious sitting room. There was no sign of either his uncle or his cousin, so he must suppose they were at the bedside.

This room was warm, a fire lit in the grate, and was expensively furnished, but with old-fashioned pieces. The bedchamber door was slightly open and he made his way quietly to it and knocked again. This time he didn't wait to be invited to enter but stepped in.

The curtains were drawn, the fire huge and the room suffocatingly hot. His grandmother was an almost indiscernible shape beneath the mound of bedding. Sitting on either side of her were two men he could not fail to recognise as his relatives.

His uncle stared at him in shock and then slowly pushed himself to his feet. His cousin moved more quickly and was on his feet immediately. It was like staring into his reflection.

'I apologise for disturbing you, but I needed to see how things stood. What exactly is wrong with our grandmother?'

'She has a fever that refuses to break. We fear she won't survive another night.'

There was no sign of animosity in his expression – indeed – his cousin looked pleased to see him.

'Small wonder she's made no improvement. This

room is stifling. We need to get her cooler, not push her temperature up.'

His uncle made his way across and seemed equally happy to see him. 'My boy, I can't tell you how relieved I am to have you here. The doctor insisted we must build up the fire and pile on the covers and sweat the fever out. Are you saying this is incorrect?'

'I'm no expert, sir, but I've seen similar cases during my time in the army and the treatment was always to cool the patient down, not make him hotter.'

As they both looked at him expectantly he took charge. 'Frederick, find a jug of water and put the fire out. Sir, draw back the curtains and open the windows. I'll remove the bedcovers.'

As they rushed off to do as he bid, he wondered where the obnoxious Bates was – surely she should be nursing her mistress?

He was shocked how frail his once robust grandparent had become in so short a time. For a heart-stopping moment he thought she might already have died but when he leaned closer he discerned a faint breath on his cheek.

With ruthless efficiency he stripped off all but the linen sheet, tossing the heavy covers to the floor without a second thought. A welcome draught of fresh air came from the first open window and late evening sunlight streamed into the room, making the candles redundant.

He went from one to the other and snuffed them out. The fire still roared and there was no sign of his cousin. Then Frederick reappeared carrying a pail of water. Without hesitation he threw it over the flames and immediately they were enveloped by choking smoke.

'Buggeration! Quickly, we must hold a comforter across the chimney until the fire is out and the smoke gone.'

His uncle snatched one from the floor and he and his son did as Grey suggested. With all three large windows open, the room soon cleared and he mopped his streaming eyes.

Fortunately they'd contained the disaster and his grandmother hadn't suffered. 'Excellent. Now we must get liquid into her and it would help if she was sponged with water. This also has proved efficacious in lowering a fever.' He recalled another thing that had been employed when officers had succumbed to the ague. 'Cinchona bark would also be useful – but I doubt we'll find any locally.'

'Grandmamma seems better already,' Frederick

said as he resumed his seat at her side. He tipped a little lemonade onto a spoon and carefully dribbled the contents into her mouth.

Grey took the opportunity to speak to his uncle. 'Where is her maid? She should be here to take care of her.'

'She too is unwell and Mama wouldn't wish to have anyone else.'

'That doesn't surprise me; she is a formidable lady. Perhaps word could be sent to the servants' quarters that the same treatment be given to her abigail? If this was my home, I wouldn't have had the wretched woman here at all but for some reason my grandmother seems attached to her.'

They both walked across to the bed. 'There's nothing more we can do, sir, but pray this is enough to break the fever. Will you allow me to take over her care whilst you and Frederick get some rest and refreshment?'

'That would be most kind of you, my boy. Neither Frederick nor I have eaten or slept since yesterday.'

20

Madeline was impressed with their accommodation and she knew that Slater and Lottie would be relieved they had separate, but adjoining, bedchambers so there was no necessity for them to work in the same space.

'You have a shared sitting room, my lady, but if this isn't to your satisfaction we can make other arrangements.' The housekeeper had the same look in her eyes as the butler.

'This will be adequate.' Madeline waved her hand in dismissal and the woman stalked off. As soon as she'd gone, the room seemed friendlier somehow.

The furnishings were old-fashioned but elegant

and everywhere was spotlessly clean. The fire had only just been lit and gave off no heat, but it did make the room more cheerful. The apartment was laid out so that Grey's room was on the right and hers on the left and both opened onto the sitting room.

The door to her chamber opened and her maid greeted her with a curtsy and a smile. 'Lottie, there should be a tray arriving shortly and as soon as it has come you may go downstairs and have your own supper.'

'I'll finish unpacking first, my lady, and then go down.' The girl stood aside so Madeline could enter. This chamber was equally impressive and she was pleased to see the door to Grey's room was ajar.

Confident they would be comfortable here, Madeline left her maid to her duties and walked to the window. Their apartment was at the rear of Blakely Hall and she could see a splendid formal parterre, which led to an ornamental lake in the distance. Built on a small hill behind the lake was a folly constructed to look like a ruined castle. This window opened onto a stone balcony and she unlatched it and stepped out, eager to see as much as she could of her new surroundings.

She peered nervously over the balustrade as she

wasn't comfortable with heights. The balcony continued so that it included the adjoining chamber.

On glancing up she saw she was directly below several grotesque carvings. Presumably they had an ancient meaning that was lost on her. In order to see them properly she would have to lean against the balustrade, and she had no intention of doing that.

The house was set out like the letter E but without the middle bar – and she was standing in the centre. Just below her was a pretty terrace, which was sheltered from the elements by the walls. The brickwork was solid – light must come in from windows on the front and far side of the wings.

There were three more balconies within this central section, which she assumed were other guest chambers. The family must have their rooms in one or other of the enormous wings. It was an unusual layout for a stately home but no doubt the original builder had been an eccentric.

She edged her way to the far end of the balcony and from here she could see there was a maze and an attractive woodland. It would be pleasant to explore those in the coming days as long as the weather remained clement.

Although the balcony was more than a yard wide she could not be comfortable so high from the ground and was determined not to venture out here on her own again.

She had already removed her bonnet, gloves and spencer and given them to her maid but had no intention of changing her gown as she wasn't going downstairs again tonight. She paced the room for a while in order to stretch her legs after her long confinement in the carriage and was about to find herself a book from the well-stacked bookcase when her supper arrived.

As always she had a good appetite but, hungry as she was, she barely touched the tray. She would have to be starving to eat what had been sent to her. Cold beef broth with unpleasant lumps of fat and gristle floating in it was not to her taste. To accompany this was stale bread and sweating cheese. The only drink offered was rancid milk.

'Lottie, come here please.'

Her maid took one look at the unpleasant supper and snatched it up. 'I'm taking this down to the kitchens right now. I'll find you something decent to eat myself.'

'No, Lottie, I don't wish you to do that. Just take it down and say nothing. I've had more than enough to eat today and can wait until I break my fast. I've no desire to cause any fuss whilst Lady Carshalton is so ill.'

The girl curtsied and did as she was told without comment. Madeline hoped she would continue to hold her tongue when she was downstairs.

Things couldn't have been made plainer. For some reason the staff intended to make their stay as unpleasant as possible and there was nothing she could do about it until Grey joined her. He would remain at the side of his grandmother until she was out of danger, so she didn't expect him for a while.

There was a knock on the sitting room door and she called out for whoever it was to enter. A young footman came in and bowed. 'May I have permission to light the candles? I have a message from his lordship.'

She beckoned him in. 'Yes, do so. How is Lady Carshalton?'

'Her ladyship is somewhat improved. His lordship has asked me to tell you he is remaining in the sickroom.'

Once he'd completed this task he bowed again and vanished. Unlike the other servants she'd encountered, his behaviour had been impeccable.

As she was to remain hungry until the morning she thought she would retire early. With luck she would sleep and forget she'd had nothing to eat this evening.

Despite the comfort of her bed she slept fitfully and was up at dawn wandering about the chamber, wishing Grey had returned during the night. She hoped this wasn't an indication that Lady Carshalton had taken a turn for the worse.

* * *

Grey watched the surly housekeeper tending to his grandmother and was satisfied that the woman was capable of following his instructions correctly.

'I'm going to take a turn outside. I'll return shortly.'

Instead of exiting through the door he climbed over the windowsill and dropped onto the terrace below. He would check that his horses were being taken care of and that his men had adequate accommodation. The six outriders could begin their return journey tomorrow sometime.

He found the stables without difficulty and was greeted immediately by both Jenkins and Smith.

'We're right glad to see you, my lord. There's something a bit havey-cavey about this place. There'd been no preparations made for our arrival, and I reckon we'll all be sleeping in with the horses tonight. No sign of any food neither,' Smith said.

'Lady Carshalton is desperately ill. I think this has thrown the place into turmoil. You'll have to rough it tonight, lads, but I promise I'll sort things out for you tomorrow.'

'Some of the stable hands seem friendly enough but others are downright rude. Squire Chorley's men need to be fed, sir, but don't worry – Jenkins and I will forage. There's bound to be a dairy or such we can raid once it's dark.' The man grinned. 'Just like old times, my lord, when I was serving King and Country.'

'I'll leave the matter in your capable hands. I take it the horses have been fed and watered?'

'No problem there, plenty of fodder.'

Grey made his way back and hopped in over the window frame. The housekeeper barely glanced in his direction. He didn't bother to enquire how his grandmother was doing but walked across to check for himself. The fever had gone down considerably and her colour was much improved. However, she was still unconscious and until she recovered her senses he could not be sanguine she would not succumb to whatever ailment she'd contracted.

He took a seat on the far side of the room,

stretched out his legs and settled himself for a long and boring night. He hoped Madeline would be better served than his men – if she wasn't there would be a reckoning in the morning.

At midnight he sent the housekeeper to her bed and took over the nursing duties himself. He was confident his ancient relative would recover from this ailment but whether her wits would be intact remained to be seen. The sun was about to rise when his uncle entered looking much refreshed.

'Lady Carshalton is improving with every hour that passes, sir, I'm pleased to inform you.'

'That's good news, my boy. Come into the sitting room so we may talk without disturbing her. There's coffee and a miscellany of items I could find in the kitchen. I expect you're ravenous.'

Once his hunger was appeased Grey was ready to talk. 'Why is it that the majority of your staff are treating us with disrespect? My men were offered no food nor a place to sleep.'

His uncle rubbed his eyes. 'I'd no idea you were coming to visit, which is why nothing had been prepared. I'd better tell you the whole. I had no expectations of inheriting this mausoleum – I have a tidy estate that brings in more than enough rent, and Frederick and I were content to live there. But when both my older brothers and their families drowned in a yachting accident everything changed.' He sighed and shook his head. 'My father was a brutal man – we all lived in fear of him – that is apart from Mama who worshipped him despite his filthy temper and domineering manner.'

'I'm beginning to understand. I take it most of the staff here worked for him and therefore view me as an interloper?'

'They did – I would dismiss them all if it weren't for my mother. She insists I change nothing and that we live here as if my father was still alive.'

'I take it you expected to inherit the title?' He nodded. 'Forgive me for asking this, but didn't it occur to you that there could be others in line before you?'

'No it didn't. I was away at school when your father left and I was told he'd died in a riding accident. Until the lawyers informed us Frederick and I were unaware of your existence.' He stared earnestly at him. 'I promise you, my boy, I would've contacted you years ago whatever my parents thought of the matter.'

Grey frowned. 'My grandmother gave me the impression it was you and Frederick who didn't want to make my acquaintance. I must have misun-

derstood. I'll talk to her about it when she's better.'
He paused and wondered if he should warn his
uncle what to expect.

'There's no need to say it, my boy. I'm well aware
that Mama might not make a full recovery. Fever of
the brain can leave a person with scattered wits.
Whatever the outcome, I'll just thank God she's still
with us.'

They drank coffee companionably for a while
whilst Grey explained about the attacks on his life.
His uncle was horrified by this information.

'You'll be safe here, my boy. I'll put my outside
men on high alert and make sure they patrol the
extremities of the estate every day. I can assure you
any strangers would soon be noticed.'

'I thank you. I can now leave knowing Madeline
will be in no danger.'

'I hope you won't depart until your grandmother
is fully recovered. She will want to thank you herself
for saving her life. The local physician is entrenched
in his ways – he would have bled her if I'd allowed
him to.'

'That would have been a fatal mistake in my
opinion. Of course I've no intention of going until
things are resolved. However, if you'll forgive me,

Uncle, I must find my apartment. Madeline will be anxious for news.'

As he stood up his uncle spoke again. 'I'm sorry you received a less than warm welcome. I can assure you that things will be better in future. You must understand that I'd no idea until your man arrived saying you were delayed that you were actually coming here for a visit with your new bride. I think my mother must have been sickening and quite forgot to tell me.'

Grey was about to say he'd received a letter supposedly from him but thought better of it. Although his uncle could not be more than three score years, he looked far older, as if worn down by life. 'It matters not, sir. I'm here now and arrived at an opportune time. I'm looking forward to becoming better acquainted with you and my cousin.' He smiled warmly. 'I've only been wed a few days, sir, so forgive me if I spend private time with my bride this morning.'

'You must consider this your wedding trip. God knows this house is big enough for you to remain apart from us if that's what you desire, and there are plenty of picturesque places to visit on horseback.'

'Then we shall do that, sir. My thanks to you.' He took the stairs two at a time, ignoring the shocked expressions of the servants he shot past. His darling girl would still be in bed and he intended to keep her there for several hours yet.

* * *

Madeline heard somebody entering her chamber and scrambled to her feet. Grey was back. She was halfway to the door when he burst through.

'Thank God! When I saw the bed empty...' He held out his arms and she threw herself in.

'I couldn't sleep, my love. I was far too worried. How is Lady Carshalton?'

He squeezed her tight. 'She's out of danger but has not yet recovered consciousness. I've learned a lot about my family, which I must tell you, but that can wait until later.'

She couldn't help but be aware that he was eager to make love and she shared his urgency. She threaded her hands around his neck and tilted her face to receive his kiss. With a noise that sounded almost like a growl, he picked her up and in four strides was by her bed.

* * *

His attentions were passionate and she responded in kind. An ecstatic time later he gave her a final kiss and then with his arm still firmly about her waist he fell asleep.

She wriggled a little to get comfortable and then, satiated by their lovemaking, she fell into a deep, relaxed slumber. She didn't rouse until she heard the curtains being drawn back. He was still stark naked beside her.

Her maid was unaware Grey was still with her. Madeline was about to call out when Lottie picked up the tray, upon which was the jug of morning chocolate and a basket of freshly baked sweet rolls, and turned to face her.

If her husband had remained hidden beneath the sheets all might have been well, but he chose that exact moment to sit up.

With a horrified shriek the girl threw up her hands as if intending to cover her eyes, quite forgetting she was holding a laden tray. The contents of the jug landed on his bare chest followed swiftly by the rolls.

Her maid didn't wait to view the results of her actions but ran with an apron over her head from the room. His language turned the air blue and she hoped never to hear such things again.

She too was unclothed but there was little she could do about it. She scrambled out of bed and racing around to the far side picked up a half-filled pitcher of cold water left over from her ablutions last night and emptied it on him.

The chocolate would have been scalding hot and although drastic she thought her action would improve matters. He thought otherwise. He grabbed her loose arm and yanked her so that she fell across his body.

For an appalling second she thought he was going to spank her. Then he tumbled her over so that she was beneath him and now as wet and sticky as he was.

His eyes were dancing with mischief. 'My darling, I'd no idea you like to experiment in bed. I've never made love to a chocolate-covered woman – it will be a delightful experience.'

The last thing she wanted was to resume their night-time activities. She raised her hands and pushed firmly against his chest. 'Don't be ridiculous. Allow me to get out of bed. You must return to your chamber and let your valet take care of you. My poor maid will never recover from this morning's shock.'

He chuckled and rolled away to stand

unashamedly naked beside the bed. 'In case you were wondering, sweetheart, the drink wasn't hot but I appreciate your misguided effort to help.'

He was about to stride into his own room when she shrieked at him. His eyebrows shot up beneath his hair. 'For God's sake, woman, what's wrong now?'

'You cannot leave my chamber as you are. I'd never be able to look Slater in the eye again. Kindly cover yourself, sir.'

He laughed at her outrage but returned to grab his shirt and drop it over his head. The tails were long enough to cover his embarrassment and she nodded her approval.

'Madeline, my dear, can I ask you not to scream at me like a fishwife? It's hardly becoming of you.'

Her answer was to snatch up a pillow and hurl it at him. He dodged easily and, still laughing, vanished through the communicating door.

No sooner had he gone than Lottie peered around the dressing room door. 'My lady, I'm ever so sorry. I've never seen the like – I didn't know where to look.'

'In future you will wait to be summoned – I wish there to be no repeat of this.' Madeline stepped out of bed and her maid's eyes widened. 'As you can see I'm in need of a large quantity of hot water. Go and see if there is enough for me to have a bath.'

Lottie scuttled off, leaving her to rummage about amid the chaos of the bedcovers to find her bedrobe. As she was pushing her sticky arms through the sleeves she understood why the girl had been so shocked at her appearance. The chocolate mess could only have been transferred to her flesh in one way. Madeline turned pink all over. This was a morning she preferred to forget.

21

Madeline eventually joined her husband in their shared sitting room. He nodded his approval at her appearance.

'Married life appears to be suiting you.' He glanced pointedly at the clock on the mantelshelf. 'I sincerely hope breakfast will still be available as I'll not be best pleased if I've missed my meal, kicking my heels in here whilst you spent several hours getting ready.'

'You've only been here a quarter of an hour yourself. I didn't have the opportunity to tell you that the food sent up for my supper was inedible. I shall be equally displeased if there's no breakfast.'

His expression changed and he looked formidable.

'That won't happen again, my love, I assure you. Now before we go there are a few things you need to know.'

When he had finished his story she nodded. 'I'm glad there's a reasonable explanation for our treatment. I'm also pleased that you find your uncle and cousin are not who you thought they were. I'm looking forward to meeting them both, especially as you say your Cousin Frederick could be your twin.'

He pulled her hand through his arm and marched her through the vast establishment. She was puzzled that he knew his way about so well – it was as if he was already familiar with the building.

The butler bowed so deeply his nose almost touched his knees. When he straightened there was no sign of his previous dislike. 'My lord, my lady, if you would care to follow me to the breakfast room, everything is ready for you.'

The tall-case clock in the drawing room struck eleven – they were embarrassingly tardy. They were bowed into the chamber and her mouth watered at the delicious aromas wafting from the sideboard. Two footmen stood flat against the wall as if pretending they were invisible.

'My lord, if there's anything else you require you have only to ask and it will be fetched for you immediately. There's chocolate, coffee and small beer but...'

Grey stopped him in midsentence. 'That will be all.' Her husband was not ready to forget and forgive just yet.

She lifted the lid on each chafing dish in turn. 'There's so much here I don't know where to start. I think I'll have mushrooms, ham and coddled eggs first.'

They piled their plates and were too hungry to do more than devour the contents. After three journeys to the buffet she was finally replete and now turned her attention to the coffee jug.

Grey was still happily munching his way through several succulent slices of ham but nodded when she asked him if he wanted coffee.

The two footmen had also been summarily dismissed, leaving them in privacy. 'I think this must have been cooked especially for us. Did you notice there were only two places set out on the table?'

'I did. Cook is trying to make amends for her disgraceful behaviour yesterday. When you're finished, darling, we'll go in search of my uncle and cousin and...'

A voice from the door interrupted him. 'There's

no need, my boy – Frederick and I have come to find you.'

Grey pushed back his chair and walked across to embrace his uncle, and seeing them together brought tears to her eyes. The man looked older than his years but was unmistakably a close relative. Then Cousin Frederick emerged from behind them and her coffee slopped over the edge of the cup.

'Good heavens! You could indeed be twins.' He grinned, revealing he had a broken front tooth, which only added to his charm.

'I'm delighted to meet you, Lady Madeline, and a belated welcome to Blakely Hall.'

Hurriedly she stood up and curtsied and he bowed. Then she was about to curtsy to Mr Carshalton when he reached out and embraced her fondly. 'I must apologise most humbly for your disgraceful reception yesterday. I expect that your husband has already explained why this happened. No excuses – those responsible are treading on thin ice and will be dismissed without reference if anything like that occurs again.'

He beamed down at her and she couldn't help but respond to his affectionate greeting. 'I've already forgotten about it, sir. How is Lady Carshalton this morning? I hope she's continuing to improve.'

He nodded. 'Her fever has almost abated but she's yet to wake up. The housekeeper is to take care of her until her abigail is recovered.' He pointed towards the table. 'Would you allow us to join you for coffee? I've sent for a fresh pot. I wish to know everything about you both. I cannot tell you how happy I am to meet you. You are a welcome addition to my family.'

The two gentlemen took seats opposite her and Grey and helped themselves to the fresh coffee that had arrived during their conversation.

'Madeline, do you think you're able to ride? I'm eager to explore the place where my father spent his childhood.'

'I don't think so, perhaps in a day or two, but at the moment I've scarcely recovered from the journey and the carriage accident.'

His expression changed to one of concern. 'In which case, sweetheart, it can wait. We shall walk about the grounds and I'll do my best to lose you in the maze.'

'If you want to go without me, then I've no objection. I'll be perfectly content spending a quiet morning reading on the terrace.'

Mr Carshalton nodded approvingly. 'Frederick and I will take you, my boy. We intended to visit one of our tenant farmers as he wishes to increase his dairy herd but hasn't the necessary wherewithal to do so.'

The three gentlemen left for their excursion and she returned to her apartment and put on her boots, as her indoor slippers would be ruined in the garden.

The bed was restored to its pristine condition but there was no sign of her maid. Presumably she was busy elsewhere. Her duties were not only to help her mistress dress and keep her wardrobe clean and pressed, but also to oversee the chambermaids and the laundry. Lottie was an expert seamstress so repairs and alterations were also part of her daily tasks.

The footwear Madeline needed had been set out ready for her, along with a wrap and bonnet. She walked to the window and decided to step onto the balcony in order to get a better idea of what she would need if she was to sit outside with her novel.

This time she was less nervous and moved about more freely. Perhaps she would sit here instead where she had such a splendid view of the grounds, rather than the terrace. There was ample room for her to place a chair and a small side table outside and there would be no necessity for her to put on a bonnet if she remained in her own apartment.

She found the bell strap and tugged it sharply. No doubt wherever her maid was someone would be sent to fetch her. Whilst she waited she examined the furniture, hoping to find something suitable for the balcony. A quarter of an hour later Lottie arrived, red-faced and breathless.

'My lady, I beg your pardon for keeping you waiting but it's ever so far from the servants' quarters. If they hadn't marked the passageways I'd never have found my way at all.' She dipped in a brief curtsy, apparently fully recovered from the earlier embarrassing episode.

Madeline explained what she required. 'There's nothing in here that would do, but I'm sure I can find something suitable. The two chambermaids can help me search – there's bound to be something in one of the unoccupied guest rooms.'

'I don't want you going into rooms without permission. I'll remain here whilst you give the housekeeper my request. I'm certain a small chair and table will be found immediately and fetched here.'

This was indeed the case and soon she was sitting happily on the balcony on a comfortable chair, her feet upon a matching footstool. A dainty octagonal table was at her left hand. Upon this was placed a brass bell and her book.

She closed her eyes, enjoying the warmth of the autumn sunshine on her face. Grey intended to remain with her for at least a week; his plans to go in search of the would-be murderers put to one side for the moment. He'd said he might as well wait until he had word from Beau.

* * *

Everywhere they rode, Grey was impressed by the excellent state of all the properties and land. His grandfather might have been a wretched parent but he had been an exemplary landlord.

They arrived by a circuitous route at the inn in Blakely village where he'd stopped yesterday. His uncle drew rein in front of the building.

'I suggest we dismount here, my boy, and take some refreshments. They do an excellent beef pasty and the ale is good too.'

'I should be happy to have the ale, sir, but I consumed so much at breakfast I've no need to eat again until dinner time.' He glanced at the sun, well used to estimating the time by its position in the sky.

'What time do we dine? It must be well after two o'clock now.'

He dropped to the cobbles and patted the neck of the horse he'd borrowed.

'We keep country hours at Blakely – but if you prefer to eat late then so be it.'

This meant dinner would be served around four o'clock. 'Please don't alter your routine for us, Uncle. My wife and I will be happy to fall in with you.'

His cousin slapped him on the back. 'I fear we're country bumpkins. I've only been to London a couple of times and that for business not pleasure. What time do they dine in Town?'

'Damned if I know – I've spent all my adult life in the army. There you ate when you had the opportunity. My wife's the person to talk to about society's rules. However, she hasn't been presented at court or had a Season because of her parents' untimely deaths.'

'In which case, my boy, we shall do as we please. It's about time I shook things up a bit. In future we'll eat at six – what do you say about that, Frederick?'

'I say that it's a good thing my grandmamma's incapacitated. Best to get the new routine established before she's back on her feet, Papa, don't you think?'

They were welcomed enthusiastically, but not obsequiously, by the landlord. His uncle and his cousin were obviously well liked. Once they were comfortably seated in the snug nursing pewter pots of home-brewed ale, he decided to mention the invitation he'd received from his uncle.

'That's strange, my boy, for I can assure you I didn't write it. As I told you last night I'd no idea you were visiting until I spoke to your man.' He was silent for a moment and then his expression changed. 'If I hadn't been in the stable yard when he arrived, I doubt I would have known you were coming. There's something going on here and my mother's behind it. I'm at a loss to understand why she should keep Frederick and I in ignorance of your arrival.'

'No doubt she will be able to explain when she's well enough to speak to you. It's of no matter – we're here now and glad to be so.' Grey drank deeply from his mug. 'Which reminds me, did Mr Chorley's men leave in good order this morning?'

His uncle nodded. 'They did, nephew, and were well-rewarded for their vigilance. There are sufficient men employed at Blakely to continue to protect you and your wife. For some reason Mama took on half a dozen extra men last year when my father died. She said she felt vulnerable now he'd gone.'

Frederick snorted into his beer. 'She could not have made it plainer. She doesn't think Papa is up to snuff. We don't match her exacting standards. I'm certain that's why she sought you out. A soldier would be much more to her liking as head of the household.'

'Good God! Are you suggesting she wishes me to take over Blakely Hall? That somehow she intends to disinherit you both?'

* * *

Madeline remained on the balcony snoozing and reading her book in turn. She'd had no cause to ring the bell, as she required nothing – she doubted she would be able to eat again until dinner time.

Eventually she went in and she could hear Lottie moving about next door. She called out instead of ringing.

'Yes, my lady? Can I fetch you something on a tray?'

'I'm going to explore the house and want you to come with me. Then I'll take tea in the drawing room and hope that Lord Carshalton and his relatives return to drink it with me.'

'I'll get the girls to bring in the chair and table, my lady, just in case it rains.'

'Do that – but make sure they replace them in exactly the same spot every day that I'm here.' She thought for a moment and then contradicted her request. 'I've changed my mind, get them to put out a second chair and place the table between them. Then Lord Carshalton and I can sit together and watch the sunset this evening.'

Lottie stepped onto the balcony. 'There's plenty of room so I'll see to it immediately.' She glanced up and pulled a face. 'Whatever are those horrible things gawping down at you?'

'They're gargoyles. I think the rainwater from the roof gushes from their mouths when it rains.'

'If it does it will make a dreadful racket when it hits the balcony, don't you think?'

Madeline enjoyed these conversations with her maid – Beau would be horrified at her informality, as servants were to be kept at a distance at all times. Lottie had joined the staff at Silchester Court when she was ten years old and had worked her way from under-housemaid to eventually become her abigail five years ago when Mama had died. They were the same age and far more intimate than they should be.

Fortunately her new husband was no stickler and was unlikely to complain about their closeness. Indeed, she'd seen Grey deep in conversation with his valet so he obviously had the same relationship with Slater as she did with Lottie.

* * *

Her exploration of the vast house took up the remainder of the afternoon and by the conclusion she was fairly sure she would be able to find her way about in future without becoming hopelessly lost. They peeped and peered in dozens of unused reception rooms as well as a magnificent library, two smaller drawing rooms and the dining room that would seat a small army without difficulty.

She had heard a clock somewhere strike three times – she was ready for tea and whatever pastries were available. 'Lottie, I'll leave you to get another chair put out on the balcony. Find me something new for this evening – I want to make a good impression.'

She gave her request for refreshments to the footman who appeared to spend his entire day in the grand hall with the sole purpose of opening doors for any of the family who might appear. Presumably he also opened the front door to any visitors.

The fire wasn't lit today and she was relieved as the day had been unseasonably warm. The long windows that led onto the terrace were open and she decided to wait there for the tea tray. The empty flagstones cried out for tables and chairs – this area was a suntrap and ideal for sitting and enjoying the view.

She looked up and saw she was directly underneath her own balcony and the overhang would give welcome shade from the morning sun. As the rear of the building faced west, the sun was shining in her face, so after a few minutes she returned to the drawing room.

There were voices outside the door and Grey strode in looking even more attractive than he had this morning – if that were possible. Without hesitation she ran to him and he twirled her around like a child. 'I've neglected you shamefully, my love, but I'm here to make amends. We are not to dine until six – my uncle has decided to take charge of the household and not before time.'

He placed her on the floor and she tilted her

face; his kiss did not disappoint. Someone cleared their throat noisily and she would have drawn away, but he held on to her, turning with his arm still around her waist.

Two footmen waited by the open double doors carrying what looked like enough food for a dozen people. They placed their burden on the large table and then vanished, not waiting to see if they would be required to serve.

'How strange – there still seems to be something odd going on with the staff where we're concerned,' she said as she prepared the tea.

'As long as they do as they're asked, and know their place, then I'll be content. But my uncle is going to find it difficult bringing them into line. They are all loyal to the old regime and that will be hard to change.'

'Cook has obviously decided we deserve to be well fed. There are sandwiches, three sorts of pastries as well as tea and coffee. I didn't have a midday repast – I was too full of breakfast.'

'And neither did I, sweetheart, so we can devour this without feeling that we're greedy. Remember, we dine at six o'clock so you have just three hours to digest whatever you eat now.'

She pulled a face. 'Kindly desist from talking

about my inner workings – you're quite spoiling my enjoyment of these delicious treats.'

He chuckled and ignored her reprimand. They both piled their plates and sat down to enjoy their meal. She regaled him with her quiet but pleasant morning and he told her about his good impressions of the estate.

'There's still at least an hour before we need to go upstairs and change.' She saw the glint in his eye and forestalled his improper suggestion. 'I don't require a rest this afternoon, my lord. I'm eager to see the maze.'

22

The next few days passed in a haze of happiness. Madeline spent the mornings on her own, the afternoons with Grey and the evenings with her new relatives. Lady Carshalton continued to improve, as did her maid, and by the fifth day of their visit the patient was back in the care of her abigail.

Madeline's hip had fully recovered and on the sixth day she accompanied Grey to the stables.

'I can't tell you how eager I am to ride again after so long. Is Cousin Frederick not to come with us today?'

'No, sweetheart, he and my uncle have returned to their estate to organise the transfer of items that they wish to have here. They've been at Blakely Hall for a year, so I cannot imagine why it's taken so long. That estate is now Frederick's and I expect he wishes to put in a suitable tenant to take care of things.'

The horses were saddled and both Jenkins and Smith were waiting to accompany them. This was a sharp reminder that their lives were still in danger, which she had put to the back of her mind during this past week.

After a glorious and exhilarating two hours galloping about the countryside they turned for home. 'I'm quite exhausted. I'll be glad to sit quietly for the remainder of the day,' she said as he lifted her from the saddle.

'We could sit on the balcony – it's in the shade at the moment. I've nothing pressing to do this morning.'

As they strolled hand in hand to the house something astonishing occurred to her. So surprised was she, that she stopped dead. 'I've something to tell you.'

He looked down at her, a watchful expression on his face as if he was expecting bad news. 'Not here, sweetheart, wait until we're private.'

By the time they reached their apartment she'd

had time to consider and wasn't sure she should speak out. If he didn't return her feelings then would he be embarrassed to know that she'd fallen in love with him? Surely any gentleman would be flattered to know that his wife held him in such high esteem?

They had spent every night making passionate love but at no time had he said that he loved her. Perhaps she should keep this information to herself and wait until he spoke of his feelings.

'I'll change my garments and then join you in the sitting room, my love. Have breakfast brought up to us and we'll eat it on the balcony.'

Her ablutions were completed and she was freshly gowned in a pretty sprigged muslin within a short space of time. The chambermaid had been sent down to the kitchen and the trays would arrive momentarily. Apart from the first evening, every meal she'd eaten had been quite delicious.

The communicating door swung open and Grey stepped through. He was informally attired, no top-coat on over his shirt and waistcoat, and no cravat around the strong column of his neck. Her bodice became unaccountably tight and his eyes darkened in response.

If she didn't move, he would tumble her into bed

and that wouldn't do when their breakfast was on its way. She skipped out of his reach and dashed to the safety of the sitting room where the footmen were setting out their meal.

He was close behind her but swore under his breath when he saw they were no longer alone. She didn't dare to look at him – she would be unable to resist and they spent more than enough time in bedroom sport as it was.

The servants knew better than to linger and left them to serve themselves. 'I'm absolutely starving. I'm going to take mine outside and eat *al fresco*.'

'I've no intention of balancing a plate on my knees – I had more than enough of that in the army.' He sounded positively cross and she risked a glance in his direction.

'Don't be so curmudgeonly, my love. You cannot always have your own way. Look, someone has anticipated our intentions and set things out so we can sit in comfort at a table.' He muttered something quite inappropriate and her cheeks turned scarlet. 'My lord, you really must refrain from using such language. It's quite shocking and I don't like it at all.'

Instead of taking umbrage, he smiled and she saw the danger signals. He hadn't quite abandoned the idea of making love to her. Hastily she loaded up her plate and held it in front of her like a barrier.

'Very well, darling, I shall behave. Take your food out and I'll join you as soon as I've got mine. Do you want coffee as usual?'

They were only halfway through their meal, chatting of this and that and enjoying the fresh air and the stunning view, when unexpectedly he reached out and took her hand, raising it to his lips. He kissed each knuckle in turn and then, still holding her hand he looked into her eyes. 'I can't believe how happy I am to be married to you, my love. Every day that I spend in your company makes me love you more...'

She didn't wait to hear any more but surged to her feet intending to hurl herself into his arms. The chair fell. In her effort to avoid it her feet became entangled in her skirts and she tumbled sideways. His reaction was lightning fast and he was able to grab her arms and pull her back towards the wall.

As he held her, there was a hideous crack from above their heads and they were engulfed in a barrage of falling masonry. The ground beneath her feet began to move – the balcony was collapsing. They were going to fall to their deaths onto the terrace below.

* * *

Grey reached out and grabbed hold of the door frame just as the floor fell away. He leaned his weight on Madeline, pinning her to the wall, praying there would be enough stonework left to hold them up.

Clouds of choking dust filled his nose and mouth. Coughing wasn't an option. He must cling on or they would both plummet to the flagstones and die. The noise was deafening. Pieces of stone bounced off his back, almost causing him to lose his grip.

He couldn't hold on for much longer. Their combined weight was becoming too much for his fragile hold. Then it was eerily silent, the debris gone past. Now he could attempt to edge his way along the remaining brickwork and in through the door.

'Don't struggle, darling, try and get your toes on the ledge. Keep leaning against the wall.'

She didn't answer but the agonising weight on his arm became less acute. She had found purchase for herself.

'I'm going to move to your left. Very slowly. The entrance is no more than a foot from us.'

He couldn't hold on for much longer – his back

had been injured – he wasn't sure he could make his way to safety. Then Slater was there.

'Hang on, sir, I've got you now. I'll get you and the lass safe inside.' His valet's grip was strong and with his help he managed to inch his way along the narrow ledge and they tumbled headlong into the room.

He landed heavily and a searing pain shot across his shoulders. He almost blacked out. 'Help me up, Slater. We both need to get cleaned up and our injuries seen to.'

He carefully kept his back away from Madeline – he didn't want her to be alarmed. There was blood trickling between his shoulder blades and his shirt must be sodden with it.

Once on his feet, he intended to pick up his beloved but as he was about to do so the door burst open and Jenkins and Smith came in.

'Thank the good Lord you're both alive. Them bleeding gargoyles came down and took the balcony with them. It's a miracle you didn't plunge to your deaths.'

Madeline's maid was hovering anxiously, as were two other unknown girls. 'We'll talk about this later, Smith. Can you stand, sweetheart? We need to get washed and your cuts need attending to.'

'I think so. I feel a bit light-headed and as if I'm going to cast up my accounts.'

Slater heaved him to his feet. Every time Grey moved it was agony, and the sooner he got looked at the better.

'Go with your maids; I'll take care of things here. Smith, we'll need somewhere else to sleep. Find us chambers in the family wing – somewhere safe.'

His man nodded. 'We'll take care of that, never you mind, my lord.'

Grey was beginning to feel decidedly odd. 'Slater, please assist my wife to her chamber. Then join me in mine.'

'I'm perfectly capable of looking after myself, Grey. Once I'm changed, and my cuts have been attended to, I'll come through to you. You have been more seriously hurt than I and Slater must see to you until I get there.'

He was about to protest, but she shook her head. Despite the fact that she was covered from head to toe with dust and debris she seemed calm – and very determined. He raised a hand in surrender and allowed his valet to support him into his room, confident his darling girl was well.

'Here, sit down before you fall, my lord.'

The next half an hour passed in a painful blur.

Slater undressed him, cleaned his injury and then stitched him up. He was relieved that Madeline hadn't come through to witness this. It wasn't the first time his valet had put stitches into him – but he hoped it would be the last.

Just as Slater dropped a clean shirt over his shoulders, the communicating door was pushed open and she came in looking pale, but composed.

'I looked in earlier, my love, but your valet thought it best if I didn't remain until he'd finished his ministrations. The girls are already packing my belongings and will come in and do the same for you when they've finished. Have you any idea where we're removing to?'

He vaguely remembered Smith coming in but he couldn't recall what was said. His valet answered for him. 'There's a dozen or more chambers empty over there and Smith's selected one that looks over the paddocks. I'll have everything right and tight for you in an hour or so.'

'Thank you, your help is most appreciated. Now, Grey, do you think you can make your way downstairs or will you remain here until we can move?'

He flexed his shoulders. 'I'll do. I've had worse on the battlefield and still continued to fight. We'll find somewhere quiet and private where we can talk.'

Her smile was somewhat lopsided. 'Dare I say that I'm still hungry? Our meal was rudely interrupted and despite drinking two glasses of barley water my throat's sore and dry.'

How he loved this girl – she was the most courageous young lady in the land. 'Give me a moment, sweetheart; I have to speak to Slater.'

She returned to her own room without question. 'I can't remember if I've already told them, but Smith and Jenkins need to investigate the reason for this sudden fall. It could be a horrible coincidence – but there's been too many of those lately. They must go up on the roof and see if there's any evidence of somebody tampering with the gargoyles.'

'It's being done at the moment, my lord. I don't see how it could have been done deliberately – for the whole lot to come down as it did it would have taken more than one person to shove it. I think this was just an accident.'

'I sincerely hope you're right, otherwise it means danger has followed us here.'

* * *

Grey collected Madeline and together they made their way slowly to the ground floor where they were greeted by both the butler and housekeeper. Their distress over the incident seemed genuine as did the reactions from the group of footmen and maids who were milling about in the grand hall waiting to show their concern.

After he'd reassured them that they were both relatively unscathed, that they blamed no one for the disaster, Grey escorted her to the terrace. 'I thought we were going to one of the smaller reception rooms? I'm not sure I want to perambulate about the garden at the moment.'

He kissed the top of her head affectionately. 'Neither do I, sweetheart, but I need to see exactly what happened and I can only do that from out here.'

To her astonishment the terrace was clear of debris – only if you looked up and saw the balcony and gargoyles were missing would you know anything untoward had taken place. 'How can they have cleared the rubble away so soon? It can't be more than an hour since it took place.'

'Quite extraordinary! The estate manager must have organised this – no doubt he didn't want to upset Lady Carshalton by leaving evidence of the disaster.'

A shout from above them attracted their attention. She looked up and saw Jenkins on the roof. 'There's something you need to see, my lord. Can you come up? I'll come down and show you the way.'

Before Grey could refuse she squeezed his hand. 'You must go, my love, but would you please come with me to find a sitting room we can use as our own.'

'Of course, and I promise I'll be as speedy as I can. Can you order us something to eat? By the time it arrives I should be back.'

They retraced their steps and a footman jumped forward to offer his assistance. He knew exactly where to take them and the pretty chamber was exactly what they wanted. He was then sent to the kitchens to arrange for a replacement meal to be brought.

'Are you sure that scrambling about on the roof won't open up your stitches?' Grey was still looking less than well and she was worried about him.

His answer was to draw her into his embrace and hold her gently to his heart. 'I'll take care, darling.

I'm a military man and used to being injured and remaining on my feet.'

She breathed in his familiar aroma and despite their near fatal experience she felt safe in his arms. 'I love you, Grey, and I'm so relieved that you return my feelings.'

When he reached out to cup her face she felt him flinch. He wasn't nearly as well as he insisted. 'How could I not fall in love with you? I can't believe you love me too – I'm the luckiest man in Christendom.' He kissed her, not passionately but tenderly, his lips showing her how much he cared.

This time she was the one to pull away, knowing he had important business elsewhere. 'You do realise that if I hadn't jumped to my feet to tell you how much I loved you we'd have been sitting at the table. Our love saved our lives.'

'You're quite correct, darling. I'm beginning to believe that a higher power is taking care of us. I sincerely hope the good Lord continues to keep watch.'

He released her reluctantly and with one of his devastating smiles strode off. Apart from his carriage being a little stiffer than usual one would hardly know he'd got a dozen stitches in his back.

Her face was sore, but she'd suffered no more than

superficial scratches. Unexpectedly her legs became wobbly and she sank into the nearest chair. Was the shock making her unwell? She leaned back and closed her eyes hoping the dizziness would pass. At the moment the last thing she wanted was to eat – should she send word to the kitchen to delay the meal?

She was jerked from her reverie by the noise of heavy footsteps running towards her. Her heart jumped. What disasters had overtaken them now?

23

Grey followed Smith through narrow passageways and up a variety of uncarpeted stairs until they reached the attic.

'You get on the roof from here, my lord. It's a ladder but not too difficult.'

'I've fought battles with more serious injuries than a few sutures in my back, Smith, so don't attempt to mollycoddle me.'

He emerged through the hatch onto the roof and one look at the face of his other man told him he was about to see something he would dislike.

'You need to hang over the parapet, my lord, and then you'll see what's been going on,' Jenkins said.

Grey did as suggested and his eyes narrowed.

'This was no accident. It's obvious someone has been up here knocking out the mortar so the gargoyles would fall when pushed.'

He straightened and turned to face his men. 'This couldn't have been done in an hour or so; they must have been up here for several nights working on it. They couldn't have achieved this without inside assistance. We were being watched so whoever was here knew when to push the stones.'

If he'd been paying more attention to the danger that surrounded them, had not been so engrossed in his wife, he would have heard the bastards working. No more. From now until this matter was settled he would be a soldier first and a husband second.

His inattention had almost cost him his beloved – without Madeline he would be bereft. Life would have no meaning.

'The perpetrators could still be in the house – although I doubt it. Search the place thoroughly and then question the staff. I'll send Slater to find you. I'll speak to Lady Madeline and then join you.'

They both jumped to attention and saluted. From now on, he would be their officer and they must follow his orders without question. He wished he had more men at his disposal but would have to make do with the five he had.

'These men are dangerous; make sure you're armed.'

He returned to the apartment, forgetting his belongings had been moved elsewhere until he burst in and found the rooms all but empty. He cursed under his breath – he needed his sword and pistols and had no idea where they were now located.

Then Slater emerged from the hidden door in the panelling. 'I need you and my weapons and I need them now.'

Whilst his valet conducted him to his new chambers Grey explained what he'd seen on the roof. 'Are you intending to leave her ladyship without protection, my lord? Do you think she's safe here?'

For a moment Grey didn't understand then his blood ran cold. Slater was inferring that his family might be behind the attempted murders. The idea was preposterous – perhaps before he'd met his uncle and cousin he might have harboured doubts about them – but they were good and decent men. He would stake his life on that.

'I'm certain she is. This is nothing to do with my family – although it's possible more than one of the staff have been bribed to help. Which reminds me, the letter from the duke should be here by now – I wonder what the delay is.'

After several minutes running through the servants' passageways he finally arrived at his new rooms. He didn't stop to admire them but opened his trunk where his weapons were stored. Seeing him with his sword buckled around his waist might alarm Madeline, but her sensitivities must be put to one side. Her very life might depend on it.

* * *

Madeline scarcely had time to scramble to her feet before Mr Carshalton and his son burst in.

'My dear girl, we came as soon as we heard. Thank the good Lord you're both unhurt by this terrible accident. I can't begin to apologise that something so dreadful should happen to you whilst you are under my roof.'

Her cousin rushed to her side and his expression was as concerned as his father's. 'Lady Madeline, I don't understand how you and my cousin were not killed. Could you tell us exactly what transpired?'

She gestured that they be seated despite the fact that they were mud-spattered from their gallop to Blakely Hall. She quickly explained how she and Grey had avoided plunging to their death and they listened with close attention.

Her uncle-in-law shook his head. 'It's a miracle you weren't killed. What a dreadful coincidence that the gargoyles should fall at precisely the same moment you were sitting on the balcony.'

'It shouldn't have happened. Although I didn't examine the gargoyles in depth, I did a thorough inspection of the property when Papa inherited it last year. There was nothing amiss then and I can't believe...' He stopped and she saw the colour drain from his cheeks.

What had upset him? Why was he looking so appalled? She looked at his father but he was in a chair with his head sunk in his hands. There was something very wrong and she couldn't think what it could be.

'Cousin Frederick, please tell me what you realised about this incident?'

'I think this to have been a deliberate attempt to kill you both – it's the only way it makes sense.' He grasped his father by the shoulder and shook him vigorously, which she thought was most disrespectful.

'Papa, whoever is trying to kill Lady Madeline and my cousin is here – has been hiding in this house for the past week. We are to blame for this near disaster.'

Mr Carshalton groaned but didn't look up. 'I know; we should have taken better care of them. I should have got rid of the old staff and employed my own people and then this wouldn't have happened.' Finally he raised his head and wiped his eyes on his sleeve. 'I've allowed myself to be trampled over by my mother long enough. The staff here must have turned a blind eye to these men and that's tantamount to aiding and abetting.'

He stood up, a militant look in his eye, making him look much more like Cousin Frederick and Grey. There was a knock on the door and two footmen came in carrying the food she'd ordered. She no longer had any appetite and doubted that her husband would either.

'Put the tray over there.' She pointed to a sideboard and they hurriedly did as she bid and then left as quietly as they'd arrived.

Before she could offer to share the meal she heard another set of heavy footsteps running towards the room. She was unsurprised when her husband shouldered his way in. She scarcely recognised him; he had metamorphosed back into a soldier and she was glad of it.

His uncle and cousin greeted him enthusiastically, and before she had time to interact with her beloved husband he snatched up a meat pasty, gulped down a cup of coffee and was ready to leave. His uncle and cousin were to help him root out the assassins.

She thought he would go without speaking directly to her, but at the last minute he pulled her into his arms and kissed her. His lips were hard, demanding, and she responded to his passion. He raised his head and his eyes shone down into hers. 'It will end today. I intend to apprehend the villains and from them obtain the name of the man orchestrating this. The house and immediate area will be thoroughly searched before we leave, so I know you'll be safe in my absence.'

His uncle nodded. 'There are half a dozen men who came with me from my estate, my dear, and two of them will remain to guard you. I'm sure it's unnecessary – but it's better to take no chances.'

'Grey, my love, take care. Don't worry about me. I'll be safe waiting here. I never thought I'd be put in the position of a soldier's wife, but now I know how they must feel every time their husband goes into battle.'

He raised her hand and kissed her palm and then he was gone. It was going to be a long afternoon. The smell of the food made her nauseous and she decided to vacate the chamber and go in search of her new abode.

This apartment was more than adequate and, although it had only the one bedchamber, it had a large dressing room and a delightful sitting room, which overlooked the meadows at the back of the house.

Her maid greeted her cheerily. 'Only one more trunk to unpack and then it's done. Mr Slater said he'll sort out his lordship's belongings tonight. I can't think why he's gone off like this; his job is to take care of his master's things not to be gallivanting about the place.'

Madeline thought it better not to discuss Slater's whereabouts with her maid so just smiled at her remark. 'As you've almost finished with my things, Lottie, could you and the girls unpack for his lordship as well? Also Lord Carshalton will need to bathe when he returns this evening so make sure this too is arranged.'

The girl curtsied. 'Yes, my lady. Is there anything else you want before I unpack for his lordship?'

'No, I'm going to sit quietly next door and read. I noticed that my books are already on the shelves.' Heaven knows what the staff would think of having to provide hot water for so many baths.

* * *

It took Grey an hour to search the house thoroughly even with the help of his uncle and cousin. The staff had been questioned but they all gave the same story – even the ones that were recently employed and held no loyalty to the old regime. Everyone denied having seen any strangers around the place and he was forced to accept the men who had tried to kill him and Madeline were even cleverer than he'd thought.

'Uncle Richard, you take three of the men and search to the north of your estate and Frederick must come with me. I need to have someone who knows the area in my party.'

'Very well, we should be able to cover the entire area by nightfall.'

Despite a thorough search and stopping to question any villagers, or labourers, they encountered, Grey found no sign of the men he sought.

'Wherever they might be, Cousin, they're no longer on our land. Therefore there can be no further attacks on you or Lady Madeline,' Frederick said as they concluded yet another fruitless search of a deserted building.

'I agree – time to return.' His back was on fire

and every muscle ached after being in the saddle for so long after his unpleasant experience that morning. 'It will be dark soon – I've no idea how far we are from Blakely Hall. Will we be able to get there whilst it's light enough to see?'

'We're no more than a mile away and will be back in good time. I cancelled dinner tonight; supper trays will be sent up to us when we want them.'

Grey pulled his horse in behind his cousin, glad he didn't have to find his way through the fading light. He dozed in the saddle, something he'd done many times before, knowing his mount was as tired as he was and would be eager for his stall.

They clattered into the yard where the stable hands were expecting them. He saw that his uncle had already returned and he was glad of that. Presumably he too had had no luck. He tossed his reins to a waiting boy and rolled from the saddle. His knees almost gave way beneath him and he was forced to steady himself before setting off for the house. 'Slater, take care of yourself. You've done more than enough today.'

What he needed was a square meal, and a hot bath, and for the first time since he was married his mind wasn't on bedroom sport. He hoped Madeline would understand.

The house was quiet. Only the sconces on the stairs and in the grand hall were still alight. The clock in the drawing room struck eight. He hadn't eaten a full meal since yesterday and was sharp-set. He hoped the promised tray was waiting for him.

He turned to his relatives. 'Thank you for your assistance today. I wish our search had been successful. I'm damned if I know where to look next.'

'It's the least we could do, my boy, and you can go to your bed secure in the knowledge you and your lovely wife are safe. Goodnight and God bless you both.'

Frederick arrived at his side. 'Do you need a hand, old man? You look done in.'

'I'll manage, thank you. But I've forgotten in which direction to go and would be grateful if you led me there.'

He thanked his cousin and bid him goodnight outside his chambers. He was forced to lean against the door frame as he stepped into the room. He'd expected it to be empty despite the earliness of the hour, but his darling girl was waiting for him.

Immediately he straightened, but too late. She

was on her feet and at his side before he could phrase a reassuring comment.

'Let me help you; I've been waiting. There's a bath next door and I've dismissed my maid so you won't be disturbed.'

'I can manage on my own. I don't expect you to be my servant.'

She ignored his protest and he was too tired to argue. He rather liked having her ministering to him instead of Slater. Her hands were more gentle but she was equally professional. The bath was perfect and although he couldn't stretch out, the warmth of the water unknotted his muscles and eased the pain in his back.

'I'll clean your injury whilst you're in here and put on a fresh dressing when you get out.' She was obviously unbothered by what she saw so he relaxed and enjoyed the process.

Eventually the water cooled and he emerged feeling a new man. She handed him a large bath sheet then stood aside to allow him to dry himself. He sat in silence whilst she took care of his wound and didn't protest when she handed him a voluminous nightshirt.

'I don't think you need a bedrobe, my love; it's still warm. Supper is waiting next door and we shall eat together. There's no need for you to tell me what happened as obviously you didn't find the men you were searching for.'

'I didn't, but we can sleep tonight knowing there's no immediate danger. My uncle has positioned men at all the entrances, which I think is unnecessary in the circumstances, but he insisted he wished to keep us safe.'

He scarcely knew what he ate but it was just what he needed. 'You look desperately fatigued, Grey – why don't you retire? I'll finish my supper and then join you.'

The bed was as comfortable as the previous one and he rolled onto his stomach and was asleep instantly.

* * *

Madeline woke early and was surprised to find her husband still beside her – she'd half-expected him to get up at dawn and resume his search. Quietly she slipped from between the covers and into the shared dressing room. As Lottie had been told not to appear until summoned, she would find her own garments. There was sufficient water left in the pitcher for her ablutions and in no time at all she was dressed in a simple pale blue muslin. She scooped her hair up into a loose arrangement at the nape of her neck and fastened it with the pins.

Grey must be allowed to sleep and then take care of his morning preparations without her in the way. Therefore she would put on her boots and spencer and take a stroll around the garden for an hour or so. However, she would carry her footwear until she was safely in the sitting room as she had no wish to disturb him.

The house was already busy with parlourmaids and footmen about their early morning tasks. She reassured them she required nothing and they resumed their work. There was a side door she'd not used before and she was about to unbolt it when she was interrupted.

'Allow me, my lady – them bolts are a mite stiff.' This must be one of the men left to patrol the passageways.

'Thank you. I've not exited through this door before. Can you tell me where it leads to?'

'The path leads to the terrace that runs in front of Lady Carshalton's chambers. You'll not disturb her ladyship; she'll have the shutters closed at this time of the day.'

The sun was just rising behind her and it bathed

the area in a soft, golden glow. Today was going to be warm again and she would insist that Grey spent time with her walking around the beautiful garden.

She was tempted to turn the other way and avoid the risk of causing offence to the occupant of these rooms, but the other direction looked less appealing as it led towards the dairy and other outbuildings.

If she walked on the very edge of the flagstones and trod softly, then she doubted she would be heard from inside. As she rounded the corner she shivered. The sun didn't reach here until mid-morning and it was dark and cold. The terrace looked decidedly uninviting although the view of the parterre and ornamental lake was attractive.

She made her way to the balustrade that edged the terrace, intending to keep as far away as she could from the building. The grass looked wet and uninviting – perhaps she would go the other way after all. As she was about to turn back a well-remembered voice called her name.

Lady Carshalton was standing by an open window staring out at her. 'Lady Madeline, what a pleasant surprise. Have you come to visit me so early in the day?'

'My goodness, I do apologise if I've disturbed you...'

'My dear girl, I've been awake this age. If you don't mind seeing me in my disarray, then please come in and keep me company.'

She could hardly refuse. 'I should be delighted but I don't know how to find your apartment if I go inside.'

'Don't worry about that. You are young and fit, surely you can scramble over the windowsill right here?'

Madeline's gown was loose enough to allow her to attempt this extraordinary request. Lady Carshalton never failed to surprise.

24

Beau read the letter that had just arrived from London a second time and shook his head. This didn't make any sense. The man they had suspected of orchestrating the attempts on Grey's life was living in the colonies somewhere and hadn't been in England for more than three years.

This meant he couldn't be behind the attacks. So who the hell was? His brow creased and he tossed the letter aside. He needed to think and the best place was outside in the fresh air.

As he strode through the house, he heard his twin brothers arguing in the drawing room and thought that maybe Perry and Aubrey might be able to offer some sensible explanation for this co-nundrum.

'I need to talk to you. Pay attention and stop bickering like children,' he said as he joined them.

Perry looked up with a laugh but his expression changed when he saw his brother's face. 'What's wrong, Beau?'

He told them the contents of the letter and they were equally mystified. They sat in silence for a few minutes all trying to solve the puzzle of who was threatening members of their family. Then he knew and the knowledge was like a fist in his chest.

'There's only one other person who might wish Grey dead – the man who expected to get his title. My God! How could I have been so stupid as not to realise? Our sister and her husband are in deadly danger at Blakely Hall and believe themselves to be safe.' Beau was on his feet as he spoke. 'We must go to them. If we ride we can be there before midnight.'

There was no need to ask his brothers to accompany him; they were already on their feet looking as grim as he did.

'I'll get Peebles to open the gunroom. Do we want to take extra men? Carshalton will have a dozen or more at his disposal,' Aubrey said. The older twin by five minutes, he was also the most decisive.

'Excellent idea. We do need more but I'm not sure if we have enough who are competent horsemen. Perry, go to the stables and find out. It's a good thing Giselle is away with her friend for the sennight so I don't have to worry her with this.'

He didn't bother to pull the bell strap but strode to the door and shouted for attention. His butler appeared at a run. 'Tell the kitchen to prepare food we can carry on horseback. We're going to be away for a few days.' He left his brother to explain the necessity for pistols and headed to his apartment. His valet was efficient and helped him change into his oldest and most comfortable riding gear.

'Shall I put a change of raiment in a saddlebag, your grace?'

A futile suggestion as all such items were kept at the stables. 'No time, I'll manage as I am. You and the other valets can follow with the luggage to Blakely Hall.'

In less than twenty minutes, he was mounted on his most powerful horse with his brothers at his side. He had managed to muster five men who could both ride and shoot, and they too were in the saddle and ready to leave.

'We must go across country – I'll lead. Make sure you keep up. We'll stop to rest the animals every two hours.'

He touched his heels to the flanks of his gelding and pushed the beast into a gallop. He prayed they would get there in time.

* * *

Grey, through half-closed eyes, watched as his beloved wife crept from their bed and made her way in the almost dark room to the shared dressing room. He listened to her moving about as she washed and dressed herself. For the first time since they'd been married, he didn't feel the urge to get up in order to protect her from unseen danger.

He was still short of sleep and another few hours' shut-eye would do him good. The matter wasn't settled – but he would wait until he heard from his brother-in-law before he took matters further. She emerged fully clothed and carrying her boots. His lips curved in the darkness when he saw she had ignored convention and wore no bonnet or gloves.

Just as the door was opening, he pushed himself up on one elbow intending to call her back. There was something he'd much rather do than sleep. Then he reconsidered. If she wished to walk in the garden on her own, then that was her prerogative. He had no intention of being a dictatorial husband.

When he woke again it was fully light and Slater was standing beside his bed. 'Your shaving water's waiting your attention, my lord, and if you don't get a shifty on you'll miss your breakfast.'

Hardly a suitable comment from one's valet, but Slater was so much more than that. They'd been together for many years and he would trust the man with his life.

Grey sat up, yawned and stretched. The look of incredulity on valet's face stumped him for a moment. Then he remembered he was wearing a borrowed nightshirt.

'I know, my wife thought it best and who am I to argue? I've no need to wash as I took a bath last night.' He stripped off his nightshirt, pleased that he was able to move both arms freely this morning. He was dressed and shaved in no time.

He glanced at his watch, shocked to find the time already past ten. 'Slater, have you seen my wife this morning? She went out for a walk before six o'clock and I expected her to return here to wait for me to wake.'

'I've not seen her, sir, but I expect she's with Mr Carshalton and Mr Frederick in the dining room.'

'Stay vigilant. I'm still not convinced there's not an inside man.'

The breakfast room was empty, but he was so hungry he decided to eat before going in search of Madeline, or his relatives. All soldiers were able to consume vast quantities of food in double quick time and he was no exception.

He searched the downstairs rooms, but there was no sign of them. He was so late coming down they were probably outside somewhere. He would try the stables first.

Smith touched his cap as Grey walked under the arch. 'Morning, sir, nothing untoward to report here.'

'Have you seen Lady Madeline or my relatives?'

The man shook his head. 'I ain't seen her lady-ship today, sir, but the gentlemen went out an hour or so ago.'

'Any idea where they went?'

'There's been an accident on one of the farms and they've gone to see what needs doing.'

A faint flicker of concern ran through him. If Madeline wasn't with them – where the hell was she? Of course – how stupid of him. She was with his grandmother.

He arrived at the apartment and banged loudly on the door. It was opened immediately, and not by the prune-faced maid.

'Is Lady Madeline within?'

The girl shook her head. 'No, I've not seen her and I've been here since seven o'clock.'

'I wish to speak to my grandmother.' He didn't wait to be invited but stepped around the girl and made his way to the bedchamber. He should have visited her sooner, he was fond of the old lady and she deserved better from him. He would spend a few minutes in her company and then resume his search.

He was about to knock when she called out to him. 'Come in, my boy, I've been hoping you would come.'

She was sitting, looking perfectly well, in an upright chair by the window. He bowed. 'I apologise for not visiting before this. I'm glad to see you looking fully recovered and hope you will be joining us for dinner very soon.'

'Unfortunately my legs no longer work as well as they used to, so I'm confined to my apartment for the moment. Sit down. I want to talk to you.' He picked up a chair and carried it across the room and placed it a few feet from her. 'I gather that your prompt action saved my life. I thank you for that.'

'I'm glad I could be of service to you, Grand-mamma. No doubt you heard about the near disaster with the balcony – we've searched the entire estate and found no sign of the men who did it.'

'Well, I'm glad that you are both safe.'

'I intend to make sure it stays that way. Forgive me, my lady, but I must go. I'm looking for my wife. I don't suppose she came to see you this morning?'

'I've not seen her since you arrived and would dearly like to. However, my maid mentioned she saw her walking in the garden earlier today.'

'Did she say in which direction she was going? I fear she might have met with a mishap and be in need of my assistance.'

'Towards the folly, if I recall.'

He bowed a second time and promised to return and visit her with Madeline later in the day. He left the room as if he hadn't a care in the world but as soon as the door closed behind him he broke into a run. Something was wrong – his beloved must have met with an accident or would have returned by now.

The quickest way to the hideous marble monstrosity on the far side of the lake was by the path that bordered the woods. When it had been built, the land around it had been cut away so the ruins appeared to be on a hill and the artificial moat could be filled from the lake by winding up a metal plate beneath the water.

He covered the distance at a run, looking from side to side, searching for a clue. The building was correctly named – it was certainly a folly – his cousin had told him that it had been built at the express desire of his grandmother. It had been constructed to resemble a crumbling castle in miniature and had a tower, ramparts, and a selection of artistically ruined walls including a deep moat.

Why it had been done in pink marble he'd no idea – it looked ridiculous. He wasn't surprised Madeline had wanted to investigate more closely. He began to call her name as he got closer, but there was no response.

He skidded to a halt in front of the folly. He shouted again hoping she would respond this time. A faint call from inside made him forget his caution and he rushed in, not waiting for his eyes to adjust to the darkness. There was a sound behind him and then a searing pain at the back of his head and his world went black.

* * *

Madeline had given up her attempts to climb out of the slippery pit she'd been tossed into. The marble walls had no crevasses or edges upon which she could gain a fingerhold. She still couldn't quite believe that Lady Carshalton was behind the assassination attempts. The old woman was obviously insane.

She'd no idea how long she'd been down here and little light filtered in from the window slits high above her in the make-believe tower. Then she heard Grey calling her name. He'd come to find her as she knew he would.

'I'm here. Inside, in the pit.' She was about to yell again when there was a slight scuffle. Before she could react, her husband plunged into the pit landing in a heap beside her.

He was horribly still. Had he broken his neck in the fall? It was no more than three yards to the top – surely he couldn't have received a fatal injury dropping from so small a distance?

'Grey, can you hear me? Have you broken anything?' Even as she spoke she thought how silly her questions were but could think of nothing else to say. She wriggled until she could get onto her knees and thus examine him more carefully.

The pit they were trapped in had several inches of water in the bottom and already she was soaked to the waist and her extremities were numb. She ran her fingers over his face and was relieved to find it warm. He was alive – thank the good Lord for that.

He mustn't remain slumped in the water. She must somehow get him upright and pray he had no serious injuries that would be made worse by her moving him. It was difficult to push him so his back was against the wall, but somehow she managed.

After a few moments he groaned and his eyes flickered open but they were unfocused and he didn't respond to her questions. As soon as he was recovered he would have a plan to get them out. They would be missed and his men would probably be searching for them at this very moment. All she had to do was remain calm.

Slowly her heart stopped thumping as if it wished to escape from her bodice. Although wet, cold and uncomfortable they were in no immediate danger. Grey stirred and she gently shook his shoulder. This time his eyes stayed open and his senses returned.

She was about to explain that his grandmother

was behind the murderous attempts when a hideous screeching noise filled their prison. What was it?

He understood immediately. 'God dammit! The bastards have opened the sluice gate. This space will fill with water. Can you swim?'

'I can't – I've never liked being immersed in water.'

'Don't worry – I'll keep you safe.' He pushed himself to his feet and hooked his boots off. 'You need to remove your skirts – they will weigh you down disastrously.'

By the time he'd finished speaking, the water had flooded up to their knees. Her hands were so cold her fingers refused to answer her command. He pushed them aside and tore her skirts from the waistband, leaving her in her bodice and petticoat.

The water was now up to their waists.

He discarded his topcoat and then turned her around so her back was to him. 'Lean against me, sweetheart; whatever you do don't struggle. I'll keep us afloat until we reach the top of this shaft and can get out.'

As the water reached their shoulders he kicked against the floor and they were floating. She tried to remain relaxed in his embrace but being sur-rounded by icy water and now out of her depth was too much for her. She tried to turn and clutch onto his neck and took them both down.

The water closed over her head and she opened her mouth to scream and swallowed a choking mouthful. She was going to die and her struggles increased as her desperation grew.

* * *

The second time she sent them beneath the rising water, Grey knew he had to do something drastic or they would both perish. When his head emerged he dragged in a life-giving draught of air. Then he wrenched her arms from his neck, held her up by her bodice and punched her hard on the temple. She went limp in his arms.

A few seconds later the moat was full and he was swimming strongly to the edge. He put his hand under her bottom and heaved her to safety. He clung on until he'd regained his breath and then joined her.

Whoever had tried to drown them would be disappointed – but not for long – as he intended to find them and put an end to their miserable existence as soon as he'd taken his beloved back to Blakely Hall.

He checked and found a strong pulse. His blow

hadn't done her serious harm – thank God! He staggered to his feet with her in his arms and then half-slid, half-walked down the grassy slope.

He swore loudly and violently. The moat was full and it would be impossible to negotiate it with her in his arms. They were trapped over here. He put her down carefully in the shelter of the half-ruined outer wall. If he removed his shirt and scrambled back to the top of the mound where the tower was built, he could wave it above his head and attract attention.

He was about to do this when he froze. Whoever had hit him and pushed him into the pit was still in the vicinity. They had only just filled the moat. At the moment they must think he and Madeline had drowned – if he appeared they would know they had failed and come across to finish the job.

They would be helpless against armed men. He couldn't risk alerting them. He would return to her side as silently as he could. If they weren't found before nightfall, the elements would finish the job the water had failed to do.

25

Beau and his entourage were making excellent progress and were more than halfway to their destination. When they thundered into the posting inn he came to a decision.

'Perry, we'll change horses here. I want to get to Blakely Hall before dark. Tell your brother when he arrives.'

Aubrey had dropped behind as his mount was blowing badly. Beau shouted for attention and immediately they were surrounded by ostlers.

'Do you have nags for us? I'll return for these in a few days.' He tossed the reins across and strode into the inn. Soon he was mounted on a massive gelding well up to his weight. An ugly beast, but strong enough to take him the next twenty miles when he would have to change horses again.

After this second halt he was within a few miles of his destination. A village clock struck four. He gathered his men around him and explained his plan.

'Lady Madeline and Lord Carshalton are unaware they are in deadly peril and are surrounded by potential enemies. All the men employed there could be dangerous. We can't give them warning of our arrival. We must approach cautiously.'

'Do we know the exact location of Blakely Hall?' Perry asked.

'I do. I got directions from the landlord here. We can approach along a little-used cart track – leave the horses and then complete the journey on foot.'

'And what do we do we get there? We can hardly shoot everyone we meet,' Aubrey said with a wry smile.

'I think we must reconnoitre and make our decision once we know how the land lies. My priority is to see that my sister and her husband are safe. Apprehending the villains can come after that.'

Aubrey walked amongst the men, checking their weapons were primed and ready to fire. His brother was becoming a man to be reckoned with – his twin seemed to be less mature and still had a deal of growing up to do.

He looked around his band of hopeful soldiers. At first glance it would be hard to tell who was duke and who was the servant. They were all mounted on similar nags and whereas he had dressed in his oldest and most disreputable garments, his men had put on their best. This meant their appearance was similar. Only when he and his brothers spoke did it become obvious they were in charge.

Blakely Hall soon became visible in the distance and he gestured that they stop and dismount. Fortunately there was a well-fenced meadow by the side of the track, which was ideal to keep the horses safe in their absence.

'I think it might be advisable to send one of the men ahead to investigate – they are less likely to be noticed than one of us.' Beau selected a suitable candidate. Then they made their way forward, making sure they kept out of sight.

Suddenly three armed men stepped out in front of them. 'Hold it right there. Stick your paws in the air. Don't any of you bastards make a move towards your weapons.'

No point in arguing. Beau raised his hands as

did the others. There was something familiar about these three. Then the man who issued the order lowered his gun.

'Beggin' your pardon, your grace, I never recognised you first off.' He touched his cap. 'Smith, I works for his lordship. This here is Jenkins and that's Slater.'

Beau explained why they'd come and the information he received in return filled him with foreboding.

'We ain't seen Lord Carshalton nor her ladyship since this morning. Mr Carshalton and Mr Frederick are frantic – I don't reckon either of them's involved,' Smith said.

'Then that means it has to be Lady Carshalton who has orchestrated these attempts. I can scarcely believe it.' Beau turned to his brothers. 'We'll confront the harpy in her rooms – she'll tell us what we need to know. I just pray we're not too late.'

He led the charge through the vast establishment to the suite of rooms the murderer occupied. He kicked the door open and charged in, his pistol primed and loaded. His brothers were close behind him – Carshalton's men followed.

There was a flash, a hideous noise and the room

was full of cordite. Thank God the bullet had missed its mark. There were two men confronting them and both had a second pistol raised. He fired without hesitation and one of them collapsed, a red stain on his jacket front indicating he'd been hit.

Aubrey took care of the second villain and it was over.

'The Carshalton woman must be cowering in her bedchamber. How many other men does she have at her disposal?' Beau directed this question to Smith.

'Six, your grace. I reckon there's another two bastards to deal with. Leave it to me and my men – no point in you toffs getting shot.'

Beau stepped to one side, as did his brothers, and the three armed men approached the closed door like the professionals they obviously were. 'What's happened to the rest of our men?'

Aubrey pointed to the window. 'They've gone round to the terrace – they should be there by now. One of the grooms is taking them. The darkness will be to their advantage.'

Before he could reply someone shouted from outside and then there were further shots. Smith and his cohorts hurtled through the door and Beau was close behind. He'd expected to see the dowager cowering in a corner now she was unmasked.

Instead he was greeted by a torrent of vile words. 'You can do nothing to save your sister or her miserable husband. They will be dead by now. My son will have the title and my work will be done. I care not what happens to me now I've achieved my goal.'

In two strides he was beside her and barely restrained himself from striking her. Instead he held out his hand and Aubrey placed a loaded gun into it. He pressed it against her temple 'Where are they? I shall not hesitate to fire.'

Her breath rasped in her throat. He pressed harder and she flinched. 'They are in the folly. They will be drowned by now.'

'Have her locked in here. She is to receive no visitors. Lord Carshalton must decide her fate. She deserves to rot in prison for the remainder of her life.'

Perry grabbed his arm. 'I can see lights flickering out there. Someone is on their way to rescue Madeline and Grey.'

Beau swallowed a lump in his throat and stepped away from the vile creature gibbering to herself in the chair. 'I pray to God that they're not too late – that this day will not end in tragedy.'

* * *

'Madeline, sweetheart, can you hear me? You need to wake up now.' Grey was cradling his wife in his arms, trying to transfer some of his own body heat to her. If she didn't wake up soon he feared she'd become too cold and never recover her senses.

Her eyes opened. 'I'm so cold. I thought I was going to drown and then you hit me.'

'I did. It was the only way I could get us both out safely. We can't walk about to keep warm but we must devise some other way if we wish to survive...'

Her fingers clutched at his shirt front. 'It's your grandmother – she's the one who's been trying to murder us.'

'Your wits are addled, my love. I fear the blow has confused you.'

'No, you don't understand. She invited me into her bedroom this morning but insisted I climbed in the window. I was half in when I was smothered by a blanket and the next thing I knew I woke up at the bottom of the tower.'

Everything that had happened now made sense. 'It was her men who made the gargoyles fall. As they weren't strangers, of course nobody reported them. I was always puzzled why she travelled with six outriders.'

'Remember that one of them disappeared and then was replaced by somebody new – that must have been because you shot the other one.'

Her excitement at this discovery was exactly what she needed to restore her. Her cheeks were less pallid and her fingers a little warmer. 'The woman must be insane to think she could get away with it.'

Whilst he was talking he continued to rub his hands up and down her arms, which was also of benefit to him. 'Why aren't you attracting attention? Someone must have missed us by now.'

He explained to her his reasons and she shrank back into his arms, looking nervously over her shoulder. 'How will your men know to look here?' She shivered violently. 'What if your uncle and cousin are also part of this? They could have everyone murdered.'

'I'm sure they're not involved. I can only surmise my grandmother so hated my father she didn't want his son to inherit.'

'I think that Mr Carshalton is more biddable and she wished to remain in command.'

He smoothed back a wet lock of hair from her

forehead and kissed her tenderly. 'We just have to remain out of sight until we're rescued. You've been missing for hours and I already had my men searching. I'm sure it won't be long before they find us.'

The sun would be setting soon and it would become much colder. He had to keep her warm and active until someone arrived. He could think of only one way and he wasn't sure making love in the open air when they could be discovered at any moment was a sensible solution.

* * *

Madeline saw his eyes darken and the telltale flush appear along his cheekbones. An unexpected bubble of laughter escaped. 'Dearest Grey, much as I love you, I draw the line at being intimate with you out here.'

His smile was wicked. He wasn't to be put off. 'We need to keep warm, darling, and I can think of only one way to do this if we're required to remain on the ground.'

His arms tightened and he pulled her closer. His head blotted out the light and for a few delicious minutes she almost succumbed. Then she pushed on his chest and immediately he relaxed his grip. Her heart was pounding and she was certainly much warmer.

'Well, that certainly worked. Don't look so shocked, my sweet; I wasn't going to take things to their natural conclusion.' He settled her more comfortably and resumed his rubbing.

'What will happen to Lady Carshalton?'

'She will be incarcerated in an asylum for the insane – we can hardly hang her as she deserves. Although her minions will meet their maker at the end of a rope.'

'I can't understand why your grandparents hated your parents so much. It's not as though your mother was somebody beyond the pale – a vicar's daughter is perfectly acceptable.'

'My father never talked about his family and my uncle could shed no light on the matter either. Perhaps she'll explain her motives before she's taken away.'

He continued to massage her limbs and she wriggled, kicked and waved on command. His intention was to keep them both alive, but as time passed she was finding it increasingly difficult to stay awake and she knew if someone didn't come soon this might be her last hour on this earth.

'I just want to say that if we are to perish, then I'm glad I'm here with the man I love. I don't regret anything...'

His snort of laughter jerked her awake. 'God's teeth, Madeline, we're not in one of your romances. I've no intention of kicking the bucket today and I'm damned sure I won't let you either.' He surged to his feet and dragged her up beside him. 'It's dark enough now to walk around safely without being seen. Come along – quick march.' He turned her and gave her a sharp slap on her posterior, which had the desired effect.

She shot forward clutching her rear end. 'Don't you dare do that again, sir, or I shall inform my brothers you're a wife beater.'

His arm snaked around her waist and she was lifted from her feet. 'You're my property – I shall do what I want with you.' Before she could protest he crushed her to his chest. His kisses were hard, demanding, and she was able to put aside her fears for a few moments.

Abruptly he set her down. 'I can hear something. Listen.'

She stilled and sure enough there was the sound of voices approaching. Was it a rescue party or the villains come to finish the job?

Grey shouted. 'Smith, we're over here, man. We can't get across the moat; someone will need to work the sluice gate and drain it.'

Less than a quarter of an hour later she was enveloped in a warm blanket and being carried through the grounds and back to the house. Grey barked questions at his men and from the answers she gathered that Beau and her brothers were here – and that they had taken care of Lady Carshalton.

The house was ablaze with candlelight and she was vaguely aware of a circle of worried faces staring down at her. There was a hurried conversation before she was taken upstairs to her new apartment. She'd expected her maid to be waiting for her, but the rooms were empty.

'There's a hot bath waiting for you, all of the fires are lit, and a supper tray will be sent up in half an hour.' He stood her by the tub and without a by your leave stripped off her ruined garments and lifted her into the lemon-scented water. Tenderly he soaped her limbs until she was quite recovered.

'You are as wet as I was, my love; you mustn't remain in those garments a moment longer.'

His smile made her sit up so abruptly the water sloshed over the edge. 'I've no intention of remaining clothed, my darling. What I have in mind requires me to be as naked as you.'

Her eyes widened as his shirt, breeches and stockings were tossed aside. His intentions were obvious. 'There's no room for two in this bath.'

His answer was to reach in and lift her out. He wrapped her in a warm bath sheet and carried her through to the bedroom. 'Dry yourself, sweetheart, whilst I remove the filth from my body. I'll not be more than a minute or two.'

With trembling hands she used the towel and somehow managed to pull on her négligée. Someone was in the sitting room and she pushed open the door to investigate.

'Madeline, little one, thank God you're fully restored. I'll not stay long.' Beau opened his arms and she ran in to receive his embrace.

There were sounds from next door – her husband was about to appear. 'I'm so glad you and the twins are here but can we talk tomorrow?'

'Of course, I'll leave you to your supper.' He strolled out and for the first time in her life she was glad to see him go. From now on the only gentleman she wished to be alone with was her husband.

* * *

MORE FROM FENELLA J MILLER

The first in another brilliant Regency romance series from Fenella J Miller, *Return to Pemberley*, is available to order now here:

https://mybook.to/ReturnPemberleyBackAd

ABOUT THE AUTHOR

Fenella J. Miller is the bestselling writer of over eighteen historical sagas. She also has a passion for Regency romantic adventures and has published over fifty to great acclaim. Her father was a Yorkshireman and her mother the daughter of a Rajah. She lives in a small village in Essex with her British Shorthair cat.

Sign up to Fenella J. Miller's mailing list for news, competitions and updates on future books.

Visit Fenella's website: www.fenellajmiller.co.uk

Follow Fenella on social media here:

facebook.com/fenella.miller

x.com/fenellawriter

ALSO BY FENELLA J MILLER

Goodwill House Series

The War Girls of Goodwill House

New Recruits at Goodwill House

Duty Calls at Goodwill House

The Land Girls of Goodwill House

A Wartime Reunion at Goodwill House

Wedding Bells at Goodwill House

A Christmas Baby at Goodwill House

The Army Girls Series

Army Girls Reporting For Duty

Army Girls: Heartbreak and Hope

Army Girls: Behind the Guns

Army Girls: Operation Winter Wedding

The Pilot's Girl Series

The Pilot's Girl

A Wedding for the Pilot's Girl

A Dilemma for the Pilot's Girl

A Second Chance for the Pilot's Girl

The Nightingale Family Series

A Pocketful of Pennies

A Capful of Courage

A Basket Full of Babies

A Home Full of Hope

At Pemberley Series

Return to Pemberley

Trouble at Pemberley

Scandal at Pemberley

Danger at Pemberley

Harbour House Series

Wartime Arrivals at Harbour House

Stormy Waters at Harbour House

The Duke's Alliance Series

A Suitable Bride

A Dangerous Husband

Standalone Novels

The Land Girl's Secret

The Pilot's Story

You're cordially invited to

The Scandal Sheet

The home of swoon-worthy historical romance from the Regency to the Victorian era!

Warning: may contain spice

Sign up to the newsletter

https://bit.ly/thescandalsheet

Boldwood

Boldwood Books is an award-winning fiction publishing company seeking out the best stories from around the world.

Find out more at www.boldwoodbooks.com

Join our reader community for brilliant books, competitions and offers!

Follow us
@BoldwoodBooks
@TheBoldBookClub

Sign up to our weekly deals newsletter

https://bit.ly/BoldwoodBNewsletter